The
Invitation

OTHER WORKS IN PROGRESS
Café Stories by Nina
Snapshots Without a Camera
Stories from the Senior Café Ha Ha
Kitchen Talks
Writer's Boudoir

The Invitation

A NOVEL

Eva Gerszon

REGENT PRESS
Berkeley, California
2025

[Paperback]
ISBN 10: 1-58790-730-5
ISBN 13: 978-1-58790-730-2

[E-book]
ISBN 10: 1-58790-724-0
ISBN 13: 978-1-58790-724-1

Library of Congress Catalog Number: *forthcoming*

*This is a work of fiction. Any resemblance between
the characters and any persons living or dead
is purely fictitious.*

*Excerpt from "Love at First Sight" by Wisława Szymborska
translated by Eva Gerszon*

*Excerpt from "True Love" by Wisława Szymborska
translated by Stanisław Barańczak and Clare Cavanagh*

*Fragments from "Labyrinth" by Wisława Szymborska
translated by Clare Cavanagh and Stanisław Barańczak*

Manufactured in the United States of America
REGENT PRESS
www.regentpress.net

*To my fiction teacher Mary Webb
for her belief in me*

TABLE OF CONTENTS

*Both are convinced
that a sudden passion
joined them together.
Beautiful is such certainty,
but uncertainty
is even more beautiful.*

. . .

*For each beginning
is only to be continued
and the book of happenings
is always open in the middle.*

WISŁAWA SZYMBORSKA (1923-2012)
Awarded the Nobel Prize for Literature in 1996
Excerpts from "Love at First Sight"

OVERTURE

Voices of Present and Past

In 1968 many of the remaining Jews in Poland who had survived WWII were expelled, along with their children born after the war. Their sole crime was having Jewish roots. Passports confiscated, citizenship revoked, families divided, they were dispatched into the unknown with just a Document of Travel classifying them as stateless, and five dollars per family in their pockets. No right to return or even visit.

A small contingent of these "remnants" — about a dozen in all — ended up in the San Francisco Bay Area and eventually found each other, by chance and with great joy, at local cafés. Periodically, they would gather with their mostly American spouses for private home parties — *prywatki* — a dying Polish tradition they still observed in a new country in a new century.

Late into the night, often till sunrise, there would be lots of drinking, eating, singing, dancing, and boisterous arguing and laughing — plus, yes, also some crying. Polish delicacies were served, notably *kabanosy* — thin sausages with a distinct smoky aroma — and *Żubrówka* — a beloved vodka infused with a hint of juniper. A legendary blade of grass from a pristine Białowieża Forest near the city of Białystok floats in each bottle. On the label, a *Żubr*, a smaller version of the American Buffalo, which presently thrives there but was almost extinct a century ago, intently peers out at anyone looking back. Without *Żubrówka* and *kabanosy*, a *prywatka* was not a *prywatka*.

These small private parties also carried a scent of nostalgia, taking the remnants back to summers in rural Poland, at Jewish Youth camps, where they hadn't had to pretend to belong where they were not welcome. Though they still carried indelible memories of growing up in Poland, they rarely spoke of the past.

This is your invitation to attend a *prywatka*, which may be Nina's last.

THE ENVELOPE

"Smell it, darling."

Feeling Good — Nina Simone

The camellia tree outside the kitchen was not yet in bloom. The beaded curtain over the open door moved almost imperceptibly, catching the last rays of sun reflected on the hundred year old house's terracotta stucco with purple and gold accents, which she had painted herself, despite protests from her husband and a few neighbors. They had bought the house when it was still affordable, a cozy place of their own up twenty stairs, with two bedrooms, one too small for their two young sons to share; but it had to do, along with a single bathroom, until they illegally converted a closet to a tiny second bathroom. She basked in the doorway in the warm October breeze.

Each room was in colors inspired by Matisse. With the aid of transparent fabrics, fishing line, and clothespins, she had filtered the sharp direct light, to her husband's vocal protests. All he needed was a bright lightbulb to read by and tables and shelves for his five thousand books, while she couldn't live without the colors and beeswax candle ambiance, or without constantly changing each room to function better, which required moving furniture up and down four steps, which she would do when he was asleep or not in the house.

Out front, there was hardly ever any traffic and she could hear friendly dog barks mixed in with shrieks of excitement by kids playing baseball and the little girl next door on her scooter, with her father encouraging her from behind. Two mothers were talking across the street, which was narrow enough so they could hear each other. Calm prevailed, one car slowly passing.

She started imagining that she was writing it all in her head (almost a lifelong habit): The magnificent leafy trees gave merciful shade when the sun shone at its most merciless, and squirrels traversed the tree branches over the street from one sidewalk to another. Children were safe playing and walking to school here, and even puppies who escaped their leashes. Nearby was a nature park, where mature dogs took their poets for nature walks.

The counter near the door was Nina's creative spot, where she smoked her first after work joint, inhaling and exhaling the freshness of the breeze's playful dance with each puff, writing it all up in her head, her chance to be her reflective stoned alone self while the kids were at soccer practice, maybe even heading from there to a sleepover. Her Irish linen kitchen towel, recently suspended with the help of two clothespins and two safety pins on nylon fishing line between two hooks, served as a threadbare, makeshift, wine stained curtain, naturally to Martin's protests. He was her steady pillar of support — a pillar who liked things properly neat and straight.

An oversized envelope had come in the mail. It was fancy and of a pale lavender hue, with a silver border. She held it near her nose and inhaled its lavender scent, with her joint in her other hand. She was cherishing her time alone before her husband's arrival and also thinking that with the kids gone maybe they could flirt in the kitchen like they did in Paris a few years ago.

She put on "Feeling Good," and danced to it in front of the long mirror, improvising, admiring herself, feeling it, puffing on her joint. Singing along with Nina Simone.

In the foyer next to the kitchen she examined her lips in the small oval mirror, applying the Merlot Wine lipstick Martin liked, plus Immortelle French lip balm, a little black mascara, and black kohl eyeliner, and she was feeling a spark of excitement as she studied the glints in her hazel eyes, trusting what she saw in them. "Feeling Good" was over. She was inhaling from a still viable roach when suddenly, inside her head, out of the blue, unasked and unwanted, her dead mother Rosa intruded, in her penetrating, profoundly mocking voice: *Ninuś! Spójrz na siebie — przecież wyglądasz jak trup na urlopie!! Jak blada śmierć! No idź namaluj sobie usta!* "Dear Mother Rosa," Nina heard her own loud voice say, provoking her mother, "shall I give you an English translation of your obscure Polish idiom — your personal creation — your idiotic compliment which you implanted in my head? Okay. It goes like this: For God's sake, Nina! You look like a pale corpse on vacation from the grave! But actually, my dear Mother Rosa, your humiliating idiomatic description of me is untranslatable, even in Polish. And it doesn't include my roach."

She moved closer to the mirror, smiling to herself and said, "So without the lipstick, I'm a pale death on furlough, but if I paint my lips I'll be alive." Her smile took on a tint of sarcasm. "And of course you are right. A Pale Death on holiday from the grave with a half dead roach hanging in the corner of my mouth, a pale lipped corpse in a torn black sweater, two different socks, a safety pin holding up the strap of a falling apart BeautiFeel shoe, and a ripped skirt held together with another safety pin! A pale lipped disheveled corpse, a homeless looking corpse on vacation out of the grave without lipstick . . . but with a half dead roach in my mouth . . . And by the way you guessed it right about my two different socks. Yes *Mamuniu*, that is what makes me an artist. Or actually am I a vacationing corpse of a pretend artist! Am I a pretend artist? An artist of feeling good? One Nina singing along with another."

She relit her still longish roach and after a deep puff produced another smile in the mirror, then with her free hand defiantly fluffed her messy (on purpose) black curly hair which she never combed. Then she screamed, really more of a shriek, in her mother's voice: "Nina! Have a look at yourself in the mirror again!"

Alive or dead, her mother had always unnerved her. To disconnect from her anger, per her yoga teacher's advice, she directed herself to take a few calming breaths, slowly in and slowly out, and she put on "Feeling Good" one more time.

With the not yet dead roach hanging from one side of her mouth, in a few dancing steps to the last of the song, she was back in the kitchen in her spot when she heard Martin unlock the front door. From the foyer, he said his usual "Hello, darling," while surveying the junk mail and starting right in with his ritual report about a difficult abstract lecture today, which sadly most of his students, didn't "get."

Martin entered the kitchen and glanced at her without a sign of registering the opulent pale lavender envelope with silver edging in her raised hand. He approached her, leaned over her (being a foot taller), and gave her a perfunctory affectionate "marital" peck on the cheek. Same every day at this time, for how many years.

Flirtatious and taunting, she fanned herself with the envelope to get his attention, but he, still oblivious to her maneuvers, left the kitchen in quick purposeful light steps and climbed the four oakwood stairs to their bedroom where he would change into the clean but same pattern blue and white small checkerboard shirt (which he wore to work and for most other occasions) and take off his sandals, because (he would explain with a strong Irish accent) his feet got "terrible sweaty," made worse by the stress from teaching a truly elegant equation to his poorly prepared students, who were not much interested in the abstract subtlety of solid and semi-solid or pseudo-expandable geometric bodies. (Robotics had just become fashionable.)

Martin was back, with a fresh pair of socks, in his home sandals. He stationed himself near the sink where every day at five p.m. he had his first drink, leaning against the counter in a static pose — a standing version of Rodin's Deeply Thinking Wise Man, one of his three variations of being relaxed, finally home in the kitchen after a day teaching.

She snapped her fingers to get his attention, turning the envelope from front to back. "Hey Marti, look at this fancy lavender envelope!" she said, sniffing it with a dramatically charming expression, her eyes half closed to savor and demonstrate her delight. He did not have a reaction yet so she, not yet too aggressively, started waving it. "Darling, it smells like real organic — or almost orgasmic — French lavender! Just smell it, darling! And you know this scent, don't ignore me. Are you afraid of organic scents? But darling, this is the same lavender perfume you like to smell on my silk panties!"

At last Martin lifted his head and his distant half freaked out fleeting gaze met the envelope, but only for a moment before his eyes returned to his comfort zone, a spot on the kitchen floor. He recrossed his feet. His strong arms, tightened in a defensive mode, were wrapped around his torso. His well defined forearm muscles and long finely shaped fingers trembled lightly. "Stop trembling, darling, you look like Rodin's Wise Man trembling statue, and *nota bene*, look at me because Eye Contact according to Dr. Butterfly is an interspecies basis for communication. And you're always preoccupied with what? Besides a static or diffuse semi-expandable equation? And does it permanently reside in your brain, darling?" She was practicing calmness, although aware of moderate intensity sarcasm invading her features. He did not look at her. "Because, darling," she attempted a smile, "I know that it keeps you awake every night, after the bloody eleven o'clock news. And you know what? I think it's a Jungian equation symbol chasing you all night long in your scary dreams, darling."

He is silent. His eyes are trained on his ritual point on the kitchen floor, and suddenly she is waving the envelope with pissed off gusto. "Darling, according to a new study reported in the science section of the *New York Times* about mind-eye coordination of an aware person from babyhood till death, Eye Contact with living creatures, along with the visual scanning of the environment outside of one's head and this floor, produces deep awareness of the external and internal worlds. So why do you concentrate on more or less the same point on the dirty floor when we are together in the kitchen? Do you think any relationship can flourish under these circumstances? Your focus for twenty years has been on the exact same point on this dirty floor . . . Marti." (Saying "Marti" reminds her not to yell.)

He looks at her with a remote, absent stare. She stops waving the envelope. "By the way, darling, do you recall what Dr. Butterfly said at Couples Intimacy group? Aren't we voluntarily committing ourselves to a self imposed, self created, marital prison of boring habits? We do not flirt. We hardly dance or even just hang out together on the couch in the living room — which feels like a dead room — and we have stupid fights about things out of place in the kitchen. Is that how we're going to spend the rest of our lives?" Just saying these words aloud she feels gloom take root inside her gut.

He gives her a look long enough to say, with an assured, superior righteousness, "Actually, Nina, in my opinion, marriage is about who puts the food on the table and who cleans up after the family cat brings a half eaten rat home. And who brings the morning coffee to bed."

She restrains herself. "But darling, pure domesticity kills, so I need to flirt eye to eye, or I will dry up prematurely — and I do not want to be dead before I die. Flirt and dance together or it's a married couple's romantic death sentence, darling!" Waving the lavender envelope she comes closer to him, waving it in his face, as if playing, just barely not slapping him with it.

He takes a step back. "Nina, I told you not to call me darling in that fake sweet voice. That is what kills love. Okay, so you want me to pretend to be interested in an envelope I'm not interested at all?" he says in a clipped staccato. "And stop pointing it at me as if it was a gun!" He pounds his fist on the butcher block, still with reasonable restraint, and immediately reaches for his whiskey glass on the shelf over the counter near the sink, where he always has his first evening drink.

"Darling, are you afraid of this especially fancy lavender scented envelope? Maybe it is about another party, with dancing, laughing, a celebration of life in old European Polish Jewish style? Too bad that you don't get it, darling, you, the genuine Irishman who doesn't want to hear nor believe unpleasant things and is afraid to experience pleasant smelling spontaneous present moment things, and whose expressive action of affection is pinching Alexis on the tail (thank God I have no tail) when she walks by. By the way, does the God you do not believe in forbid you to dance and openly laugh showing your teeth? I think Somerset Maugham, whom you refuse to read, would call your smile a difficult tight lipped one."

"Hee, hee, hee. I like that. A difficult smile is interesting. But it's not interesting to me when at your parties you all sing your supposedly funny vulgar songs in Polish and laugh like crazy. It's just too much unnecessary whining, Nina. And if you'll recall, Dr. Butterfly also said we need to be nice to each other and put a variety of LOVE stickers with flower pictures on the refrigerator every day, hee, hee, hee." He laughs without looking at her and his upper and lower lips are squeezed as if he is hiding something — an equation? — inside his mouth.

He is at the fridge. "But Nina, this true Irishman is thirrrs-tee now, and needs his chaser and whiskey, so stop torturing me with your amateur psychoanalysis." He notices the roach hanging from the side of her mouth. "And stop smoking that weed, it makes you exaggerate everything. In fact it makes your face look a bit crooked too, hee, hee, hee." He opens the fridge door.

She takes the roach out of her mouth and the envelope is at peace in her hand. The fridge door is still open when he comes up to her and kisses her on the forehead. "How romantic, darling," she says. He is back at the fridge reviewing different beer bottles. "Marti, are all the real

Irishmen romantic like that? Or are they more romantic after they quench their Irish thirst? Oh, and darling," she says sweetly, "what is the normal starting ritual to quench a real Irishman's thirst, a real Irishman who drinks no water for thirst, a special issue of an Irishman with the balls of a proud Irish bull. So is the ritual beginning with whiskey or beer? And for a lass he desires, maybe a shot of French cognac to put her in a mood so maybe then she will give him a Genius Blow Job?"

"Hey, Nina, calm down, the kids may come back early." Sudden worry spreads across Martin's face.

"Don't be perturbed, Marti. Of course I meant after they're asleep."

"That's for later. For now, I need a chaser." He pulls a bottle of Sierra out.

"But darling, in proper English, you chase after, not before, right?" Nina says, watching him search for the bottle opener in his messy gadget drawer, overfilled with corks from countless wine bottles. "And what does the Oxford English Dictionary say is the meaning of the chaser? Before and after?" She gently fans herself with the envelope, her smile a provocative smirk. "And incidentally, Marti, did you know that bilingual writers are allowed to create new words which are not in the Oxford Dictionary? Mixed languages words, for example? And I am a writer in English thinking in Polish half this and half that."

"Ni-na, I've told you many times that if the word is not in the Oxford Dictionary, it is not a word." He is still

14

looking for the bottle opener.

"Hmmm, darling, and I also read in the Times that there is scientific evidence that routine lack of Eye Contact between humans, or humans and animals — or even humans and plants — eliminates the chance of universal passion and could lead to zero growth in population. And the ideal intimate Eye Contact distance is six inches. And your penis is about eight to ten inches, isn't it? And according to the latest evidence, six inches is quite enough for at least six minutes of an intimate shared time, and six inches is a recommended distance between lovers' eyes, and that must come first, before the proud engorged Irish ten inches takes over." She stops the fanning, anticipating his response.

"Hee, hee, hee." Suddenly he unzips his pants and pulls out his penis. "See, for you it's beautiful and not bent nor crooked," he says. Then, after a few seconds of admiring it, he puts it away, zipping back up. He doesn't look at her. He gives a love pat to his erect penis through the fabric of his pants. (He does this in the kitchen from time to time when the kids are away for the evening.)

"Hee, hee, hee, Nina, you might like to check for yourself if my ten inches is ready for your Genius Blow Job? Hee, hee, hee. And you should take advantage of it while it is still standing proud and beautiful for you. Before I get too old."

"Very romantic," she says with a note of mockery and puts the almost dead roach back in her mouth, relighting it and greedily inhaling one last puff, watching him. Eureka, he found his bottle opener! Now he is studying the bottle label. "Darling, I wish your eyes were studying me the same way they study that bottle label. So intently, so tenderly. Maybe it would lead to passionate sex . . . not with the bottle, darling. But at least the good news is that you are not wasting your Eye Contact on our unswept kitchen floor. You can't sweep the floor with your eyes, but with your eyes — and Dr. Butterfly says so too — you can sweep someone off their feet. Ain't I clever, darling, for a foreigner? "

"Nina, can you stop throwing slogans around? Or at least make them more poetic like Szymborska does?"

The envelope, still in her hand, is not moving. In a defiant pose, she leans against the counter in her spot by the open door, cooled by the early evening breeze, a bittersweet half smile on her face.

A minute of mutual silence. She watches him. He releases his solar plexus from his tense self embrace, recrosses his large sandaled feet, takes a long sip of his chaser, and resumes the same protective embrace. His fingertips with neat, self manicured nails are tapping each other. His eyes go back to the floor. The envelope is static in her hand. "What are you thinking of, darling?" she says, intending no malice.

"Nina, if you really want to know, I'm thinking about how to avoid being a victim of your raging emotions and your ranting, raving, and complaining when I do not want to go to a party. I don't like parties. Period. Too much hoopla for me." He punctuates his conviction with a long swig of beer, from the bottle.

"But darling, you do like to go to an Irish wake where there is plenty of whiskey to drink! You can bring your flask of whiskey to any party and a slip of paper to write your equations on when you get bored. A slip of paper in case of a sudden insight, like James Joyce says — just a slip is what one needs when an inspiration hits . . . more or less."

"Not a bad idea, Nina."

"Hey, we are making progress, we agree on something, darling."

His whiskey glass sits on the butcher block table. Suddenly his fist pounds the butcher block twice, making the glass hop lightly two times with no spillage; the two ice cubes in it make a cooperative clink clink clink.

She resumes a mildly provoking fanning action with the envelope and can feel that her pasted on smile is contorted by a mildly sticky venom: "Darling, by the way, so you didn't notice my new lipstick? Why did I put it on for you? And when was the last time you initiated even a few seconds of continuous Eye Contact?"

"I saw that you have a new lipstick on. But stop your nonsense, Nina." His narrow lips assume a tightly squeezed shape. And alas, his eyes go back to a random but apparently deeply meaningful to him point on their unswept kitchen floor. She is not quite boiling inside, for the moment, and attempts to be kind. "Marti, don't you want to see who is this envelope from?" And with a more appealing seductive and lightly teasing smile, she fans herself with the envelope in a gentle feminine way. He doesn't look at her, nor the envelope. "Marti, darling," she starts, with surprising to herself patience. "This floor will never get truly clean no matter how hard you examine it." She doesn't let her irritation show and doesn't speak too loud, running her fingers coquettishly through her curly black hair, never combed to preserve the natural curl.

The object of his fear, the lavender envelope, is still in her hands. She is relentless: "Also, Marti, notice the pretty Polish calligraphy our names are written in." She opens her eyes to their exaggerated fullness of expression. "It looks like Sylvia's elegant writing in royal dark blue ink — and it's addressed to you, Professor Martin Didn't Notice, and to me Nina Little Biting," she says pointing to their names with mock pride. "And darling, look at the four archival collector postage stamps. Don't you like collectible stamps and historical plaques of important wise man with professorial beards like yours? But only in civilized parts of the world? Like Paris or Rome?" Her eyes are question marks.

He is not looking at the stamps. In an annoyed voice through compressed lips, he says, "Stop pretending to be nice, Nina!" Then he pounds the butcher block three times with his half full whiskey glass. The two almost unmelted ice cubes in it clink as if in resignation. A tiny bit spills. He hits the butcher block once more to emphasize the level of his annoyance.

He tops off his whiskey. The three-quarter full whiskey glass (with two ice cubes) sits undisturbed on the butcher block while she examines the back of the envelope and says, "It's from Queen Sylvia and her Doctor Smart Alek! You know what? I bet it's to celebrate their marriage to be!"

"What? What kind of celebration are you talking about, Nina?" he says absently and takes a small sip of whiskey. "Would you like some cognac after all? I think it's better for you than that awful foul smelling illegal weed."

"Darling, you know I thrive on dialogue resulting from increased not decreased awareness in life. And weed gives me that vibe and has no calories. And what if inside this envelope is an invitation to just a simple celebration of being alive? Are you afraid of being alive?" Her eyes open wide again, trying to pierce his, which are not available. "And darling, didn't you say that you're happy when I'm happy!?"

No response. Again his eyes are on the floor.

Her energetic fanning with the lavender envelope resumes, now more intentionally.

"Hey Nina, can you please stop waving this envelope at me as if it's some kind of a weapon?" He recrosses his feet, and his forearms around his solar plexus resume trembling, now more distinctly. He tops his whiskey off again with just a "little spoonful" — his expression with a tender Irish accent. "But tell me, Nina, what's so great about your privatke, where nothing new happens and no one new ever comes? It's boring to me." He replaces the whiskey bottle cap.

"For Christ sake, darling, I said you can take paper and pencil and entertain yourself. And a flask of whiskey. No it won't be a morose Irish wake, with plenty of whiskey for everyone and talk talk talk about the weather and those unaccompanied old Irish laments you love. At Sylvia's it's Polish-Jewish style, not an Irish wake and definitely not a stiff American university soulless small talk department party where people laugh anemically, or with boisterous artifice. What the fuck is wrong with laughing for no reason, darling, or for a very stupid reason, and why not drop the feeling of shame about me looking like a homeless person, and how about not worrying about what's right and what's wrong? And who are you to judge us all? With your history of Irish Catholic suppressed childhood? Professor Martin Didn't Notice, an intellectual and rational man who claims that shame is a most important emotion — which is not considered an emotion by those emancipated, and it is not sexy at all! So darling — if you don't want to go to this party with me, I'll go alone!"

She threw the envelope on the counter, still yelling. She crossed the room in defiant rapid steps. It was getting dark and cold outside. She slammed the door shut after her.

INTAKE NOTES – PT. 1

This couple has been together for 20 years. They have 2 sons in their early teens.

Martin was born in Ireland. He says he must be buried in County Kilkenny on a green hill. He is a tenured mathematics professor at a reputable state university. Nina is visibly proud of Martin's academic success in his field. In Group, she said he is a poet of equations and then kissed him with affection.

Nina was born in Poland and forced to leave with her family because they were Jewish. She came to New York City at age 16. Soon she was introduced to marijuana in Greenwich Village. A peak experience was hearing Leonard Cohen play his songs in a café.

A part-time home health Occupational Therapist, Nina still sees herself as an "irresponsible bohemian" who aspires to be a writer in her time off work.

A source of considerable friction between them, according to Martin, is that when he is not home, she paints their house (inside and out) in odd, loud purplish colors, which once incited a near riot on their street, culminating in a petition demanding that she keep the color scheme of the neighborhood. (She kept the balusters bright purple.)

Martin was voluble on the subject, stating that she has also transformed all the rooms to resemble "gypsy tents," with transparent shawls. According to Nina, the shawls mellow the sharp direct light, but Martin does not notice romantic ambiance nor romantic décor, and maybe that is why they do not have much sex. To Martin, who is well over six feet, his wife's decor also presents obstacles to his head. He calls the shawls "shmatas" (Yiddish, derogatory for rags.) All of this amounts to an outsized issue in their marriage.

———————

THE UNVEILING

"You don't look so pale anymore."

Zefiro Torna (Madrigal with sweet soprano)
— Monteverdi

It was the next evening. With a bewildered expression on his face, Martin peeled garlic to go with the steak for a family dinner. The boys were still at basketball practice. Nina was in the kitchen, playfully indulging in a few more inhale-exhale sniffs of the still unopened lavender envelope.

He put the garlic in the frying pan, stirred it around in the heated olive oil, and covered the pan, freeing his eyes to examine a new random inspiration spot on the kitchen floor.

She was turning the envelope from back to front, smelling it and honing in on her husband's focused downward gaze. "Marti," she said rather sweetly, "what's that on the floor? Could it be a speck of a hint to the solution for your elegant new equation, the one you were dreaming about last night instead of me?" He looked at her as if he'd never seen her before. "Darling, don't look at me like that, like when you think I'm weird and you are about to call 911. I made nothing up. In fact, you told me about your scary Jungian nightmare where an equation is physically attacking you. A battle to the death?" she inquired with a sticky sweet empathetic feeling.

"Hey Nina, I couldn't sleep all night. And don't talk about death." Martin took on a grave expression and for a moment averted his eyes from the floor.

"But this dream seems to be recurrent, darling. You wake me up screaming and flinging your arms. I say, 'It's okay, Marti,' and you go back to sleep."

"I don't remember that."

Monteverdi was playing and the envelope in her hand did not move, but she felt its restlessness. Martin, as he was stirring the garlic and shallots in their good nonstick frying pan, threw her a distrustful glance. "I think you're plotting something, Nina."

She made a face of absolute innocence and walked to the counter where his yellow legal lined pad with an equation written in pencil was, and put the fancy lavender envelope — unsealed by her yesterday in secret — right next to it. He quickly made a single step and grabbed his yellow pad and placed it a few inches away, as if to protect it from the envelope. Nervously, he covered the frying pan and poured himself the rest of his chaser into a medium size wine glass.

"Marti, this envelope is not plotting against you like your equation is in your dreams. Are you afraid that it might poison your yellow pad?" Her eyes opened in exaggerated surprise. The chaser sat on the butcher block and his eyes resumed looking at the floor. Seemingly deep in thought, the muscles of his forearms trembling, he recrossed his feet, assuming one of his three Rodin-like statue poses (a variation she'd named Her Trembling Darling Statue).

He lifted his eyes off the floor. "I don't know what are you talking about, Nina. Do we have more garlic?"

She did not lose her cool. "Yes we do, another head." She pointed to a bulb in the vegetable basket.

"So, you want me to be excited about what is in this

en-ve-lope? Is that it?" Martin spit out in his clipped staccato.

With two cloves peeled, chopped, and sautéed, Martin took another sip of his half full chaser. "Actually, Nina, before this fancy party, if that's what's in the envelope, I think you should get a haircut or at least comb your hair. Or God forbid, are you going to go to this elegant, I'm sure, privatke stoned and looking like an unkempt homeless person? With that shoe strap hanging on with a safety pin?"

She looked at him with a witty smile and once more ran her fingers through her hair. (She liked it to be a curly mess — not just to annoy her dead mother Rosa and her husband Martin but more importantly to cover her not so shapely from the profile chin.)

"Let me explain something, Marti. First, I'm a creative authority on my hair. It's true that I'm not an artist as defined by you — one that has paintings in well known galleries, but I'm an artist like a child because I'm wearing two colors of socks at this moment, darling, and I will go anywhere the way I like it with at least one safety pin crucial to my existence. Don't worry, no clothespins will be on me as a décor item. Hey darling, the Polish word for safety pin is *agrafka*, which comes from Latin. *Graphia* . . . graphite . . . writing with graphite as before printing was invented? Marti — it's my nom de plume! Nina *Agrafka*. How does that sound, darling, for your writer of a moment wife?"

"I don't understand, Nina. Why Agrafkie?" He stirred the veggies. "Could you play "Zefiro Torna" again? I like the sweet soprano, not like yours when you yell."

"*Agrafka*'s function is to join, and joined letters make chains of words inside and outside of my head. On a practical note, it — the safety pin — can also hold together old ripped linen towels or shirts and skirts and straps of my still alive on my feet dancing shoes — and yes, the most important role of *agrafka* is to hold together my ripped conscious and subconscious thoughts. Best in writing because no one can shut me up, darling. Anyway, so you're ready for "Zefiro Torna" with a sweet soprano, not my yelling? But about *agrafka*. For your information I intend and will use words the way I like! Because I'm an authority on my own expression! And I don't care if it doesn't live in the Oxford Dictionary."

"Zefiro Torna" was on, but soon he asked her to turn it off because it was too loud. She obeyed. He stirred nervously in stony silence while intermittently looking at her as if acknowledging her ridiculousness.

She tried not to show her hurt at his wordless dismissal, nor to blow her rebellion out of proportion, so instead she fluffed her hair again with a convincing provocative flourish, and redirected herself into a positive frame of mind, thinking that he was Irish after all (and in fact he had told her that the Irish always like a little insurrection with their dinner).

Another clove was ready for chopping (he liked a lot of garlic). "The fact is that you do not understand, Nina, that nothing is wrong with a nice big erect penis in the kitchen when the kids are gone. And hey, tell me, who said that a little marital fun is not good for you after a good dinner? Ask your friends, hee, hee, hee. And actually you have nothing to complain about. Am I not cooking a good dinner for all of us?"

She took a step toward him and gave him a little peck on the mouth. "Well, you know, darling, that the kids prefer my macaroni with extra Velveeta, and I don't like red meat, nor big meaty engorged penises directed at me for a blow job on demand and not for any erotically romantic reason in the kitchen when the kids are gone. But I'll eat the veggies and potatoes."

"The kids and Alexis like the steak if it is well done," he retorted, recrossing his feet and shrugging his shoulders once. He picked up a knife and started to chop the extra garlic clove.

She left the kitchen — four steps down to the dark laundry room, where she kept her rolling tray and where she smoked and wrote in her private diary, hiding from the kids, or to avoid Martin's preemptively anxious coughs and paranoia about the neighbors smelling it and calling the police.

Back in the kitchen in her spot, she is in a fortified mood thanks to the Purple Shit pure sativa buzz and he is probably on his third whiskey.

"Oh, where were you, Nina? I didn't hear you come back. Hey, you don't look so pale anymore. It must be your new lipstick."

"Do you like my lips better now?" She picks up the envelope.

"Of course I like your lips but the lipstick could be more red. But if I kiss you, I'll ruin it."

She gently waves the envelope. "Darling, I refreshed my lipstick especially for you. And by the way, Dr. Butterfly did suggest that husbands not plant paternal pecks on their wives' foreheads. Kiss me on the lips, darling! And by the way, you yourself don't look as pale as before! Is it the aroma of extra garlic? Or is it a hope of. . ." The envelope in her hand acquires a renewed vigor.

He takes a big gulp of his whiskey and puts it on the counter. "Nina, I already asked you to please stop waving that envelope at me as if it was some kind of a weapon," he says with forced calm, emphasizing his point with his fist, pounding the butcher block once and then again for extra effect. She writes it all down in her head (in cursive in her Moleskine notebook, with a gift from him, a Pelican dark blue ink old fashioned fountain pen).

Martin seasons the meat with salt and pepper. "Nina, I hope you will have a little steak. You need protein. And your hair does look better now. Did you comb it with that comb I gave you?"

"Don't pretend you don't know that I do not comb my hair but mess it up artistically with my fingers. And did you have an extra whiskey while I had my Purple Shit half joint?"

"But Nina, seriously, I hope you aren't going to go to a fancy party in these old shoes with the strap hanging on a

30

safety pin!" He points at them like they are defendants in a courtroom.

"The steak is cooked, Nina. Rare the way you like it." He downs the rest of his whiskey and puts his empty glass with two ice cubes almost unmelted on the butcher block without agitating them. Abruptly he picks up the envelope, looking at her with a distant expression. His left hand with its immaculately shaped nails is stroking his too short and too carefully trimmed (for her taste), auburn beard with few silver strands. He studies the stamps on the envelope — he doesn't notice that it has been unsealed already — puts it down on the counter and again moves his yellow legal pad away from it and closer to him, and with his well sharpened number 2 pencil scrawls a few more symbols inside the new double parenthesis.

He moves his drained whiskey glass to another spot on the counter, picks the envelope up again, and with a courtly flourish, ceremoniously hands it to her. "You read it Nina," he says.

"So are you ready for your death sentence, Marti? Or do you need one more last chaser?"

"Don't say things like that Nina. It's not nice to talk about death. It gives me bad dreams."

"So don't be afraid of this envelope, darling. This is not about death." She gives him a more affectionate than usual marital peck on the mouth, opens the envelope, and reads aloud:

ZAPROSZENIE

COME TO CELEBRATE ALMOST FORTY YEARS
IN OUR NEW COUNTRY AND IN THE
SECOND (HAPPIER) HALF OF OUR LIVES

THERE WILL BE UNLIMITED ŻUBRÓWKA!!!

SZCZĘŚCIA!!! HAPPINESS!!
MAZEL TOV!!! JOY TO US!!!

WHEN:
SATURDAY NOVEMBER 12, 2005
STARTING TIME: 7PM
ENDING TIME: WHEN THE SUN COMES UP

PLUS ALL NIGHT
DANCE YOUR HEARTS OUT

(& UNLIMITED ŻUBRÓWKA TILL DAWN!!!)

SYLVIA AND ALEK

"Fine!" he spits out in resignation, a man beaten, his fist playing a supporting role in his expression of terminal submission. "Okay, fine!" he repeats in the same tragic manner. His fist makes contact with the butcher block again.

"Fine what?" She drills her eyes into his.

"I'll go to my doom if it pleases you, Nina! Like I always do," he says quietly and doesn't avoid her eyes. The butcher block absorbs a last full of resigned finality thump with the empty chaser bottle. "For now, though, Nina, go wash your hands, the kids will be back any minute and we'll eat the steak before our beast of a cat takes it down to the floor. Hee, hee, hee."

"But Marti, darling, how about you go to this *prywatka* — *with* me, not *for* me — like romantic married lovers do in Chagall's *Blue Lovers* painting," she said, smiling.

He lovingly kissed her on the lips. She kissed him back. A little more than a marital peck.

Dr. Angela Butterfly, MSW, Ph.D
Intimacy Specialist
INTAKE NOTES – PT. 2

Nina reports frequently feeling more alone with silent Martin than when she is alone by herself. Martin seems to pretend not to hear her, and when he doesn't know how to solve a problem, he still won't involve her in problem solving. She and her older sister agree on this – and they agree on little. (The sister named this "all-too-common" condition WHD – Wife Hearing Deficit.)

He always has to be right, Nina says. She acknowledges that Martin is responsible and loyal – a true "pillar of support." He is more than fair, always giving money to the poor. She admires him for these qualities. And for his strong arms, shapely legs, and firm buttocks. Sex was good in the early days of marriage. Her feeling of love was infused with passion. She was "in love" with his blue eyes, and his gentle voice turned her on.

To illustrate Martin's "proud Irishman bearing," Nina recounts at length how, 20 years before, at their wedding in NY they received about $2000 dollars in checks (traditional wedding gifts from Polish-Jewish friends of Nina's parents). Martin was very drunk and afterward set fire to the checks with his cigarette lighter, b/c "a real Irishman does not accept charity from strangers." Nina told her mother, who told her friends the checks fell into the fireplace, and they wrote new ones. Nina hid them from Martin and bought a set of crystal wine glasses. He is still angry at her for going behind his back.

She is vocal about their cultural differences (Irish silent style vs. Polish-Jewish expressive style), which lead to fights as well as the "dullness of a long-term self-imposed marital prison of pleasant habits, such as breakfast in bed." She complains that Martin dances with her only at their New Year's Eve party, and only to show off to other guests that he remains interested in her. He says of course he finds her very attractive but as for dancing: "Once or twice a year is enough."

Substance Abuse:

After work, when home alone, Nina uses medical marijuana (a joint or two per day). It is her "pacifier." She also writes in her diary. She wishes Martin was "brave enough to alter awareness together and dance with me in abandon." To her, that kind of togetherness is sensual and romantic, a prelude to passionate sex.

Martin does not believe smoking marijuana is "wrong" or "evil." But he does disapprove of Nina smoking it with their sons in the garden. "It is illegal." Martin is a self-styled "whiskey man, in the Irish tradition," along with beer chasers, and when there's no alternative, wine. He reports drinking an average of 2 to 3 shots of whiskey per evening after work, and more on weekends.

———————

A DUEL OF OPPOSITES AT DUSK

*"What would happen if Rousseau and Descartes
lived in the same century and had been
a couple, darling?"*

Madrigals of Love and War — Monteverdi

Martin was at the wheel, as always, claiming he would throw up otherwise, which suited Nina, because she liked to have a joint on the way to any adventure to magnify her enjoyment of an inspiring landscape, or, today, to hopefully suppress the angst in her gut and the fumes of gasoline in her lungs as they passed a mostly cement colored treeless suburban sprawl, separated from the car noise and stink by high, equally cement colored walls.

They had already spent a full hour on the always polluted ten lane always crowded highway, which she hated and he thought was just fine. But to smoke a joint, she would have to open the window and inhale the poisoned air while he coughed and complained, claiming to be choking from the smoke.

So far, the focus of their discussion had been elegant rationality, by Martin, versus irreverent irrationality, by Nina, and the discourse was pleasantly animated unlike their routine, sometimes quite cleverly delivered verbal blows. "Hee, hee, hee, Nina, in fact out of control irrationality leads to chaos, which is what you require to be sufficiently entertained, or you'll be unhappy." He didn't look at her when he repeated his normal monotone hee, hee, hee in a kind though mildly mocking manner (through partially clenched teeth).

"Marti, I'm not seeking chaos like you have in your Equation Studio, but doesn't regimented, reticent, emotionally suppressed life sort of die when it's fed only by necessary routines? And darling, you're driving too fast, go slower, so we don't get the police on our ass, because you know I'll have to have a joint very soon. But aren't you glad, Marti, that we don't have to drive this highway daily? Like poor Lila does. And Marti, by the way, at the party you'll have Lila to talk to about the benefits of rationality. Don't you respect women with rational brains like Lila? As opposed to mine, polluted by weed to enhance my kind of chaotic need you don't approve of, darling?"

From above the steering wheel he shot her an anxious glance. "What? Nina, are you bringing joints to this private party?!"

"Just one big one, half before and half after, darling. Don't you have your chaser before and after whiskey? You know my routine for mood fortification is also before and after."

"Okay, Nina. But Lila shouldn't drive alone in the dark. Explain to me why your sister and her unfortunate husband, who live close to Lila, wouldn't give her a ride?"

"Gertrude and Douggie? Because they need privacy in their car. By the way, Lila is about to launch her own startup, something biotech I think. And you know that Gertrude likes to be asked, and Lila does not like to ask for any favors . . . Darling, why look so surprised? My older but younger looking sister, perfect Gertrude, and her obedient husband, not only prefer to be private in a car, but also when it comes to sharing favors."

"Hee, hee, hee, you nailed it, Nina."

"And Lila is proud to be independent and make her own decisions since she left her American husband."

"Okay, Nina. Please, no dark details on Lila's husband. But remind me who else will be there. The same old crowd? No one new has come in ten years — and you've forced me to go to almost all your privatkes as a matter of fact."

"Yes, darling, I know you're a martyr and that you aren't going *with* me, but *for* me, to please me. Like a good martyr. Not like a lover from the Chagall painting. And it is what I need."

"So no one new will be there?"

"You know them all." Stylish and proud of herself Gertrude and Douggie."

"I just hope she doesn't bring Douglas on a leash, hee, hee, hee."

"And Queen Sylvia, the hostess with the mostest, will be beaming with self satisfaction and new diamonds, and her Dr. Smart Alek will be sporting his new tie with his constantly elevated gallant charm and superior wisecracks."

"I hope Sew is coming, so we'll have some real laughs, hee, hee. It could be quite boring without him. And by the way, hostess with the mostest? That doesn't sound correct. And you sound jealous Nina?"

"Not jealous. And I'm not into suburban anything, and frankly darling I prefer a *prywatka* at our own Bohemian Queen Nina and Irish Whiskey Man's house."

"You're right about that, Nina. And Gertrude's parties are too restrained for me. But don't tell her that I said that."

"The ambiance is too bourgeois and it's always cold and Gertrude never lights the candles. Hey, we agree on something!"

"Sure Nina, you and your candles! But I'm afraid that one day you'll burn our house down. Gertrude has a knack for elegance and elegant table setting, and you're a bohemian with safety pins no matter how fancy the party is. But I do not believe you're not jealous of your sister. You act like you are."

"Okay, I'm jealous of her energy and discipline, and her strong athletic body, and her flat stomach. And her skin. No wrinkles at all. And her neck. And her hair. But not of her eyes. I prefer my own."

"So what are you expecting to happen tonight?"

"Sew will tell his vulgar jokes and after we drink enough from the Promised Unlimited Bottle maybe his penis will stick out from his red shorts, but we'll pretend not to notice, or not notice and he will say that its out for a breath of fresh air. And we'll talk Polish too loud for your ears, drink more *Żubrówka*, and dance Polish folk dances with abandon, and despite that Gertrude and I don't like each other we will be dancing together having great fun, and even sing vulgar Polish songs — hey, it's good that you won't understand them, they're too peasant for your cultivated taste, darling. But Chopin was inspired by these peasant Polish folk dances like the mazurka, the polonaise, and the waltz. What else do you want to know about tonight, Marti?"

"Hee, hee, hee. So more of the same. Sew will tell his stupid jokes to impress you girls. And Nina, that story about how Sylvia and Alek met at a fancy café and fell in love from the first bite of a honey drizzled fig — will I be hearing it again?"

"Maybe, darling. By the way I have some more details to that story. About Dr. Smart Alek's very useful qualifications. Per Gertrude. Apparently Dr. Smart Alek is highly regarded in his specialty — treatment of Polish Jewish inexplicable female hysteria. Isn't that something you may be interested in, darling? So you may not be too bored. Plus you have your equation."

"Nina, I have enough hysteria live in my kitchen."

"So you're not interested in Dr. Smart Alek's theory?"

"I'm more interested in how this highly regarded doctor fell in love with Sylvia as they licked honey, and honey thoughts, off of each other fingertips. So all of you girls are fiercely jealous of Sylvia's great luck?"

"Not just Great Luck. Apparently also a Great Fuck. They speak the same language and laugh at the jokes they both understand without having to explain anything. That works especially well in the bedroom, darling."

"So Nina, correct me if I'm wrong, Lila and Sew and Sylvia are now free of their American exes and can find true soulmates while you and Gertrude, the less lucky sisters, still have more or less viable husbands but are victimized by our lack of Polish sophistication with Jewish gesticulation. You two are stuck with, respectively, a clueless American CEO with a respectable graduate degree in business and a primitive Irish peasant become professor."

"A darling Irish peasant become professor."

"Right Nina, and what could be worse than being stuck with an unsophisticated Irish peasant like me?"

"There are some benefits, darling."

"But tell me again, Nina. I can't keep your stories straight, how did you meet Sew? And I do think he is a better fit for you than I am."

"At Café Med. He was with his current girlfriend arguing with a group of various smelly long bearded local Communists. Oh shit, Marti, I hope my joint is in my bag in that tarnished cigarette case you gave me. But darling, please don't start your preemptive cough yet! But if I opened the window, the pollution would choke us both!" She reached for her small scuffed up no longer black Coach bag (from the late seventies before they'd met). "Hey, Marti, but I may need to take a few mood fortifying tokes soon. I can tell that the ugly highway angst attack is about to hit me."

"Nina, there is nothing wrong with a well designed freeway which gets you where you need to go as long as there is no traffic. And the traffic is moving okay now. And you'll be fine at the party, unlike me. I hope Gertrude won't show off Douglas again like a show pony. I don't understand how he lets her bully him the way she does despite his doctorate."

"Marti, Gertrude has a doctorate in real estate law, and in bullying since childhood practice on me. And in my opinion, you, darling, with your usually friendly Grand

Equation in your head will be occupied even if nothing new happens at Queen Sylvia's. And I have a joint to fortify my chaotic head and observe the 'nothing new' which is happening for you. And I'll try to record Sew's most inspired jokes because he is an Artist of the Joke — but paradoxically he paints sad close up portraits no one buys, so when he's done with high school teaching art, lately he also does minor plumbing jobs for old ladies. Hey, I bet he's going to wear his red shorts, with a tiny bit of his big thing sticking out. I saw it recently when I met him jogging on the sidewalk." She was about to open the still working magnetic clasp of her Coach bag.

He kept his eyes on the road and for a while there was silence. "By the way, Nina, you should not embarrass your friends in your book."

"So I should not be a writer?"

"I didn't say that. And you should realize that you and Sew and the others who speak Polish belong there, but I'll be a fish out of water like I always am at your private parties your privatkies. To me it sounds like private parts by the way, hee, hee, hee, but I'm just an Irish peasant."

"Marti, *nota bene*, you said you were but an Irish peasant the night we met. You don't remember? Or just not responding, Marti? At LaRue's Bar, you said something else but I don't remember and I liked your voice and I felt a warm surge, and I turned around and saw your face. So handsome, blue eyes — and your red beard! How many cognacs did we drink that night?"

"I probably had whiskey. You had the cognac."

"But do you remember the three grungy hairs on your neck? The same ones you always mention every time before you leave the house for the university? Darling, the three hairs sticking out on the back of your neck caused you concern even then. You complained that the wind was moving them and tickling you unpleasantly, besides ruining your image with your students. You don't remember. And do you remember after we made love that first night we met? I knew you would be the father of my children and I was not afraid to say it at the door when you were leaving to teach a class. And I was entranced by your clean lavender soap scent. We had chemistry. Maybe still do? We both like lavender . . . hmmm. Marti, don't you think that most men would run away from me right then, when I mentioned fathering my children right off the bat? And you did not. But now you don't seem to understand and absorb that even though a woman needs a man to be a father to her children, she does not need him to be a motherly father to her. But I must have intuited at first sight that you were a steady pillar of support. Was it love at first sight for you too at LaRue's Bar? Or did you want to escape my clutches?"

A smile flashed across his face. "I only remember that LaRue herself was working the bar and winked at me when I was standing behind you drinking my whiskey. No, I didn't want to escape. I escaped my village and my parents. To come to America."

"An Irish peasant became a professor. But not an

American. And me? A Polish Jewish city girl became Un-Polished and doesn't feel American."

"How many times have you told me? So, who do you think you are now, Nina? A founder of your own unpolished thought?"

"Exactly, darling. Sometimes you can be so perceptive. I am Un-Polished and unpolished, a writer of the moment, unpublished at the moment, with a Polish unpolished accent. On purpose, so that decent, polite readers will not think I'm American."

"Nina, you are American, you have an American passport. And by the way, it was LaRue who fixed us up. And I liked your voice. But I didn't hear you yell that night, hee, hee, hee."

"Marti, I didn't yell because you hadn't irritated me yet. And for your information, again, an American passport does not make me an American. A piece of paper does not make you anything other than what you are inside. Of course you, darling, need a slip of paper to write down an inspired Grand Equation, a permanent resident inside your genius head. And you think it isn't weird? But I'm weird and irrational. Like right now, I detest this highway, and *that* is why I need a joint. And according to you there is nothing wrong with this highway, so as usual we are on different wavelengths, a double disjoint. So I need a double joint, darling. And paradoxically, I'm double-jointed, which means flexible. And you? Stiff when needed darling?"

She leaned toward him, gave him a little peck on the

cheek and opened her Coach bag (that she had bought with her first Occupational Therapist real full time job money).

"Marti, aren't you an Irish bloke with overly restrained immoral instincts, so you drink whiskey to quench your thirst and squash the fear of the unknown stripped of excessive morality? No?"

"Hee, hee, hee." He took one hand off the wheel and put it on the inside of her thigh. "But if you want to, you could feel my nice erection. Hmmm, you're wearing my favorite Victoria's Secret black nylon real silky sheer stockings with seams. Hmmm." He moved his fingers appreciatively. "These are almost as smooth as the ones my mother used to wear." He moved his fingers up and down a few more times before he returned his hand to the wheel.

Through his black polyester pants she was touching his erect penis. "So darling, when you were a boy in Ireland, you loved to touch your mother's nylon stockings hanging to dry on the line in the only bathroom in your house, and you touched yourself too. An early fetish? Wow, if your mother had known, would she have hit you with her kitchen broom? But darling, I'm actually getting turned on now thinking about seeing you jerk off in secret into my Victoria Secret wet nylons, in our bathroom. Did you make it more slippery with soap? By the way, when you were a boy, did you confess anything to your priest?"

"Definitely not. I never liked my parish priest. Hey, Nina, I hope you're not going to put that in your book. Too many private details in my opinion is not a good idea."

"But it's a normal behavior for young boys, not only you, for boys any age all over the world. Nothing to be ashamed of. Creative masturbation is a good thing."

"But you don't need to put intimate details in your book, Nina."

"Life is intimate. And is a fictional story interesting if it doesn't follow life?"

"That is flawed logic Nina. Fiction questions life in my opinion."

"That's very true, so in your opinion what shall I call myself? What would be a good pen name for me? A Jewish Polka dot.com? Isn't it a good email address for me, darling?" she smiled.

"Hee, hee, hee, just one dot and she comes? I wish that was true, hee, hee, hee." He resumed stroking her inner thigh.

They are nearly halfway there. "Hey, I need a smoke to figure out who I am before I enter the Palace of Queen Sylvia and her lucky Smart Alek husband to be. Ouch, shit . . ." She removes his hand from her inner thigh.

"What now, Nina? Is something wrong already?" He shoots her a quick perturbed glance.

About to open her bag, she says, "Nothing is wrong yet since I'm pretty sure I have my tarnished with age of sin cigarette case, a present from you, in my bag. And I'm pretty sure my big joint is there. I told you I would need to fortify my angst-ed soul on this disgusting highway and before our entrance to the Palace of Queen Sylvia. But do you know why I have an adverse reaction to all types of suburban ambiance?" She opens the magnetic clasp of her Coach bag. Her joint is in her tarnished silver cigarette case and her red mini BIC lighter is there too.

He coughs his customary preemptive dry cough three times. "But don't smoke it in the car, Nina, it makes my throat dry."

Relieved to locate her special big joint in her tarnished silver cigarette case, she takes three calming yoga breaths. "I'll open the window for fresh air when we are on a smaller road. I'll just smell my joint for now. Uhm." She inhales. "Great Purple Shit from our neighbor, Maurice Roach." She closes the cigarette case and puts it back in her bag. She snaps the magnetic clasp closed, opens it and snaps it closed again.

They silently approach the gates of the upscale could be anywhere American suburb. It is dark and cold and Nina feels a renewed unsettling sensation. "Doesn't this evening feel somber?" she asks in a manner of impending gloomy doom.

"Nina, let me concentrate. I need to check the directions. Maybe this is not the right gate. And don't exaggerate, it's not that bad." He shoots her a fleeting look of concern. "And what now? Are you going to start complaining and criticizing me again?" he says sharply, clearing his throat as he watches her open and close the magnetic clasp of her scuffed up old bag again. "Why are you getting so moody, Nina? What I'm afraid of is that it is going to be worse after you smoke."

He coughs once and drives slower, looking at the printed directions.

"Darling, are you about to start a preemptive protest coughing episode? But I haven't smoked yet!"

"So don't." He performs three throat clearings.

"Okay, I'll wait till we get there . . . But Marti, wouldn't you agree that at least when it's dark you can't see the sanitized boredom of the suburban setting?" Looking out the window, she is stricken by another dose of gloomy angst. "Martin, I talk to you, and you don't respond, and that means lack of connection, and for me it means an empathy deprived angst attack is coming on. So why don't you talk to me? Remember the Almodovar film, *Talk to Me*?"

"Stop this connecting bullshit Nina! I have to concentrate on directions. I can't talk."

"Okay. I see that. And how about listening to *Madrigals of Love and War*? By the way, darling, this kind of suburban ambiance of catatonic catatonia has a dampening effect on my creativity, and a Purple Shit sativa can counteract it. Marti?"

"Hee, hee, hee." Three doubting beats with his teeth hidden behind his tightly squeezed no teeth showing lips. "Where did you hear that unsupported nonsense, Nina? And in my opinion, there really is nothing wrong with the suburbs. In fact, the majority of people in this country like it."

"I'm the one that made up this unsupported nonsense. And what kind of unsupported nonsense is your assumption that I should like suburbia because the majority of Americans do?" she says, raising her voice.

"I'm not an American, nor a majority!!! And don't argue about what I say I am. Accept it that an American passport doesn't make me American, because I don't feel and think American, darling." She ends on a calmer note, snapping opened the magnetic clasp and fumbling in her handbag.

"I hope I have my mini red BIC lighter." She puts on *Love and War Madrigals* and turns the volume up, up, up. They don't talk till the end of the disc. (Upon a repeat fumbling examination of her handbag, she'd made an unexpected find: an extra fine roach besides the Purple Sativa joint was hiding in her tarnished cigarette case. She has decided to keep it secret from Martin.)

Just past the plain cement colored entrance gate to Sylvia and Alek's subdivision there is a large sign: Bright Moon Springs. Martin stops and reads the name aloud in an animated tone, which causes Nina anguish. It's a bald faced lie, a fake promise of a picture book moonlit bucolic setting, and she has a magnified response of sheer distaste. Before she can say anything on the subject he knows she's about to raise, he proclaims in his irritating, cajoling manner: "Hey Nina, I bet you didn't know Descartes was quintessential in the development of rationalism, and Rousseau, who was a bit like you, hee, hee, hee, was the founder of Romanticism, which is irrational at its core."

"And what irrational entity am I founder of darling?"

"Hee, hee, hee, Ninaism, of course." He leans over and plants a rushed peck on her lips.

"Sounds like Naïvism . . . Ahhh, so that's why you treat me like a naïve child who needs to be advised of decent behaviors since she is never embarrassed about anything? Ninaism, darling, is about confronting preferably without crude sarcasm, but with elegant sarcasm as needed, unaware individuals who are afraid and resist change." She feels irritation getting control of her.

"And that's why, darling," she says in a sticky fake sweet tone, "I am going to have an irritated irrational attack, and to counteract it I will need at least one half of my good joint."

"Hey, Nina, you can suck on something else anytime, hee, hee, hee." He points at his crotch.

"Without Eye Contact, darling? Just like that? While you're driving? Like we did before the kids? But what if the husband of now with a beautiful specimen of an Irish endowment in his pants doesn't get romantic with her, because Irish don't know how? It's no one's fault, it's nature's trick to get two beautiful kids out of us, opposites, sticking together for too long. Hey, darling, you look perturbed. Hey, about our Rousseau–Descartes discussion: Are you Descartianly or abstractly afraid of my imminently to be enhanced hyperawareness?"

He looks at her, positively freaking out.

"Darling, why not a response? Ah, yes, of course, instead of really responding, you'll start feeding me some important objective information about why I should like highways and suburbia. Right, darling? And more about how I'm an American?"

No response. He resumes his snail pace. No muscle in his face moves and she takes three deep breaths and opens and closes the magnetic clasp of her Coach bag, not too desperately. She opens it again, with its usual sharp precise snapping sound; on her fingertips she feels the reassuring coolness of her tarnished silver cigarette case. She breathes deeply — inhale, exhale — reassured.

"Darling, you don't want me to have an early onset 'angstrum,' do you?" she observes without malice.

"What is 'angstrum,' anyway? A new word for a new calamity you're scheming, Nina?" He doesn't take his eyes off the road, even though there are no cars on the street nor people in the driveways, no one on sidewalks.

"Darling, an 'angstrum' is a physical measurement of an objective unit of angst tantrum, nothing romantic at all, and I made it up — it's not in the Oxford Dictionary yet — to address my being irritated by your constant advising me how to be and what to say. What's the word for that? I complained about this to Dr. Butterfly once when you weren't there. But how was Rousseau romantic?"

"Be real, Nina, you can't put this angstrum in your book. I have advised you time and again that a word not in a dictionary is not a real word."

"Darling, and I agree with you that I'm not real. Because I'm not a word in a dictionary. And I have another excuse for new words. Brought in thanks to immigrants like me. Aren't we emotionally labile foreigners entitled to make up words if we don't find them in the Oxford Dictionary? But Americans take foreign accents as proof that we're dumb or deaf. I'm just one example. After forty years in this country I'm still being asked in a slow, very loud voice, 'And Nina, how do you like it here?' So I tell them quietly but distinctly and slowly that having a foreign accent doesn't mean I have bad hearing. And they say loudly, 'What did you say?' So why shouldn't I make up dumb words since I'm a dumb foreigner? It's a rational conclusion by your irrational wife. So do I sound like irrational Rousseau, darling? But actually rationally speaking — what would happen if Rousseau and Descartes lived in the same century and had been a couple, darling?"

Martin laughs a triplet of hee, hee, hees in his restricted jolly yet very tame manner, through his clenched front teeth, his mouth barely open. "I don't know about their personal lives, but I think Rousseau and Descartes would have had a lot of fun with each other if they'd lived in the same century."

"Darling, like us in this century? After a few whiskeys and after a few joints?"

"I don't know what Descartes drank, Nina, but he definitely excelled in elegant rational thought. And I think I have to turn right very soon. "

"Just like you, darling, excel in elegant rational thought?"

"Like I aspire. He was a rational genius."

"As opposed to Rousseau, who was his irrational opposite, like me. We're an archetypal case of a Drunken Patriarch Scientist versus a Stoned Childish Artist. And of course the Patriarch Scientist always has to be right. So the irrational wife must always be advised and corrected to think correctly." She looks at him, expecting an answer. (Shouldn't he be able to respond while keeping his eyes on the empty street, going only five miles per hour?)

"Stop talking and twisting things, Nina. I have to concentrate on the directions." He slows down, checking Sylvia's address against his map.

"But Rousseau," she asks quietly, after waiting for him to get his bearings, "despite being a man, was more like me? Empathetic, close to nature, to feelings, and to intuitions?"

"More or less, Nina. And stop being so self referential. Rousseau along with more feminine sensibilities was above all also a great thinker."

"I see. So Rousseau, despite being an artist was also a man and above all a great thinker. And I am but an Occupational Therapist gone cuckoo to imagine I am a writer. But of course I am not a great thinker. Right, Marti?"

"Actually Nina, you're misquoting me. I said not *despite* but *along with* being artistic Rousseau was also a great thinker. You, on the other hand, seem to already be writing fiction and assassinating my character by twisting what I say. And anyway, I admitted that Descartes and Rousseau would have been a good fit."

"But, darling, you said they are like us, so if they'd lived in the same century, they would have killed each other in a duel! A Duel of Opposites in the Dusk." She resumes fumbling in her bag.

"Hee, hee, hee, not bad, Nina."

They have entered the wrong gate and must backtrack to the MOONLIT PARADISE gate on the other side of the highway. She is quiet so he can concentrate. They finally arrive at the correct gate and Martin is about to park in front of Sylvia's and Alek's.

He pulls up to the curb. "As a matter of fact, opposition is actually complementary and needed in my opinion, hee, hee, hee." He gives her a little cheek peck.

"Darling, you can't help opposing any opinion except yours. And that's why I start irrational fights about your rightful rationality. And by the way — is it rational to have to be always one hundred per cent right?"

"Hee, hee, hee, I guess it's some type of an adaptive response."

"Adaptive to what, Marti?"

He turns off the engine and actually looks in her eyes in a more direct way than she is accustomed to. "You're the writer, Nina. You figure it out." An uncommon mischievous expression appears in his eyes.

"I asked you first." She returns a quick peck on his cheek. "But characters should speak for themselves so that writers don't have to figure them out, darling."

The houses on this street look the same as the houses in the other gated subdivision. This disturbs her, and again she fiddles with the clasp of her old scuffed up bag.

"But darling, in this somber darkness of opaque moonless catatonic doom suburbia, I'm in need of mood fortification," she says in a languid way.

From her tarnished silver cigarette case came out her special joint and her red mini BIC lighter, her life savers, for when predicted or unpredicted random angst might afflict her. She clicked the lighter. It was still good to go.

N appreciates M as a devoted father/husband but says communication was already lacking early on. M was mostly silent on their first date and she had to fill in gaps. N reports that while they dated she had "several short enjoyable sexual affairs" she did not hide from him. Again she mentions that she married him b/c he was "a stable pillar of support," and she was attracted to him, and she was ready to have children.

I asked M, "How does this make you feel?" He did not answer, saying only that he has no desire to cheat on his wife.

N: "If you tell your partner that you have an affair, you are not cheating." M looked at the floor.

I tried to draw M out, but he was reticent. When he does speak, N often cuts him off.

Overall Impression: A dependent attachment with an inability to express positive emotions, partially due to cultural differences. A classic 20-year marriage midlife crisis where she feels resentful about him not knowing how to be romantic and spontaneous, as opposed to his assessment of – as he states – "her problems." M states that she denies him what he wants – and deserves – about twice a week: oral sex.

She states that she does not provide barter sexual services for his inspired cooking. She needs romantic foreplay.

Difficulties exacerbated by alcohol and marijuana, respectively.

Immediate Plan: Agreement to try to keep daily bickering in the kitchen to when their teenage sons are not at home. Nina to curb her complaining to 15 minutes per week.

Long Term Plan: Encourage to moderate their mutual substance abuse and commit to 10 sessions, as allowed by their provider, including one-on-one sessions. M makes it clear he is not interested in seeing me one-on-one, repeating that N is the one with "the problems."

_____

THE KITCHEN WINDOW

*"But really I am not
a Normal American, darling."*

Dziwny Jest Ten Świat (Strange Is This World)
— Czeslaw Niemen

They sat in the car, facing the panoramic floor to ceiling window to Sylvia and Alek's sumptuous modern kitchen. Stiff looking formally dressed people, maybe a dozen of them ("not any of us" noted Nina) stood around in small groups sipping from oversized stem wine glasses, their lips moving sans expression.

An unlit joint and the red BIC lighter were in Nina's hands. She was waiting for Martin to say that the smoke would make him choke, or for him to start coughing even before she lit up. But he didn't cough and appeared settled in his quiet resignation, as if he actually understood that it was time for her to fortify herself in front of this stifled ambiance window, and against the angst of suburbia's dark gray uniformity illuminated by a harsh neon light.

"Darling, aren't you going to cough to oppose my degenerate habit? Or do you fear that if I don't smoke, my mild dysphoria may turn into a full blown episode in the predictable repertoire of my unpredictability? It's a line I'll put in my book, darling." She smiled provocatively.

"Who coined this line? Dostoyevsky?"

She laughed. "No, I do all my own lines. I, your wife, darling." She didn't light the joint. "So Marti, did you hear me ask if and why you're not going to preemptively oppose my degenerate habit?" (This time she asked in a sweeter way.)

"Actually, Nina, I prefer not to deal with the consequences of your dissatisfaction, so just smoke your joint," he said without looking at her.

She opened the window and lit the joint, waiting for his more robust — in content relative to context — response. She tried again: "But darling, doesn't the stale, cold, and eerie calm of this gated suburbia — and the scene in this kitchen's panoramic theatre window — infuse you with a weird sense of unrest? She moved toward him and looked directly into his eyes. "Well, Marti? What is this gated suburban ambiance doing to *you*, darling?"

He repositioned his thick lensed glasses on his nose and from behind them threw her a disturbed sideways glance. Something on the other side of the street distracted him and his thumb, index, and middle fingers stationed themselves thoughtfully in their ritual position on his neatly trimmed beard.

"Darling, what are you looking at and what are you deeply thinking about? Or are you just worried about me smelling of weed? I have my verbena lavender essential oil on me. It'll mask the smell."

"He took a tentative look toward the window. "Hey, Nina. Just smoke it and don't let the people in the kitchen see you. And don't forget that children live on this street as well . . . and in my opinion . . ."

She interrupted, mockingly imitating him: "And in my opinion, Nina, since you have lived in this country for enough years, you should know that satisfied people who do not rant, rave, and complain can actually coexist peacefully in the suburbs with nice new asphalt streets without holes that ruin your tires. In fact, most Americans *like* nice suburbia, so stop ranting, raving, and complaining, Nina, making excuses about why you need a joint!"

She smiled. "Right, Marti? And the good thing, darling, for you and me, is that I have this medicine for when an expected and specific suburban cement and asphalt angstrum may afflict me. But not to change the subject, look — this kitchen scene really is surreal."

"Don't exaggerate, Nina. What's surreal about normal people in the kitchen?" He sighed with resignation. "But you should know, Nina, that in fact most Americans would like to live in upscale suburbs."

"But, Marti, you know by now that I am not a Normal American. Do I look like these normal looking Americans? By the way, in correct English, can you purposefully employ a double negative when you want to emphasize the absurdity of a concept like expecting me to feel like a Normal American? Would the double negative be wrong or right in some cases, darling?" She fired her red BIC. He gave her his mildly bewildered look as she took the first long puff, expecting him to cough. But he didn't!

She took two deep puffs with smoky exhales, and he didn't cough, and still he didn't cough while she was observing the kitchen scene intently — as if inhaling it with each greedy drag.

"Darling, you're not watching this kitchen scene because you don't like to spy on people. But I feel as if I'm secretly watching a silent stiff American kitchen party film. As if it was staged," she said in a reflective voice.

"Nina, it's not nice to eavesdrop on strangers, and you should not be so obvious." He gave the panoramic window a fleeting, and maybe a bit guilty, inspection. "To me, Nina, it's just a regular good size kitchen window with normal people inside. Just finish your joint."

"Darling, this is a silent film, so I'm not eavesdropping, I'm watching it. But why aren't you coughing yet? For real, Marti! Don't you agree that these people in this sparkling kitchen look like uncomfortable stilted cardboard figures holding the stems of identical oversized wine glasses? And they seem to be quite trapped in polite small talk about the local real estate market and the weather. And football. No one is laughing. Real or surreal? Hey Marti, do you hear me? Marti, these are the decent American looking people. By the way I am sure that they'll leave before the real *prywatka* starts, because I know something about this. They are Sylvia's workers from her fancy jewelry business and they were paid for the cameo appearance to celebrate Sylvia." Demonstratively, Nina took an even deeper drag on her joint.

Martin made his signature three coughing noises (at last!) and said very quietly, "Hey Nina, if you really want to know, I feel like turning the ignition back on and going back home right now." He moved his head to look through the rear windshield.

She said tenderly, "But why, darling?" and put her hand on his thigh. "Darling, cheer up, Lila is coming. And you like her — a true intellectual who knows biotech stuff and politics. Subjects I'm not passionately into. And I bet Lila will be wearing her high heel sandals and will smell of Chanel N°5, which reminds you of Marucella Malbec, who *nota bene* was a much better match for you than I am. Too bad she is married. But her husband would kill you anyway. Do you remember how hot you were for her? No? You forgot? In our red dining room? You were drunk already when you came down from our bedroom and you were naked under my torn silk robe and you opened it to show us (Marucella and I were enjoying her good Malbec) your less than half erect big thing and very quickly you pointed to it and said proudly but delicately, 'Nina, make it hard for Marucella.' And she couldn't believe that you, the serious decent professor, were saying that! So if you're bored, darling, you can get drunk and flirt with Lila and smell her Chanel N°5. And Lila is not married."

"Really, Nina, so you won't mind if I flirt with Lila?" He seemed to receive a sudden jolt of hopeful energy. "Hee, hee, hee, I don't believe you."

"Marti, of course I wouldn't mind. Dr. Butterfly thinks it's a good idea for marital long term prisoners to flirt with others. I would like it. I'm not competitive. And it gives me permission."

"Hee, hee, hee." He laughed less tight lipped than usual. "And since when do you need permission, Nina? But could you just please finish your joint and let's go in. We are already fifteen minutes late."

"You know that I don't rush anything loaded with

pleasure. And by the way, a double permission as opposed to double negative is certainly better, darling." She took two good puffs in a row.

"So, who else will I know besides Lila? Hey, maybe I will flirt with her since you don't mind." He laughed with a bothersome certainty.

"I told you who you'll know. Weren't you listening? And why not try flirting with Gertrude too, darling. I don't think Douglas minds. I think she loves him in her way, because when she's affectionate, she calls him 'my husbie Douggie'."

"Hee hee, with her Polish accent it sounds like doggie."

"Doesn't it? But only when she feels affectionate, of course. But I think she's right to be pissed off when you act like a Patriarch and call women of your age *girls*."

"Nina, do you think Gertrude will be showing her husband off tonight? I really hope poor Douglas will not make an idiot out of himself for her amusement." Martin seemed concerned.

"Martin, Gertrude will definitely showcase her husband's unique talents tonight."

"Sure, Nina. You're right. Why would Gertrude control herself? You Polish women know how to put down your husbands! Anytime, anywhere." He coughed three times (and she was wondering why always three, but never four).

"Hey, Nina, just finish your joint . . . I'm about to choke from the smoke."

"You can wait outside the car, darling. It's not too cold

yet." She inhaled very deeply. "But I agree with you that my entitled, logical genius in proving she's always superior beautiful sister cannot restrain herself from exhibiting her wit. However, do you like my Nina wit? About you. How is my Dostoyevsky style?" She pulled out her Moleskine notebook and read:

The predictability of her husband's past, present, and future ritual of hee, hee, hee's irritated his wife to the bone. He didn't realize that the poetry of romance is in the spontaneity of the present, and not in stinginess of any expression and not in morose fear of the unknown with travel plans only to places he had already been before — places with historical plaques of important wise men . . . That was her future with him.

"Didn't I nail it, darling?" she said, as he opened the car door. "As for the past, darling, isn't the past just a fictionalized, selective, and embellished memory in the hippocampus? "

"If it's not scientifically proven and reported in the science section of *The New York Times* — it's unlikely, but in the case of your family . . . possible." One exasperated cough. "But be real, Nina," he spat out. "Take the example of your mother and your sister, and you — maybe a hundred percent of Polish Jewish women can't stop themselves from complaining — combined with routinely putting down their husbands."

She suddenly felt a most unpleasant acid injection in her esophagus at the level of her solar plexus. But she didn't yell. "Darling, is this a generic or genetic put down by the Patriarch Irish husband?"

"No, Nina. it's a factual statement based on being with you half of my life. But I'm about to choke from the smoke," he said as he stepped outside. "So hurry up, Nina, and please don't make up another story about the kitchen window."

She finished her joint, listening (acid feeling past) to "Strange is this World" as she continued watching the silent movie scene in Sylvia and Alek's kitchen.

Soon, she was standing beside Martin who was leaning against their car. A stump of her roach was at the corner of her mouth.

"Darling, do you want to know who else will be at the party? A Russian Jewish couple, neighbors of Sylvia." She fixed him in her gaze. "Marti, please remove your glasses. I need to check if your eyes are still blue like they were when we met and you began romancing me not just with your unique specimen of a true Irishman, the engorgement of which is proportional to the silkiness of silky panties and stockings you want to feel on me. Remember when I had a red haired pussy and your beard was a truly auburn flame?"

"I hope you don't put the words dick and pussy in your book, Nina," Martin said before obediently removing his eyeglasses and letting her look into his eyes. Then he replaced the glasses on his nose and coughed three times, right on cue. "This weed I smell on you really makes me choke, Nina. And stop putting down the people in the kitchen. What makes you think, Nina, that agreeable American politeness is not okay?"

"But Marti, on the way here you informed me that opposition is necessary for growth of population and of ideas. So, leaving each other alone politely leads to what? To being together in a dreadful silent boredom and loneliness? Not for you, because you're married not just to me but more so to your abstract equations in your head. But I too can be abstractly logical, and actually you do know that I came up with a new unit of measurement, not of tantric but of a transient tantrum of angst attack — remember how I came up with it when after twenty years together you still couldn't distinguish nor recall a place to put small, medium, and large plates in our kitchen, *where we eat every fucking day*? So, darling, I credit you with my expanded definition of angstrum! A marital fighting unit causing a tantrum attack ignited — or inspired — by you, and there isn't yet a word in any dictionary describing this condition and severity in response to no response, or to you not being able to distinguish between small, medium, and large plates among other gadgets we both use in our kitchen. That would piss off any kitchen or marriage partner! And I know your opinion already — it's somewhere in the kitchen. And if it's not in any dictionary, neither the word nor the human condition exists. And why then talk about things that in your opinion do not exist? But in my opinion, if the hero of the story is naïve, or pretending to be a naïve foreigner, he or she is entitled to make up a word and pretend it's a foreigner's mistake." She was about to light the stump of her roach.

"Don't burn yourself Nina. So what's next? So one unit of angstrum per one joint? So you plan to have two of those one angstrum units?"

"Yes darling. And I will put my angstrum unit in the Oxford Dictionary!"

She lights her minuscule one or at most two puff roach, takes a prolonged toke, and looks straight into his eyes behind his thick lenses in their no frills stern rectangular frame. "And darling, if you believe in the growth of ideas and in the growth of your member properly attended to by your proper wife, why not contribute to the Oxford Dictionary together? Original words are often created by foreigners, and maybe combined with Irish concepts they might one day be in the Oxford Dictionary, darling."

"Hee, hee, hee, Nina, I never said you have no imagination. Even your mother and father said you didn't have enough brain power for real life but that you had a great imagination." Martin gives her a little marital peck, and fingers the car key in his pocket. "But again, in my opinion no made up words should be put in a book, because that confuses the reader. And if you write in English you should obey the rules."

"And what if a stoned foreign writer writes whatever she wants, darling?"

He takes a tentative glance at the scene in the window.

"Hee, hee, hee, since you are a stoned writer now, can you tell me who are these early arriving cameo performers?"

"I already told you but maybe you didn't listen." She is about to put the expired roach away in her cigarette case, for the way back (another puff may be left). "But Marti, what I'm about to tell you again is not verified, because I only have my information through gossip. So, do you still want to hear it, darling? Without a rationally objective proof?"

"Don't bother, in that case," he sniffs. "Anyway, Nina, put that roach away. We are more than twenty minutes late. We should go in."

"But Marti" — now she is exasperated — "you asked me a question, so listen. The workers from Queen Sylvia's diamond business are local Americans. And according to gossip they were invited to admire the splendor of their Diamond Queen and to witness the charm of her husband to be, Smart Alek, a much better match than Sylvia's first American husband. Gertrude knows more about these workers. Apparently they may have been *ordered* by their Queen to come before the properly invited guests to make a lively crowd impression. But I've already told you that to me they look like polite talking stiff cardboard figures sipping wine from the bottom of huge wine glasses. As if they were *hired* to perform on the kitchen stage — a one hour performance. Gertrude overheard something when Sylvia was talking on her brand new flip phone. But I'm not going to tell you. You're not into gossip, right?"

"Hey Nina, I've already told you that the stuff you

smoke makes you see things weirdly. Are you sure you're not cooking up another pure fiction story? Seriously, I don't believe that Sylvia would hire and order her employees to stand in the kitchen and sip from oversized glasses of wine and look bored. Really, Nina, it's all in your head." A freaked out expression escapes from behind his rectangle rimmed eyeglasses.

"No, I'm not cooking anything up in or out of my head, I only report what I've heard from Gertrude and what I see in this full screen cinematic window. But, darling, how is it that you suddenly know what's in my head? You've said many times that you don't want to go into my head, nor to know what's in it, and you don't want me to go into your head either, which however is the basis of relating apparently, and the main contributor to sex happening by the way. So why are you making up what's happening in my head right now? Are you writing fiction, darling!? Or maybe it is you who does not want to accept this reality? Maybe it's not just a genetic Irish fear of unknown sights, tastes, and smells, maybe it's the suburban small talk that you fear as much as I do. But what is it that makes you not see what I see? Out of or in my head? But thanks for noticing that I can be creatively logical when I'm stoned." She puts the expired roach away.

"Nina, hee, hee, hee, that's what you think! But let's be quiet now and let's make sure you closed the cigarette case properly. I don't want the guests to smell it on you. And you are right. I'd rather not know what's in your head. Too fuzzy for me."

"In my head you'd find many knots in an unending spool of unpredictability. But I'm not asking you to untie my knots. This work belongs to me. But your lack of interest in what's in my romantic head via my eyes is a primary reason why I don't suck your specimen. Lovers pry into each other's eyes before they fuck — a communication we lack, and the result is *nothing interesting* to feed my pages with, so the readers for sure will get bored with neurotic Jewish Polish female monologues competing with what's there in your Mathematical Head — the thing that festers and reigns night and day: an Almost Perfect Equation, your true and Constant Companion I do not understand. Not only your students don't, but everyone else, I mean no one else, except only six professors in the whole world understand. So don't repeat yourself with your ranting complaint that I deny your beautiful *member* a Genius Blow Job after you cook me a good dinner. Don't pretend you do not remember, darling, what Dr. Butterfly taught us, or tried to! About how to spice up a routine, in our case your routine that doesn't go into each other's heads nor eyes, and about how to accept a fucking feckless marriage!" She glares at him with her eyes wide open. He returns the glare with a clearly disturbed uncomprehending expression.

She continues: "I see, darling. Of course you don't get it. I see fear in your eyes. And you must be worrying that I didn't properly extinguish my joint ashes in the car ashtray. And that our car will catch on fire from it. A perfect example of your engorged paranoia! Don't you remember

Dr. Butterfly's advice, darling?"

"What is it, Nina, you're going to blame me for now?"

"Marti, it seems I have to repeat what you've already heard. Without yelling, so neighbors don't hear. She advised us that direct Eye Contact from an intimate distance — which is six inches — comes first, at least for a duration of a few minutes, before the six to eight or maybe ten inch stubborn Irish bull specimen comes in thirty seconds in the mouth! Prolonged eye contact comes first! Darling, *that's* what she said."

"Since you're a Genius of Blow Jobs, Nina, I'm sure you must like it and I'm also sure all your ex-boyfriends liked it too. Oh, and," he said quickly, "Lila really should not drive alone late at night, it's dangerous for a woman. She needs a man."

"Most women need a man who fucks their deep insides — not just the oral cavity in and out — and a man who talks. But most men need a woman to be quiet, to be quiet and suck their dick, right Marti? And I need a joint, my pacifier, to shut me up. Peace." She pulls out her next to nothing roach from her cigarette case and puts it between her lips momentarily, then takes it out: "I wish the roach was longer, darling . . . No hee, hee, hee? And by the way Marti, I offered Lila to catch a ride with us but she said she wanted to drive. So she does not need a man driver."

She sticks the roach back in her mouth and takes it out again: "Hey, darling, and what if there is a man at this party to flirt with — for Lila, and maybe for me too? *You* do not flirt with me. So am I not entitled to flirt? You don't dance with me, so I learned to dance alone. I know you think you're entitled to a Genius Blow Job on demand, simply because we're married. So am I not entitled to what you have no interest in? For example, a romantic fig drizzled with honey date? I also want to lick honey thoughts from each other's fingers. It's how Sylvia and Smart Alek fell in love." She returns her stump of a roach (she can't part with it!) back into her tarnished cigarette case and snaps the magnetic clasp of her bag.

He takes a step toward her. "Nina, actually I'm romantic." He kisses her on the cheek.

"An Irish kind of romantic, darling?"

"Yes, I make Irish stew for you. I bring you breakfast in bed every morning. Doesn't that count? But hurry up and make sure you put that roach away correctly. We're close to the car, so I don't want it to catch on fire. Did you close the lid of that cigarette case properly?"

"Darling, this *is* a prime example of excessive paranoia. I think I'll put it in my a la Dostoyevsky description of you!"

"Nina, stop changing the subject and pretending that Sylvia and whatever guests will not smell marijuana on you. They will."

"Reality of a Descartes Rational Man, darling? Or a fictional worry example?" she says, angrily opening and closing and opening again the magnetic clasp of her handbag, with her cigarette case (his gift) and the infinitesimal stump of a roach in it. She pulls the roach out and holds it a few inches away from his nose. "Marti," she says daringly, "how will this double positively dead roach catch the car on fire?"

As she questions his reality, her eyes assume a theatrical expression of wonder, and to add to it she combs her fingers through her hair, admiring the feel of it — having washed her hair on the occasion of this special party with his good shampoo, so for a change it's not at all knotted. She fluffed it too, to make sure it's in the correct disorder of curls (that she would never brush with a comb for fear it would straighten them out).

"Marti, is my messy hair going to embarrass you too? And I happen to like the mixed smells of marijuana, verbena, and lavender!"

"Hee, hee, hee." His stifled laughter is emitted through his partially clenched teeth. "Nothing embarrasses you, Nina. That's why your friends like you."

A long ten seconds of silence.

"Darling, but before we go in, don't you think, Marti, that this panoramic window kitchen scene does seem surreal?"

"No, I've already told you it looks normal to me. Nina, when will you realize that your perception is altered with that stuff?"

"Describe normal to me, darling."

"I see nothing abnormal, Nina. It's in your head."

"No — it's in the window. Take a focused twenty second look at these cardboard figures pretending to be engaged in small talk. Like on a Real Suburban American Kitchen Party movie set."

"You're projecting, Nina. But you know who really feels out of place here? Me. Does it ever count to you how I feel?" A quiet worry has entered his voice.

"Marti, why are you afraid of unpolished Polish ha ha ha's?"

"Nina, I wish you would realize how some of us feel when you all get together. We don't understand Polish and feel like strangers."

"Like foreigners in the country they don't belong to? But Marti, you won't be alone feeling like a stranger. Douggie will be there. Besides, why worry? You're never alone — you've got a partner permanently residing in your head. A lightheaded buzzed up skeleton of an idea budding from its roots in your brain. And of course you have a Joycean slip of paper for when inspiration hits! An unpredictable event is exhilarating! Darling, do you realize that we've always actually had a threesome: You, the Equation, and Me. Don't you have a slip of paper in your pocket? In Sylvia's kitchen, after the normal Americans leave, if the two of you are bored, you can let the skeleton escape and note an enhanced idea on the Joycean slip. You have your No. 2 pencil sharpened in your pocket, don't you?"

"Hopefully, they have some whiskey. Hee, hee, hee." (Martin's laugh has a jovial hint!)

"By the way, Marti, I've never heard you laugh robustly with a true zest . . . even after enough whiskey. Is it a genetic

Irish modesty? Propriety?"

"Whatever you say, Nina. One thing I know is that whiskey helps for sure."

"Enough of it in fact might help annihilate your Irish propriety," she says sweetly and gives her husband a brief marital peck on the cheek. "Remember how you ordered me to make you hard for Marucella Malbec? Where was your modesty hiding then?"

"It's getting cold Nina. Let's go in. But do you really think they'll have whiskey? And when do you expect the Zuperofska hoopla to start?"

"Don't you have a flask in the pocket of your jacket? You'll need it. The *Żubrówka* frenzy will not start properly till midnight, so could you please, darling, try not to drag me out of there till the sun comes up? Okay? Darling? You said you're happy when I'm happy, right?"

No response. He watches her (irritated by his no response) opening and closing the magnetic clasp of her scuffed up Coach bag. He coughs three times. "Nina, in my opinion you've really had enough of that stuff. In fact, you still smell of the smoke." (He clears his throat three times.)

"Then, darling, just let me go back to the car for a little while for the smoke to wear off. I'll watch the surreal kitchen scene some more. And I will listen to "Strange is this World." And you can wait for me in your Rodin Thinking Serious Man pose. But zip up your jacket darling, so you don't freeze your ass off."

She exits a few minutes later, warm in her ankle

length soft purple wool coat from Zara in Paris (which she'd altered and ripped a bit, to Martin's chagrin about 'homeless person style'), and in her black shawl, which she knitted for herself from soft Alpaca wool. Martin is relaxed, leaning against the driver's side door in the same focused static Wise Man Standing Rodin pose. Except his fingers are stroking his beard now and his head is slightly bowed, his eyes downward on the newly resurfaced street, as if the answer resides there, on the blackboard of the black asphalt.

She stands on tiptoe in her black comfortable medium heel BeautiFeel shoes with one ankle strap held by a safety pin, and gazes into his eyes.

"Darling, any Eureka hints on this perfect blackboard of fresh suburban asphalt illuminated by suburban neon glare?"

He glances at her lips. "Just getting my ideas organized. You look good, by the way. Did you put on more of your nice red lipstick?"

"Yes, I did put on my lips my nice red lipstick and I am sufficiently fortified to enter the Palace of Queen Sylvia and Smart Alek." She recites this as if it were a line from a play. "Are you and your Grand Equation ready yet, darling? Hopefully, there is whiskey and you'll be fine."

Through the kitchen window, the tableau is unchanged.

"My equation," he says excitedly, out of the blue, "is the same equation I've been trying to solve for days. No one has ever solved it, Nina. I would be the first. I have to write it down before I forget." He strokes his beard restlessly.

She is still on tiptoe looking into his eyes. "But isn't the skeleton of your idea already embedded in your elongated genius heavy head? It's why you can't lighten up, darling."

She takes one step back and looks at him. "Did you know, Marti, that despite this nauseating pukey bright neon light in this American gated suburb, your beard is still Irish auburn, and very handsomely peppered with silver strands? It looks distinguished, just like you are, darling." She opens her lips in anticipation and he readily delivers a warm marital plus kiss. "That's all, darling?" she pouts, opening her lips for more.

He moves a step away from her. "Nina, we are in a public space. And someone in the kitchen may see us, and you still smell of that illegal stuff."

"Of course you don't want to be embarrassed, darling!"

"That's right," he whispers and cautiously looks out onto the empty street. "And we already know that *nothing* embarrasses you, Nina."

"And everything embarrasses you except your dick, Marti!!"

At the door to Sylvia's house a somber silence sat between them. Thinking that the stern look on his face was unsexy, she placed a hesitant peck on his lips to lighten his mood, but he anxiously turned away.

"Darling, so you think mature kissing married people on an empty suburban street at night are indecent?" she said, dripping resentment.

From her handbag she extracted her compact mirror, inspected herself, and refreshed her lips with Merlot Wine lipstick.

"I'm ready to make my Grand Stoned Entrance," she said and fixed her husband in a rebellious gaze.

DR. ANGELA BUTTERFLY, MSW, PH.D.
INTIMACY SPECIALIST
(2nd Session)
6/1/05

Before I'd even settled into my seat, N started in, in an animated tone. M can't understand why she gets so frustrated when she can't find her only spatula or knife or lemon zester in the kitchen. She quotes M: "Obviously they didn't leave the kitchen."

M held his head in his hands. Then changed the subject, saying quietly that she still moves furniture and rugs around almost every night, keeping him awake. He then laughed a restricted shy multi-part giggle, before reverting to looking at the floor.

N complained that M studiously ignores their lack of communication, that he doesn't like to acknowledge things that are painful. He was brought up in County Kilkenny not to dwell on pain, and definitely not to talk about it. Not to express his feelings, for fear of being shamed. M responded that N can't keep her feelings to herself, and doesn't even try, and that's what he likes about her, except not when she yells.

M then said, "It's almost five. I need a drink." N responded that he has at least four drinks per evening (contradicting his self-reporting), which he did not deny, saying his intake is "normal for an Irishman." (A previous therapist told N that a drunk man is not present. At that time she'd been thinking about leaving M.)

When I asked M to define intimacy, he laughed a non-emotive giggle and said, "Intimacy is a thing girlfriends are good at, therefore they should go to a café and talk to each other about it."

N dramatically lost her cool and, to M's quiet outrage, took out a half-smoked joint and put it between her lips. I calmly informed her it is illegal, medical prescription notwithstanding, and while I do not personally disapprove, I would end our work together immediately the next time she did so. N had tears in her eyes.

Then she loudly informed her husband that his unwillingness to talk is precisely the simple reason why she is not interested in sucking his penis. (She used the word "dick.") I was taken aback by the strength of her resentment. Our time was up.

———————

IN THE FOYER

"Okay. Okay. I'll make a fool out of myself, the fool I already am."

Distant Non-Invasive Generic Elevator Muzak (wafting from the living room)

Radiant Sylvia, in a cream silk dress voluptuously wrapping her body, opens the door. Warm smiles and kisses on the mouth, at first careful, so as to not disturb lipstick, then on both cheeks in a more effusive Polish style. Nina inhales Sylvia's intoxicating perfume near her abundant décolletage adorned with a single sparkling diamond of impressive size and quality. Surrounded by resplendent black mascara enhanced eyelashes, Sylvia's eyes emanate a deep green mist of definite happiness . . . and the dreamy satisfaction of a woman who has everything, Nina writes in her head. Martin gets a brief hug and no kisses.

Sylvia's husband to be is not at the door but his booming voice can be heard from the kitchen. Regal Sylvia graciously welcomes arriving guests, and stoned and mesmerized by Sylvia's eyes, Nina continues taking mildly bewildered steps farther into the foyer, where she admires the glowing amber lights and feels a tiny bit off balance in her medium high heel BeautiFeel scuffed up black flamenco style dancing shoes, hoping the right ankle strap held by one safety pin will not break.

The walls of the foyer are lined with cherrywood framed raw silk antique gold crepe panels, and the center point is an opulent oil landscape of autumnal Northern California hills in vibrant sunset hues of unreal quality. Next to it is an exquisite black marble mantelpiece with an intricate natural gem inlay, and Nina, relieved that there is a place to stop, stands at the mantelpiece, admires the painting and feels slightly less out of place.

Her fingertips caress the marble and feel its cool smoothness as she observes the scene at the door and writes it all in her head: Smart Alek appears, kisses Sylvia, and they await new arrivals. Alek is handsome and distinguished, and predisposed to boisterous joviality. He towers over everyone, even Martin (who also looks handsome in his slightly worn Irish tweed jacket over his usual blue and white checkered shirt with no tie). Alek wears a crisp freshly pressed blue striped shirt with a bold multicolored tie. If the guests speak Polish, he will make silly jokes in their native tongue, the crassness of which will vary with the guest. Intermittent laughter will follow, somewhat forced from the polite guests. Nina ruminates, while her fingertips continue to delicately tap the marble.

Lila arrives. She approaches me at the Italian marble masterpiece in light energetic steps. Her eyes are clear blue, wide open. An expression of warmth all over her face welcomes me. We kiss each other with affection (but carefully, so as to not smear our lipstick) on the mouth, then on both cheeks, then Lila looks into my eyes and in a hushed voice says, "But Nina, why do you look so solemn?"

I push her hair away from above her ear and whisper, "And you look solemn too, Lila. Why?"

We continue communicating into each other's ears, while Lila touches the marble with her fingertips. "Brrrr, so cold." Her teeth nearly chatter. "Nina, do you think the warm glow here is real or is it fictional? You should know — you're a writer. Because I'm really cold. Brrrr."

"The glow isn't really warm and this marble is really cold . . . yet it is really soothing to touch . . . "

"Hey Nina, but couldn't you please not say nasty things about Sylvia tonight? She has very good taste. But I really could use a fur muffler, brrrr."

"Sylvia's taste needs to show off how special she is. But don't tell her I said that. And don't tell her the ambiance here is glowing with a surreal cold glow which doesn't warm you or me."

"I didn't ask you about the ambiance sur-reality, Nina." Lila displays her annoyance in my ear. "And you shouldn't talk like that about Sylvia if you care about other people's feelings. But, yes, I really feel cold too."

"It's a paradox of an entitled life, isn't it? An expensive cold . . . a chilled expensive cold in fact." My whisper has an air of mystery.

"Stop it Nina, be loyal to your friends!" Lila's anger is not in control and she moves her ear away from my mouth. Her angry eyes meeting mine, she says very quietly but distinctly, "But what kind of paradox do you have in mind?"

"A fancy expensive cold . . . a stoned paradox — too fuzzy to explain."

"Hmmm." Lila's eyes are trusting. She places one very cold hand on top of mine and the other on the cold marble.

And together we watch the scene at the door.

A quiet prolonged reflecting "hmmm" escapes from Lila's mouth and she whispers, "But Nina, do you know anything about what's up in the kitchen? I went there to get a drink of water. The people there don't speak Polish and look serious."

"A surreal stiff still from a silent film scene, right? But Martin thought that the weed made me hallucinate."

"Nina, just skip your hallucination and tell me what you know. But please don't whisper so loud."

"These are workers from Sylvia's office, here to stay for one hour. I think she hired them!"

Lila's eyes open in disbelief, and her cold fingertips with red lacquer on her prettily shaped nails, which sympathetically touch the back of my hand, are suddenly removed. "Nina, please stop gossiping. Nothing good comes out of it."

I put my hand back on top of hers. "But let me warm your hand, you're shaking. Don't you think this mantelpiece would be a warm place if instead of marble there was smooth warm rich wood? But maybe bourgeois taste is supposed to be cold elegance. Like Gertrude's."

Lila's blue eyes with their long black eyelashes are displeased. "Nina, this is a very rare natural Italian marble and I've already told you, don't put down Sylvia. She earned it. Are you jealous or what?" Her whisper is curt. "But all right, I agree Nina, the marble is too cold for my fingers," she ends in her quietly reflective manner.

We continue whispering. Our cheeks almost touch, and our fingers stroke the cool marble in joint choreography. We watch the front door, where in a restrained manner the normally ebullient Alek welcomes a young couple in proper sounding English. Sylvia stands slightly to the side, smiling with pleasant slightly superior politeness.

"But actually this glow is freezing," Lila says and puts both cold hands between my palms.

Gertrude appears at the door and suddenly Lila removes her warmed hands from my palms just as I whisper very close to Lila's ear: "Gertrude — in her full splendor festive iridescent look at me stylish retro and on sale in the charity shop royal blue metallic fabric jacket!"

Sylvia and Gertrude exchange animated, but at the same time cautious, kisses on the mouth and on both cheeks (careful not to disturb the lipstick) and immediately start with a few — a routine to them — couture admiring comments in excited Polish. Gertrude smiles. Her smile is a mix of admiration edged with not entirely camouflaged hints of jealousy. She bends down to examine the freshwater pearl beaded lace hem of Sylvia's cream silk dress.

"Watch what happens next, Lila," I whisper. Lila moves her ear away and her blue eyes open wider.

"Just watch, Lila, Gertrude will be up and down examining the shimmering silk of Sylvia's very expensive designer dress on Sylvia's voluptuous body," I whisper with an air of definite prophecy.

Douglas stands behind his wife, watching her perform

a few more focused down and up touch feel assessments of Sylvia's dress, which Sylvia is clearly enjoying. Now Gertrude seems ready to focus on Sylvia's neck — where the spectacular single diamond, as if in sync with the more than happy self adoring misty satisfaction sparkle in Sylvia's eyes, and with her self satisfied smile, is making a proud and bright glamor statement. Gertrude's smile has now become a three part mixture: dubious admiration plus a pinch of jealousy plus an added pinch of indignation.

Douglas, slim and muscular, compact and handsome in a stylish steel gray cashmere sweater (chosen for him by his wife), is wired with energy, as if ready to burst; static for now, he is by the door with an uncertain polite and slightly amused as if unsure of itself smile fixed on his delicately boned youthful face, his beard fashionably trimmed and shaped by Gertrude. (He is always stylishly dressed by his wife, who buys good quality clothes for herself and him and their two sons at department store sales and upscale secondhand shops.)

After Sylvia has looked Gertrude up and down without seeming overly impressed, and they are finished with the mutual inspection, Douglas's pent up energy springs into action, wholeheartedly — if not a bit over enthusiastically, probably out of nervousness about the right thing to do. He gallantly sidles up to Sylvia and kisses her on the mouth and on each cheek (Polish style) and I report it all in my head till I am interrupted.

"You know what, Nina? I wish we were as energetic and

good natured as Douglas is," Lila comments quietly.

"But according to Gertrude there are problems. Douggie suffers from an irritating variant of Generic Male Condition — which requires a woman's supervision or nothing ever gets done right," I murmur and Lila covers her mouth to muffle her giggles, giving me an opening to go on. "But Douggie really tries. Hey, look at his attempt at expression, not exactly confused, but as if he doesn't know what it should express. On the bewilderment scale: 90 out of 100. But notice, that at the moment both of Douggie's eyes are open for a change! It means that he is actively awake now, but later you'll see that he will have only one eye half open while the other one will be resting fully closed. According to Gertrude, in an emergency Douggie can develop a third eye." (I say all this without stopping for a breath, to prevent Lila from interrupting me.)

"Stop talking, Nina. Poor Douglas, he has a hard time staying awake in the evening," Lila sighs.

"Hey, Lila, are your hands getting warmer yet? But let me tell you what I think. I think he'll one day outsmart Gertrude . . ."

"How? What do you have in mind?" Her whisper is full of curiosity.

"Did you notice that he almost always has at least one of his eyes half open to keep track of things so that he doesn't annoy Gertrude more than he already does? Each eye, one at a time, has a function of a guard. Like in some ducks and geese, one hemisphere sleeps and the other is awake with an eye open on guard for possible danger when they fly. I read it in *National Geographic*."

"Oh stop it, Nina! That's enough, I already told you I don't want to know any more such details!" Lila warns sternly in my ear.

Suddenly, a not quite cautious grimace appears to be trying to settle into place on Douglas's face. "Lila, watch how Douggie is trying to figure out an appropriate expression to plaster on his face for the occasion."

"I see that. You're right Nina, he does seem to be not sure what he is supposed to look like."

As if trying to look jolly, but not knowing what jolly is, not quite a smile and not quite a pleasant grimace is stuck on Douggie's face. Just then, Smart Alek (a bit restrained till now near the door), towering more than a head above Douggie, approaches him with a loud gregarious guffaw, and yells, "Good to see you Douglas!" He jovially slaps Douggie's shoulder. Douggie's nimble compact stature responds, slumping significantly on the side of the slapped shoulder. But he recovers quickly, and a sheepish half smile, half grimace, appears as if it has been stuck by someone else on his face.

Smart Alek's deep bass voice is booming: "Dear Douglas, I will tell you a joke in English with a few Polish lines. Unfortunately for you and all the other spousal foreigners here who don't speak our language, we have very specific idioms in Polish which are impossible to translate into English and thus inadvertently are lost on some of us." Smart Alek ends his short exuberant lecture and looks around laughing with an expansive gusto. (At parties he always speaks in a joking manner and laughs sans restraint. His eyes also laugh. Everyone likes Smart Alek.)

"Hey Lila, do you think Doctor Alek makes his silly Polish jokes when he has sex with Sylvia?"

"Stop it, Nina!!!"

Smart Alek continues his up tempo speech: "And it is especially sad for some of our foreign spouses who will never quite get our sophisticated idioms, and our sophisticated wives, and our sometimes idiotic lines." He ends with more gregarious laughter.

Martin, who has been hiding in plain sight in his cautious ready to flee position, is on the opposite end of the foyer not far from the door. Upon spotting him, Smart Alek bounds over and lights up in a joy of great surprise (or joy for the opportunity to make fun of Martin): "But Oi Vei!" Alek bursts out. Martin has a guarded expression, and just in case takes an instinctive getaway step back from Smart Alek's big palm, which is readying itself to slap his shoulder. "Look, there is our Martin!!! He is a fine smart chap professor. *He* does not mind the untranslatable idioms. The proof is that he is with his dear wife Nina for how many years?" Alek extends his arm to shake Martin's hand, and with a closed-lipped faint smile Martin shakes hands without any further retreat and laughs, hee, hee, hee under his nose.

"See Lila? Dr. Alek diagnosed me. I'm Nina, an

untranslatable idiom! And Martin puts up with me!"

"Hey Nina," Lila whispers, "your Martin is quite handsome in his classic Irish tweed coat. And the blue and white checkerboard shirt looks good on him too. You should be aware that you've got a special man. A man who takes care of you — and he does have a strong body. Does he exercise a lot?"

"Lila, he has never been to a gym in his life. He was born a farmer and is naturally strong without exercising. He only walks from the parking lot to his university office, and in the morning he also exercises when he runs up and downstairs from the kitchen to our bedroom with coffee, toast, cheese, and banana for our breakfast in bed with the boys and my black cat daughter. On the other hand, Martin constantly exercises his brain in which an Elegant Equation to be perfected is in permanent residence."

"You don't realize what a treasure you have, Nina, you really shouldn't complain."

Gertrude bends down yet again to more specifically assess the hem of Sylvia's cream silk dress. The door to the house is closed now; it's getting cold. Alek suddenly becomes all gallant, showering effusive attention to Sylvia and Gertrude.

"But ladies and gentlemen, here is our Gertrude — Douglas's charming wife, not yet released by Sylvia, my charming wife to be!" Alek hugs Gertrude with affection, all the while laughing even more frantically.

"Smart Alek knows how to be happy," Lila whispers.

"Maybe the happy ones can teach us how," I quietly say and continue a report of here and now in my head: Smart and happy Alek is kissing my beautiful sister Gertrude on both cheeks and on the mouth, making loud yum noises of delight. Gertrude is accepting this display with a partially disguised superior annoyed kindly tolerant look in her eyes indicating that out of politeness she is forced to put up with Smart Alek's exaggerated fits of mock affection. Quickly enough, Gertrude disengages herself.

A young English speaking couple is welcomed at the door by the host and hostess in a markedly reserved English accented manner. They linger nearby and witness more of Alek's jovial and crass expletives in Polish. There are some laughs. The couple seems shocked or lost and proceeds into the foyer. They smile when they see me and Lila, and before going further they stop near us to take in the oversized landscape of autumn hills bathed in amber light.

"Hey, Nina, Gertrude as usual looks gorgeous." Lila moves her head closer to my ear.

Gertrude doesn't see us yet. I'm watching my older sister (with jealousy, viscerally felt). Why can't I take care of myself like she does, and discipline myself to exercise instead of rolling and smoking joints? Would the skin on my face and neck be as spotless and wrinkle free as hers? Would I have no sagging arms and no unshapely chin?

"I agree, Lila. Gertrude is elegant in whatever she wears. Why weren't we born naturally elegant and athletic like Gertrude?"

"Like what? Why? What did you say?" Lila seems not to hear.

"Gertrude is always slim and has a flat stomach and watches what she eats, and exercises and works a lot, and makes a lot of money though she hates her job, and I'm jealous of her flat stomach and that she looks younger than me, but I don't care about the more money than me she makes. And I prefer my own eyes. Hers are always in a suspiciously cynical mode. I trust and like my eyes. And your blue eyes, Lila, believe me, they're really striking with your lovely long lashes. Your eyes are full of curiosity . . . And positivity. Opposite to Gertrude's. Did you ever see her look at me with pure disdain? I think it's because she thinks I'm lazy, undisciplined, and too fat. She even looks down at our cat because her stomach sags when she walks." And I say louder (close but not into Lila's ear): "But I wish I knew how to make myself motivated to exercise and be disciplined like Gertrude."

"Nina, we shouldn't be focusing on what we don't have. You and Gertrude are attractive in different ways. It's true that Gertrude is always tastefully dressed, but you could change your black only style if you wanted to. And I do not understand why you insist on a ripped dress, for example? Try colors! At least a scarf."

"But I like tastefully ripped black. I'm a punk."

Lila stops me from talking into her ear and points to Gertrude with her eyes. Gertrude is definitely done with adoring Sylvia and approaches Douggie, who at this point has a more confused and even more shy expression on his face, as if he doesn't know what it should express. Gertrude places her hand inside his cashmere sweater and pets his wrist as if to reassure him.

Suddenly, Gertrude sees Lila and me at the marble mantelpiece. An animated smile of recognition spreads all over her face. She strides toward us in long confident steps accompanied by heel clicks of her in fashion pointed black patent leather boots with dramatic silver clasps (most likely from a big sale in an upscale consignment store in her neighborhood).

Of course a ritual of Polish style kisses on cheeks and mouths (or is it mouth first and then cheeks?) follows, warmly with Lila and more restrained and cold between us, the sisters. Next, Lila is admiring Gertrude's iridescent classy royal blue jacket, while I ponder more on the subject of my jealousy of my beautiful and brainy sister. Do I feel envious right now? I ask myself. I don't like Gertrude's iridescent jacket — it's stiff and loud. Around Gertrude's smooth wrinkle free neck is a necklace that features a disproportionately large piece of amber the size and shape of a medium large egg. It hangs on a heavy silver loop. Gertrude's taste is not to my taste.

Lila is pawing the metallic silver threads in the fabric of Gertrude's vintage royal blue jacket in perfect condition, and Gertrude is visibly pleased with Lila's attention and pretty much ignores me.

Finally, Gertrude is ready to acknowledge my presence

with a specially reserved for me — her younger sister — look. A look stingy of positive emotion, and just in case, somewhat critical and suspicious.

"So, Nina, Lila, do you two have any observations about this party so far?" Gertrude inquires discreetly.

"Gertrude, but don't you have something to tell us first?" I say controlling my provocative self.

Lila perks up. "Gertrude, you must feel this marble, how smooth it is. And we should stop gossiping."

Gertrude looks at Lila and briefly touches the marble. "It is very tasteful."

"I agree with you, Gertrude, though I prefer the warm feel of wood," Lila says. "And I'm still freezing, brrrr. I definitely need a Polish muffler for my hands."

"Hmmm." Gertrude touches the marble again. "I never had a muffler. In my opinion this mantelpiece is stately and elegant, and I'm sure quite expensive. Sylvia likes expensive things," she says with conviction.

"By the way Gertrude, you know better than me, what's with the strange kitchen guests?" I say quietly, while Lila keeps tabs on the people at the door. "Lila wanted to know . . . but she doesn't like gossip."

"Well, why don't you two give me your observations first?" Gertrude shoots me a blank look.

"But we asked you first," Lila livens up, and Gertrude's eyes are getting more suspicious.

Gertrude looks at both of us, shrugs her exquisite shoulders, and her eyes shift to the tips of her pointed boots with big silver clasps. "Ouch, I think my boots are slightly scratched. Can you see the scratch on them, Nina?"

I look down to examine the spot on my sister's pointed shining leather boot with the silver clasp. The spot is tiny, hardly a scratch at all. "Gertrude, I don't think anyone would notice."

"Nina has a weird theory about the kitchen guests," Lila says slowly while looking at me.

"So do you have any accurate information, Gertrude?" I question with an air of innocence.

"Well, actually, I was wondering what do you two think?" Gertrude continues to evade my question. Her words have a mildly condescending tint, and the usual hue of mistrust is back in her green with specks catty eyes.

"Let's skip the gossip, let's be positive," Lila offers. "Let's admire Sylvia for the skills she has instead."

"The skills we *don't* have? I agree, we don't," I throw in.

"What do you mean? What great skill don't *we* have? And can you speak for yourself?" Gertrude's curiosity has a bit of outrage, I note, and do not skip a beat:

"For example, Sylvia succeeded in business and in new happy love. Did we?"

"Nina, are you talking about Sylvia's good luck in being her own boss?" Gertrude gifts me with her usual somewhat camouflaged dose of disdain.

"Not just good luck. I admire her energy and optimism," Lila says.

"She is lucky to be with someone who speaks and jokes

in the same language, so there is no need to translate the jokes which cannot be translated!" I contribute.

"It's true — none of these happened to us," Lila says.

"But Gertrude, isn't it lucky to be with someone that understands jokes in Polish?" I repeat and wait for my sister to agree with something I say.

"I'd rather not speak Polish," Gertrude retorts flatly. "I just teach my husbie a few practical idioms. But Nina, why are you so stuck on Polish sentimental pseudo-philosophical slogans? In my opinion you can do better than that. And actually I was wondering if you are going to make an official declaration tonight that you're a writer of the moment? I'm really hoping that you will finish something and publish it finally." Gertrude has thrown down the gauntlet, challenging me with her normal dose of spite (which painfully reminds me of our father and mother and gives me a sinking feeling in my gut).

"Actually, Gertrude, I write for fictional pleasure. But the surreal kitchen window, with stiff but normal according to Martin, American looking people . . . I just wanted to get it right so I can put it in my book. That's why I'm asking you about it. So I get it right."

"Oh Nina, but I thought you wanted to know how is it that when Sylvia decides to be happy, she makes it happen, no matter what it takes and some of us are not capable of doing that. Isn't that the theme of your unpublished book, Nina?" Gertrude says (with a note of mocking she keeps in constant reserve for me).

"Oh please, Nina, Gertrude, please don't fight." Lila is quietly begging. "But I do want to learn what Sylvia knows — what it takes to be happy." Lila looks very thoughtful.

Martin appears at the mantelpiece. "Hee hee hee. And I hope I can learn it too." He kisses Lila and Gertrude on both cheeks, and places an affectionate peck on my lips. Then, as if on automatic, he proceeds (unasked) to help me take my coat off with its uneven slightly ripped and jagged hem line, the one he says I look like a homeless person in. Then, from my neck he removes my long scarf of soft black alpaca wool, which I recently knitted. "I will put these in the closet, Nina," he says, bestowing a peck on my cheek and walking away. Gertrude's eyes make an unpleasant contact with mine.

"Nina, can't you take off your coat and scarf by yourself?" Gertrude addresses me in a mocking voice.

"Gertrude, the reason why I didn't take my coat off is because I was cold."

Martin is back. "So girls, shall we go into the dining room? I really need a drink." He smiles (lips sealed) and takes my hand without checking if I am ready to go with him or not.

"Hey, Martin, when will you realize that we are not *girls!*" Gertrude says sharply. "Are you and your professor colleagues *boys*?"

I pull my hand free. "You're not my father, Marti, so don't treat me like a child," I protest calmly. Martin ignores my outburst, lets out a hee, hee, hee, and explains to Gertrude that *girls* is just a common American expression of fondness. He puts my hand in his again. Gertrude glares at Martin, shrugs her shoulders, and approaches Douggie near the door.

Gertrude commences to affectionately stroke her husband's chin, or rather the fashionably shaped — by her, to save money — short beard. He does not object. In fact he closes his eyes, his face relaxes, he opens one eye. His face is trying to express calm amusement, maybe. Gertrude moves her hand from his chin to his lower arm and she strokes the inner aspect of his forearm from under the sleeve of his cashmere steel gray sweater (that she got for him on sale at Banana Republic).

Gertrude surveys her audience: "Douggie is shy, but he is actually quite capable and talented," she announces to everyone and no one, and looks at her husband with mock real tenderness. "But don't be shy, husbie, be a good husband and show off your Polish." She looks at her husband in an encouraging way. "He is modest, but the results are promising so far, because he is studying Polish a lot lately." She sounds as if she is praising an obedient child or a dog who deserves a prize. Douggie opens one alert eye and produces a sheepish smile with a look of apologetic resignation. "But," he stutters and pauses. "I'm . . . not at all sure if my Polish accent is even passable, much less good enough to satisfy my wife." Gertrude's smile is not entirely kind as she pets her husband's inner forearm under the sweater. He tries to crack a witty smile.

"Oh come on, Douggie, tell them that important Polish idiom I taught you! You worked so hard on it." Gertrude is beaming and looks around to gauge interest level while she delves deeper into the soft cashmere sleeve and pets more intensely the inner aspect of his forearm, feigned tenderness in her eyes shining in anticipation. She laughs briefly at her wit and turns to look at Sylvia and Alek to assess their reaction.

Alek approaches Douggie again and slaps him lightly on the other forearm, now free from Gertrude's ministrations. "Hey, my friend Douglas, I'm sure your wife provides you with expert guidance, so don't be afraid, just do it, for isn't the goal of life to laugh and have some fun?" Alek guffaws. Sylvia joins him. Douggie laughs too, without conviction and not at all loud. Martin is near him and is quiet and his face looks half freaked out.

"I bet Gertrude taught Douggie something stupid specifically for this party," I whisper in Lila's ear.

"Nina, I hope he doesn't do it, oh God help him."

"He'll do what she wants him to do, to please her, and she pleases him by wearing tight miniskirts and tight fitting jackets. I think she's getting a little lifting repairs on her face. But I don't know. She says it's private. Maybe a secret expensive magic cream . . . Lila — you're still shaking from cold. Do you want me to puff some warmth into your palms?"

"Nina, please stop whispering in my ear and grabbing my hands before someone sees us?! Okay?" (Lila is being short with me.) "Just be quiet for a moment and try to be nice. You have only one sister. But do you happen to know who is the great plastic surgeon she has? I wouldn't mind a consultation, but of course I can't afford this kind of a thing."

"You don't need it yet, Lila. But I could use a chin fix. Hey, watch, I'm sure Gertrude will make an Idiot Clown out of her poor Douggie to amuse herself at his cost," I manage to whisper before Lila moves her ear away.

"I said don't talk anymore about anything, Nina." Lila's irritated whisper is without its veneer of patience, till she says softly, "Poor Douglas. But you know, I'm still freezing. Brrrr. I do wish I had my furry Polish muffler right now," she sighs.

"Just rub your hands together, Lila."

A sheepish grin returns to Douggie's visage and he takes a step forward to face his audience in a gesture of obedient resignation. "Okay, okay, I'll make a fool out of myself, the fool I already am!" he announces with a not quite pretend tragic finality and moves to the center of the foyer, as if he is stepping onto a stage.

"Lila, it's all over. Poor Douggie is ready to face his slaughter!"

Martin moves closer to Douggie. "Don't, Douglas, it's not worth it," he advises in a secretive voice hardly audible to us from the distance of the mantelpiece.

Gertrude removes her petting hand from her husband's cashmere sleeve and Douggie appears mildly embarrassed.

He is attentively listening to Martin. But is there any way out? A gallant humor returns to Douggie's face: "I don't mind making a fool out of myself as long as I can please my very discriminating wife!" Douglas speedily exclaims in a resigned burst, assuming a comical posture of tragic readiness. His lips are pursed, his eyebrows knitted. "I'm trying to look the part!" He laughs tensely. "Okay! So are you all ready for me to make a fool out of myself in Polish, just to please my sophisticated wife?" He nervously shifts from foot to foot, a sheepish undecided but bashful smile plastered across his face.

Gertrude is close by, an amused smirk on her lips, an anticipatory gleam in her eyes. "Don't be afraid, husbie, show them your superior Polish accent!" Her tone is softly cajoling.

"Look Lila, poor Douggie is about to open his mouth and disgrace himself to please Gertrude!"

I hear Martin's desperate warning. "Don't do it!"

"Hey people, I have nothing to lose! I am lost already! So here goes." Douggie takes a deep breath. "*Ja jestem głupi chuj!*" He mouths each word deliberately and distinctly.

Lila's eyes widen and she raises her eyebrows; her mouth opens almost all the way in a display of outrage. "Nina! Can you believe it?" Her whisper is exasperated.

"Yes, Gertrude made him practice that at dinner with my parents. Actually, his Polish accent is quite impressive for an American! Don't you agree, Lila?"

"Stop, don't joke like that, Nina. So why does Gertrude

105

need to teach her poor husband those humiliating insults?"

"The question is why does he cooperate? *That* is the question of the day! And I bet no one is going to ask him that. Lila, do you think he asks himself?"

"I really could not say. But I do not like what I see or what I hear," Lila says quietly.

Gertrude looks around and is quiet now. Anticipating applause? A not knowing what to say look (of disbelief?) appears on the faces in the foyer.

"Gertrude," Martin is gently pleading, "Let's not translate for us foreigners who do not understand. In fact, we're better off if we don't."

He addresses Gertrude but throws the remark toward Smart Alek, who approaches Douggie and gives him another friendly slap on the (already slapped) shoulder. "Hey, Professor Martin is right as usual!" Alek says, his voice booming — I wonder if he uses that voice only at parties. He slaps Douggie on the other shoulder, but not as hard, and Douggie retreats one small step. A familiar (his signature) not knowing what it should be expressing grin settles itself on his lips and in his eyes.

Gertrude's eyes are lit up with a gleam of pleasure. She turns to her husband with an affectionately victorious smile and resumes petting his inner forearm. "Douggie is well trained. He can translate it himself!" Pleased with herself, she throws her habitual quick glance around her, to judge the effect of her cleverness on others.

Alek's hand is still on Douggie's other shoulder. "I

agree, Douglas is expertly trained by his talented wife and certainly he does know the meaning of this very Polish Idiom!" Under Alek's large confident hand, Douggie lowers his shoulder as if driven by a protective instinct to avoid another friendly slap.

Sylvia, in her high heel designer silver sandals with her toenails perfectly manicured red, takes a few seductive steps closer to Gertrude, puts her arm around her waist, on their faces smiles of mischievous expectation. They are watching Douggie.

Alek removes his heavy hand from Douggie's shoulder and Douggie titters nervously, clearing his throat. He seems not to know what to do next. "Okay, okay, okay!! but don't laugh at me," he utters with the desperation of surrender. "It's my wife's idea — anyway it's only a joke." Clipped words come out of his mouth at a quickened pace.

"Come on, Douggie, don't be afraid, translate it for them," Gertrude says, still reassuringly petting his inner wrist under the soft cashmere sleeve of his tastefully chosen (by her) steel gray sweater.

The young English only speaking couple is not that far away and on and off they throw shy glances at the scene before hurrying away toward the dining room.

Douggie makes a step away from his wife, and rubs his palms — a self encouraging motion: "So there . . ." (louder and faster): "Hmmm . . . so since I've already decided that I'll make a fool out of myself . . . Ahhh . . . uhhmm . . . so it means in English . . . Ahhh, hmmmmm . . . *I am a stupid dick*!" he finally lets out with tragicomic finality. "And being who I am most of the time, I just can't help it, but. . ." He looks at Gertrude as if for confirmation. "It's just a joke, right Gertrude? So do I get a good mark? Did I give a decent performance?"

Alek and Sylvia laugh politely. Gertrude emits two short, animated bursts of self congratulatory laughter. Douggie appears to be quite uncomfortable now, and Martin is hiding his discomfort by averting his gaze down to the floor.

"Let's go to the dining room. I really need a drink, Nina." Martin was impatient.

"Darling, did you go to the kitchen to check if the host has whiskey there? And the cameo performers, are they still there?" she said sweetly.

He whispered, "Shush, Nina. Don't insult the host. I didn't see any whiskey in the kitchen, and all your surreal normal Americans are already gone."

"But if you're a lucky darling boy," Nina said more sweetly, "there may be some whiskey in the dining room, at that little booze table." He looked into her eyes with a brief show of affection, placed a brief kiss on her mouth, and repositioned her hand inside his warm palm. She didn't protest.

Dr. Angela Butterfly, MSW, Ph.D.
Intimacy Specialist
(3rd Session)
6/15/05

After informing me by phone message that he was "too busy at work" to attend the session, M showed up a few minutes before N did.

We spent considerable time discussing ways to facilitate communication, by identifying new habits of positive impact.

Until N threw cold water on positivity by stating, "Can a stale marriage be salvaged?"

I suggested that they surprise each other by putting LOVE sticker messages on the refrigerator, or other loving signs, such as hanging favorite lacy silk panties on the post of the shed, or a green color signifying willingness to engage in foreplay or mutual massage. (M stated that he is too ticklish and doesn't like to receive massages. N, on the other hand, loves to be massaged, but says M does not have a feel for it – too hard or too soft, too slow or too fast. And when she itches, he always scratches her in the wrong place.)

I also suggested a couples massage class (with M's ticklishness communicated to the instructor), and counseled them not to attempt cunnilingus or sexual intercourse at this point, but to focus on sensual exercises to find out what both of them like for mutual foreplay.

To avoid misunderstandings, I suggested that they do not use words, and that it is ok to close their eyes and open them when it is comfortable to do so. (M has difficulty maintaining eye contact when intimate issues are raised.)

Next session is with N solo.

―――――――――

IN THE DINING ROOM

"Darling — let's overcome the fear of the unknown together."

Ramo Verde — Radio Tarifa

The long rectangular dining table covered with white lace cloth is overflowing with all manner of silver and crystal platters filled with inviting Polish delicacies. A small round table across the room has bottles of wine. Martin makes a beeline for it, and after a short pondering, pours white for himself and red for me, returning with a glass in each hand.

"Marti, look at the centerpiece," I announce. He puts the glass with red wine in my hand, but I set it down on the edge of the table. He throws a very quick unexcited look at the largest and fanciest *kabanosy* platter.

No one else is in the dining room.

"Shit, Marti, no whiskey for you on the little round table?"

"No, but there's good wine. A nice merlot for you." He attempts to put the wine glass in my hand again. "Is there a problem already, Nina?" He lowers his voice and looks around. I put the glass down, again, on the edge of the table.

"Not yet, darling, but I'm warning you in advance that I want to wait for *Żubrówka* and am not mixing it with wine, and please don't drag me out of this party when I'm not ready to go, just when we the Un-Polished Polish Jews are about to start the *Żubrówka* thing at midnight till the sun comes up, as is promised in the Invitation, and those that do not belong will be bored or should be home in bed," I say sweetly.

"Hee, hee, hee," he laughs under his nose. "Nina, you mean a hysterical Zuperofska extravaganza, I think." He places the glass of merlot in my hand yet again and yet again I put it down on the edge of the table.

"This extravaganza, darling, requires unlimited *Żubrówka* to induce unpolished, unrestricted, randomly hysterical laughter — a catharsis — for us. Un-Polished by Poland."

"Hee, hee, hee. But I'd rather not be around any hysterical outburst. And I'd prefer . . ."

"Yes, I know. To be home where the whiskey is, with a Sierra Nevada chaser on our butcher block table, and double that to celebrate a perpetually to be perfected Grand Equation which inhabits the inside of your head 24/7, the one you wrote on the blackboard with that special Japanese chalk that doesn't make dust. And triple celebration is for when for a change your students understood!" I deliver all that into his ear. (We are still alone in the dining room.)

He swirls the white wine in his glass, not looking at me. "Stop putting down my little victories, Nina. Don't you like your wine?" Again he puts the glass in my hand, surveys the room, and is satisfied that no one can hear him and without looking at me he says in a very private tone, "Nina, just taste the wine." And before I can put the glass down, he firmly moves my hand with it closer to my mouth.

The young couple appears at the other side of the table. I stop Martin's hand with my free hand and say in his ear, "Darling, you know that I suck no one's dick on demand. But watch this young couple on the other side of the table." He throws a brief hesitant glance in their direction and says, "Stop spying on people, Nina, just drink your wine." He pushes my wine glass closer to my lips, I keep them shut and push his hand away gently.

"But observing isn't spying, darling," I say in his ear, "and don't push the wine to my mouth, just watch the young ones at the other end of the table — their cheeks are touching, their eyes are in unison, focused on the platters with unknown delicacies. Watch how they survey the unknown together and without fear. Or with a little fear. And to me, that's romantic. I bet they have great sex, too."

On the other side of the table, the young couple give each other 'what the fuck is this thing on that plate' mildly perturbed questioning looks.

Martin's focus returns to his wine and his nose is busy sniffing the rim of his glass. He takes his first sip as I watch him. A steady unchanging ritual of his, to pause and ponder over his verdict about the wine, repeated twice, then another pause and more pondering till he's fully convinced of his opinion. The final verdict is delivered in a most serious appreciative voice. "Hmmm, not too bad at all."

When he finishes this final prolonged appreciation sip and verdict, I say discreetly, "Darling, it could be that the innocent young ones are afraid to try what they don't know. Or will they overcome the fear of the unknown together? To overcome the fear of the unknown together is intimate. So maybe you and I . . . darling . . .?"

"Do *what*, Nina?" Martin's furrowed eyebrows lift above his narrowed in mistrust eyes. "What's up your sleeve?"

He swirls the wine in his glass. Finally, I do take a tiny sip of my red; it is sour and I make a face. He takes a long swig of his white.

"Don't worry Marti, no deviousness of any kind, darling . . . I was just thinking it would be a good thing for the foreigners here if there were explanations in English by each platter of unknown Polish delicacies." I toast my idea with a second sip. The wine still tastes sour, but I don't complain. Martin, encouraged, brings his wine glass to mine, our glasses clink, then he throws one of his quick checks around the dining room.

"If you want to know, Nina, I feel more and more like a total foreigner here," he says very quietly and takes another large swig of wine. "But the wine is not too bad, not bad at all."

"Marti . . ." I look in his eyes and smile my nice smile. "But you don't need written explanations for our Polish delicacies. I'll translate for you so you know what you will be eating. But can you see what the young lovers are examining now?" I say *sotto voce*, so as not to increase his anxiety. "It's *śledzik*, something you might like. One of the most cherished Polish appetizers: pickled herring in sour cream sprinkled with green onions and chives. And vodka is next to it. Did you know that vodka is a universal Polish disinfectant and is always next to *śledzik* per longstanding tradition? You drink it chilled in shot glasses with each bite of *śledzik*. And here are sautéed plum brandy infused and smothered to smooth pulp chicken livers with garlic salt and pepper, garnished with fresh cilantro. That's *pasztecik*. Next to it is *rybka wędzona*: smoked trout, my favorite. And *kiszone ogóreczki* — cucumbers affectionately pickled in salt dill and garlic, never ruined by a drop of vinegar. And I forgot to mention another Polish specialty." I point to a bowl of cucumber, sour cream, dill, and chives. "It's called *mizeria* and it tastes very good despite sounding like misery. Like our long term marital prison, darling, of what some call love . . . are you listening, Marti?" I say louder and take a third sip of my wine. It tastes more sour than ever, but I still don't complain nor make a face.

Without looking at me Martin takes another sip. "Nina," he says quietly and impatiently, "I'm listening and also focusing on the wine."

My eyes devour the large oval platter with the high pile of *kabanosy*. "Darling, would you like me to once more explain to you the *kabanosy*? The sausages in the fanciest platter in the center of the table? See it, darling?" I'm pointing to the oval platter but he is still distracted by the wine. "Marti, it's the most important Polish delicacy!" I lower my voice. "So you're not interested? But you're interested in putting in my mouth, in our kitchen, your big sausage, when the kids are away of course. Not exactly a spontaneous unpredictable unknown. But to overcome the fear of the unknown together, first how about a brave cautious look at the *kabanosy*, then come closer and smell them from about a six inch distance, as recommended by Dr. Butterfly. Smell it, darling!" (I was very sweet.)

"Stop it, someone may hear you. And I don't know what you're talking about, Nina," he whispers and takes a fleeting look around.

"Darling, you need to smell it because it is a quintessential Polish thing. Hey, if you smell a *kabanos*, I promise to smell your favorite duck sausage, darling."

"Jesus, Marti," I murmur . . . At the same time, I keep an eye on the young couple at the other end of the table. They are quietly conferring. "Darling," I address my husband with an air of mildly flirtatious irony, "you — as a connoisseur of objective truth, the absolute proof of which is your opinion — shouldn't you realize that one can't smell or taste the words on the page? Plus, taste and smell are subjective, thanks to our irrational limbic system, and so cannot be objectively described. Thus, since you're an objective scientist of abstraction, don't you need an empirical personal proof? And isn't a personal proof valid only when a doubtful scientist personally experiences what he desires to know in order to write an original poetic equation that solves this subjectively objective abstraction? Maybe Proust can make you experience his madeleine on the page, but I can't do that with a *kabanos*, darling. But we can take a closer look and smell it together. Like in a romantic play." I take another sip — I'm getting used to the merlot — while he swirls his . . . chardonnay I think, and takes two more sips. More like gulps, actually. "And Marti, if you want to understand the very unique Polish idiom, which roughly translates as heaven in the mouth, you have to experience the *kabanos* that produces it. There is no other way, darling,"

With his hand over his mouth, Martin muffles his hee, hee, hee to avoid the young couple's attention. "But you're a writer, Nina. You can do it!"

"If you're hungry, darling, eat a piece of juicy rib eye steak dressed in silky French lingerie sauce," I retort. "And you can chew it to your liking. Steak doesn't complain when you bite too hard, darling." I pretend to nibble his ear.

"Stop it, Nina." He scans the room to check if someone could hear. "And what's wrong, Nina, with me eating something I like and you sucking my dick like a wife should?"

"Eating *what* the way you like, darling? The way a husband is entitled to?"

"That's right, ask other husbands. And what is wrong with the fact that every man likes to have his dick sucked. Be real, Nina. I don't see what's wrong with you appreciating a good size sausage in your kitchen, rather than this puny kibanossie hee, hee, hee." (Very discreetly, in my ear.)

"Nothing is wrong, darling," I say flatly.

"So Nina, why not use your rare talent on me and eat my sausage the way you — Nina — like it. And I get a Genius Blow Job."

"In barter for a good dinner? You consider that romantic? But Dr. Butterfly and I agree that foreplay comes first. Remember the definition? Eye to eye fucking is *first* at six inches, before mouth on sausage or on pussy or on steak

119

in an erotic lavender sauce."

"Hee, hee, hee, And what else, Nina?"

"That in my opinion a routine of a long term what's for dinner loving marriage is a killer of romance." (These last words came out a bit too loud, causing Martin to move a step away from me.)

"But actually, Nina, what I ask you for is what a normal wife does when her husband comes home tired from work. An idiot husband like me, who cooks dinner for you and the kids too. Why don't you ask Lila and Gertrude when and if a husband deserves a blow job and how often. Lila will tell you the truth."

"Lila will tell me her truth about sucking dick??? Be real Martin, Lila doesn't ever even say this word! Ask her, darling. And Gertrude does not talk about private things. But my truth is that a normal woman, even an American woman, would be totally turned off by your idea of treating her pussy like a juicy steak with proper sauce, darling."

"Hee, hee, but a proper sauce always improves any dish!" Suddenly, an affectionate marital peck is bestowed by my husband on my mouth (followed by his dining room inspection).

"And you know what? In my opinion, cooking dinner for you and the kids is actually romantic. Ask Lila. And Gertrude can tell you too."

I smile, barely. "Your definition of the romantic, darling? Hey, Marti, maybe I should interview this young, sensually vibrant looking couple — look, still cheek to cheek at the other end of the table!"

He becomes alarmed. "Oh don't, Nina. That would be impolite. But maybe you can pull it off, nothing embarrasses you, hee, hee, hee." His glass of wine is almost empty. (Mine is almost full.)

"That's true, Marti, nothing embarrasses me except my dirty bitten off fingernails if someone looks at my hands. And you know that Lila doesn't like any embarrassing things and Gertrude will shut me up on principle. But we got off the subject that it would be a good idea to make signs in English to let the foreigners know what they will be eating."

"Please nothing vulgar, Nina." His perturbation is fortified with a next to last sip and thoughtful swirling of the rest of the wine in his glass.

"Look, Marti," I whisper, "the young ones. They are cheek to cheek like Louis Armstrong sings. They will be fucking tonight . . . No, not fucking here and now, don't look so disturbed, darling, later on, in private."

He sends the young couple a fleeting glance. "Hey, stop spying. I have a better idea." His whisper becomes animated. "In your book, you really can try harder to describe these kabanosees for me, so I don't . . ." (His teeth are showing just a little.)

"Darling, you're repeating yourself. But I will smell it and taste it *with* you. But not *for* you. In my opinion, if one takes responsibility for recognizing one's hidden desire for the things unknown, maybe one's erection will also get spontaneously enhanced. Isn't the erotic magnified by taste of the exotic? So Jesus Christ: At least smell it, Marti!" My patience is wearing out.

"Hey Nina, stop yelling your slogans in my ear. Fine, I may try it — but only if you convince me with a rational explanation. First, though, finish your first glass of wine."

"There is no convincing rational logic to the unknown, darling. It could be a randomly unpredictable spontaneous joy. Like an orgasm for example."

"Actually, Nina, do you want to know what I think? I think your mind is extra illogical from that stinky weed you smoked. But the wine will help," he advises.

"What, the wine helps in not being weird? Will it also censor my too weird to be expressed thoughts? Too weird for public consumption and of course for you — just a regular Irish bloke?"

"Hee, hee, hee, you figure it out. I tell my students that no one can figure things for you but if you want to, you'll learn for yourself!"

"Exactly! So we agree that no one can smell the unknown for you. But the courage increases with togetherness." My lips provocatively brush his mouth.

"Okay, so tell me more about these kabanozees, Nina." Martin throws a shy glance toward the piled high platter.

"I've been telling you this for how many years now! A perfect *kabanos*, darling, is even sexier if it is not cut into smaller pieces. An original *kabanos* is about the length of a horse's thing. Here it is cut in middle finger size pieces for ease of consumption." My smile is broad and my eyes are perplexed question marks.

Martin takes a step closer to the *kabanosy* but doesn't seem convinced; his eyebrows furrow, and his eyes throw shy glances toward the platter. "That sounds almost tempting, Nina. Maybe I'll try that later, but I need more wine. And don't force me, I don't want my stomach to be upset. And how do you know if they are freshly made?"

"I can tell, I can even smell them from here, so I know that they are freshly smoked. Anyway, I've told you about the Polish remedy for any type of stomach discomfort. A shot of Wyborowa is recommended with each *kabanos*, and some say that this premium clear potato vodka clears your gut from reacting badly to all kinds of unknown potentially unfresh ingredients. It's ancient knowledge, darling. And Wyborowa is also recommended to accompany the *grzybki marynowane*." I point to a small tureen of marinated Polish mushrooms. "Just in case there's a nasty one among them. But *kabanosy* are smoked just after being made, and I trust our local Polish butcher Kruk. Plus my nose provides the subjective proof. And I trust the Wyborowa because it is 100 proof."

"Hee, hee, hee. So the Polish mushrooms — khybki, is that what you call them — can they poison you? And only one or two or three vodka shots are recommended to accompany them?" His hand covers his mouth and he pretends to be serious, but I can tell he's suppressing his laughter under his nose.

"*Grzybki marynowane* are marinated chanterelle

mushrooms, freshly picked after the rain in the Polish forest. And I feel true nostalgia for the Polish forest. So it is the taste of my childhood."

"Wait, Nina, I'm ready for another glass of wine. But do you know the person who picks these mushrooms?"

Martin doesn't take long, returning with a glass of a different red wine. I take a small sip of mine; it isn't too bad. "So Nina, you don't know the person who picks these mushrooms? So how do you know that you can trust them?" He tries to pronounce *grzybki marynowane* three more times, puts his glass down, swirls my red wine, and takes a sip of it. "Not bad at all. It matures when it breathes." Satisfied, he swirls my wine around a few more times and takes another sip. "Nina, why don't you write this all up for a food magazine? That's my advice. Period." He delivers his opinion firmly, with an air of absolute conviction (as if he knows better than I do what is good for me, which always irritates me, often to the point of very vocal hysteria), and picks up his glass of wine, swirling it as prescribed for a connoisseur of wine.

"Hey Marti, I'm not a food writer and before I expire I'd like to waste my time how I want, on inspired writing about nothing that is important to you. And inspiration is always fresh, doesn't expire and is crucial to life — as is expiration, which expires at the end of it. And good weed enhances awareness of any reality, and makes it fictional or fuzzy. Plus, darling, even your kiss tastes nicer." I illustrate the foregoing with a brief kiss on his mouth, which he accepts, though his eyes scan the dining room. The young couple are inching closer to the *grzybki marynowane.*

"Nina, but why do you need to assassinate my character, pretending it's fiction?"

"No, darling, I'm just trying to get you to smell before you taste the unknown together with me, because togetherness brings us closer. Closer to heaven." (I'm feigning innocence.)

He takes the first sip of his red wine, puts it down, then moves his tongue inside his mouth, assessing it. "It needs to breathe some more. But it's not bad." He lowers his voice and places his hand over his mouth. "But Nina, just stop forcing me to do what I don't want to do. That is called bullying." He braves a fearful peek at the platter of *kabanosy.* "And by the way, Nina, you're the mother of two teenage sons, so why not worry about them instead of wasting your time on your fictional insults. If you're a real writer, prove it and describe the kabanossie for me. Or write stories for gourmet travelogue magazines." He swirls his wine nervously.

"And frankly Nina, I only need to go to Ireland when I miss the emerald hills and my father's golden barley fields in Kilkenny. And that's all the travel for me until I die. And you'll bury me there in a nice oak coffin. But let me bring you a glass of a better merlot." (My glass, on the edge of the table, is still about three quarters full.)

"So Marti, when are we going to Ireland?"

"The golden barley fields are ready for harvest in the third week of August. We'll take the kids, of course. And I'm sure you'll also see the red poppies in the fields that remind you of Poland. The kids will play hurling." He almost downs his glass.

"And you'll be quenching your thirst with a fresh Guinness stout in every pub on the way?"

"And why not, Nina? An Irishman is always *thiiiiirsty* for fresh Guinness! But first, let me pee and get you a better merlot."

"I'm stoned darling. I don't need more wine."

"Did you pee darling, while I was pondering your fear of the uncertain unknown resulting in non-experience? Yes, I'm repeating myself, darling, because I'm an ignored non-conformistic-confrontationalistic and at times ballistic monologist! And think about my readers. Wouldn't they eagerly await a spontaneous dialogue response from Martin! Bored students are the worst nightmare for the professor, right? Bored readers are my nightmare, darling."

He doesn't respond and the volume of my whisper in his ear increases. "Darling, are you holding off? Maybe you need to go pee again? Or haven't you peed yet? And you might relax better if maybe you find a bottle of Irish whiskey to quench your Real Irishman's thirst . . . because you need to deny your fright filled awareness of my increased fuzzy weirdness." I smile. Martin doesn't notice. He's too busy taking what he must think are well disguised concerned glimpses around the room.

"You're right, Nina. What I need now is to pee again, and then what I need is a piece of paper to write the skeleton of the new equation I'm working on. Fortunately, our hosts have plenty of wine. Not all so good, however. But Nina, please don't repeat that to them." The fear in his whisper is quite real.

"So after you pee once again, you'll get better wine to booze up your loyal Equation, darling, your steady partner, the one that occupies your head day and night? So you will not be bored." I am in control of my whisper. "Because I'm staying till the end of the *Żubrówka* histrionic melancholia abandon, which in your opinion is an unnecessary communal hoopla. And maybe I can sneak out and smoke my extra roach. And you can just commune with your Equation!" My voice in his ear has become almost militant. He moves his ear away and seems perturbed in the extreme. His eyes open quite wide and look at me petrified.

"What, Nina, did I hear you correctly? Are you planning to smoke *more* of that weed *here*, to fortify your hoopla and your mood against me?" A truly disturbed look fills his eyes.

"Darling, go pee again, then get more wine," I say to calm him, and then say in a soothing whisper: "I probably won't smoke my roach till six in the morning, on the way back home. But turn your head to the right a little. See who is coming straight to the *kabanosy*!"

"Is it Lila? I don't want to turn my head, or she may see me looking at her." (He makes no movement at all.)

127

"Oh darling, but why don't you want to look at Lila with an undisguised admiration of her charms, why so shy?"

"You tell me what you see, Nina." He turns his eyes away.

"Lila is coming over to where we are in dainty steps, with her youthful spring, her feet in pretty high heel sandals, toenails bright red. Her petite figure is all grace in an understated and elegant blue dress."

"That's enough. I told you it isn't nice to spy and gossip, Nina," he says very discreetly.

Lila is almost at the *kabanosy* platter.

"Hey Nina, Lila is here," Martin announces loudly, turns on a dime, switching to his jolly mode of social behavior. He is about to start chatting with Lila, in her blue minidress that invites a glimpse into her delicate black lace adorned décolletage showing off her shapely breasts, but Lila's eyes are focused on the festive oval silver platter.

"Uhm, *ka-ba-no-sy*," she utters and her eyes turn upward as if in thankful reverence to a Higher Being. Her face a mere few inches above the *kabanosy* platter, she takes two elated inhales of the smoky scent.

Looking up from the sacred platter, she registers our presence. "Hi Martin and Nina, so you're here already? But why are you two looking at me like that?"

"Just watching you inhaling heaven, that's all." I smile.

"Martin, seriously you should smell these too!" Lila is genuinely excited.

"As a matter of a fact, Lila, I was just trying to get Marti to smell the *kabanos* from the recommended intimate distance of six inches, which is ideal for exciting the sense of smell, medically recommended and validated in studies with humans and animals. They all say the intimate distance is about six inches. So I wanted Marti to smell it from this distance, then progressively to reduce his fear of the unknown, decrease the distance, to help him overcome the fear of *kabanos*, so he can eventually understand what *Niebo w Gębie* means. In short, I wanted Marti to appreciate the flavor of the unknown — or Heaven in the Mouth, because no one can do that for someone else."

I look first at the perplexed Lila, then at my husband, who is holding three empty wine glasses.

"Marti, weren't you going to get some better wine? And Lila, I've already explained to Marti clearly that an unknown smell or taste cannot be described in *words*, so must be *experienced*. But Marti is afraid of anything new, so I tried to convince him to experience it *with* me. He says if I'm a real writer, I should be able to come up with a poetic metaphor that can stimulate his olfactory sense and salivation, and his desire to taste an unknown. The *kabanosy* in the present case, but he thinks words can smell and taste on the printed page. So the question is, can words imagine the flavor of something they have never tasted before? What do you think, Lila?"

Lila listens with no smile while her starkly blue eyes guarded by black eyelashes with perfect mascara are piercing mine. "I hope, Nina, that you're done with your mouthful, because I didn't get much of it either." She pronounces each word with precision in nearly unaccented English.

She still doesn't crack a smile but looks at me uncomprehendingly. She turns to Martin.

"Did I say something inappropriate, Lila?" I ask.

"Lila, don't pay too much attention to my wife, that's how she is, hee, hee, hee. But of course, you know that already." Martin isn't looking at me.

Gertrude approaches. "What is it that's happening here?" she chimes in from the vicinity of the *kabanosy*, with her uncamouflaged politely mocking expression and a coldly sustained look directed at me.

So I let myself go: "Gertrude, Martin has quite an interesting opinion regarding what a wife is for. She is a *girl* of course." I unfurl this with an air of pure innocence.

Lila and Gertrude look at each other. "Wait till Seweryn comes," says my sister.

"Seweryn will make a joke of anything, the more stupid the better, just to laugh," Martin says supportively.

Gertrude's cold stare chills me. "But since Seweryn the clever joker isn't here yet, Nina, there is no need for you to show off. Or we may be in imminent danger of being too disgusted and not be able to stomach any of these great appetizers here." She doesn't smile.

And Lila's elated smile, which she had bestowed on the *kabanosy* platter, disappears. "I agree with Gertrude. Just please stop it Nina, you really are going too far," she throws in, a bit annoyed.

"But Nina thinks it's funny," Gertrude says, looking at Martin. Then with the tap taps of her heels, as if to spell out her disregard, she walks toward the other end of the table. (The young couple is nowhere to be seen.)

"That's how Nina is, she can't distinguish between public and private," Martin says, turning to face Lila and looking away from me.

"But do you want to hear something important?" I say to Martin and Lila.

"What now, Nina?" they say in unison.

Gertrude must have overheard it and is back. "Well, Nina, you can tell us as long as it does not involve hanging out your dirty laundry in public. Do you think you can do it, Nina?" She is seeking Martin and Lila's support.

I stay silent, calming myself — trying to prevent a potential burst of noxious sensation brought on by her dismissive tone. (Both her silence and her comments have always had that effect on me.)

Very quietly, I say, "Gertrude, my husband likes only clean sexy silky underwear, and he likes to wash and hang it out himself. Right, Marti?"

Martin shrugs, the three empty wine glasses in his hand. "I'll be back with some better wine for you *girls*. Gertrude, a glass of red?" are his parting words.

"Hmmm, Martin and his *girls*," Gertrude says and her gaze at me is charged with her customary contempt.

A perplexed look shows up on Lila's face. "I don't follow you, Nina. Your thoughts are disjointed. And Martin is a nice man even if he says *girls*. And frankly, we've had enough of it, so let's change the subject. Let's not spoil a nice occasion, okay?" Lila is looking me straight in the eye, drilling holes through mine. Then she looks at Gertrude.

Gertrude is watching and pitches in, her tone fake friendly, "And I have some good advice for you, Nina. Exercise more if you want a flat stomach like mine — and if you want to disclose fictional details, why don't you go to a café and write in your notebook? You can be as dirty or as hygienic there as you so desire. I agree with Lila. Let's change the subject." She looks at Lila, seeking agreement.

Martin is back with four glasses of wine, two in each hand. "Hee, hee, hee, my wife is addicted to cafés," he offers. "And she writes in the notebook which unwisely I gave her, after she smokes her illegal stuff on the way in her car with loud music blasting. And she doesn't get it that she shouldn't smoke in decent neighborhoods, or on streets where other professors live. It's derelict. So don't pay any attention to your sister, Gertrude, she smoked right in front of Sylvia's house. Ignore her, she makes no sense! But here is the wine!"

"Oh! I see!" Gertrude is livening up. "So my exhibitionist sister is sharing with us all the unasked for nonsense in her head as bait, so later in the café she can put our responses in her notebook? So we are her puppets?" An increased portion of scorn inhabits Gertrude's blank stare (the scorn of a smarter older sister for her younger sister, not as smart nor as well exercised, and not as elegant as herself).

Martin puts the four wine glasses on the edge of the table. "Hee, hee, hee. I think, Lila, you will like this chardonnay?" (Lila always drinks chardonnay.) "But you *girls* should know that my wife can be dangerous. So I advise you not to take my wife seriously, because she will write or say anything that comes to her head, mostly inappropriate for public consumption. In conclusion, when my wife smokes that illegal stuff, she has no concept of decency."

I take a few more calming breaths. In, out, in, out. Gertrude tastes her wine and says, "I think I would prefer the chardonnay today, Martin."

"Sure Gertrude," Martin says and dutifully leaves for the booze table.

"What's up, Nina, why so quiet suddenly?" Gertrude's words are like a jab. Then, with a slight indignant shrug of one shoulder, and without waiting for a response, she strides toward the other end of the long rectangular table, her heel clicks accompanying her indignation.

The young couple is there now and Gertrude says something to the woman, who is touching the edge of her iridescent metallic royal blue jacket. I'm fingering the fine white lace cloth on the table. Gertrude and I don't exchange any long distance looks. Lila sighs deeply.

DR. ANGELA BUTTERFLY, MSW, PH.D.
INTIMACY SPECIALIST
(4th Session – Solo with N)
6/29/05

We started out concentrating on N's insights about herself and her tendency to overtly confront and challenge M. Where does it come from? Did her mother do that to her father? Negative modeling after parental style discussed.

N acknowledged her inability to accept M's silent style along with his need for zero degree of ambiguity as part of life, and his fear of experiencing the unknown.

N: "He is an Irishman and always right and with big proud balls!"

I advised her to stop tormenting her husband about tasting what he doesn't want to taste. Polish delicacies, and African/ Turkish cuisine. Food is very personal – maybe just too exotic for him. Can she learn to accept that there are some people who like only what they were exposed to in childhood? If she's patient, M may yet acquiesce to her desires to try new things, and to travel to places other than the ones he already knows.

Last 15 minutes of session: N very emotional, tearing up and claiming her older sister is constantly putting her down, and further, insisting M and I are "ganging up" on her. I assured her otherwise but will self-examine.

KABANOSY

"For now it's just foreplay."

Bolero — Ravel

At the most ornate oval platter Lila is fully engaged smelling the *kabanosy* from a distance of about eight inches. Martin, back with more wine, watches her. I can't resist: "Marti, see how enchanted Lila is? As if she is inhaling a taste of heaven. By the way, darling, the scent of the real *kabanos*, for us who grew up in Poland, produces an explosive salivatory response."

"Hee, hee, hee, and next is Kabanozee Orgasm!! Hee, hee, hee. That's a perfect title for the finale of an Italian opera!" Martin laughs at his own witticism, revealing more teeth than usual. He puts two glasses of merlot on the edge of the table. "Actually, not a bad title at all, Nina." He laughs some more under his nose while handing me a glass with the better merlot. Lila's nose is still near the *kabanosy*, and Gertrude, from across the long table — by the group of herring platters — is on silent alert; or maybe she's just searching for a hook to better put me down. Then, in her shiny leather pointed toe boots with proudly shining silver clasps, she strides toward the *kabanosy*, her always confident and sleek click click clicks full of appointed superiority.

With an air of innocence I address my older sister: "Hey, Gertrude, but the good news is that Marti may believe us *girls* that the Heaven in the Mouth exists — if, of course, we demonstrate it to him properly. And it may be difficult because he is a devout scientific proof atheist — but he used to be an avid Catholic. So there is hope."

Gertrude emits a sneer colored with a dose of mildly

contemptuous attitude. Lila lifts her head. Her strikingly blue eyes, surrounded by her long eyelashes with perfectly applied black mascara, open wider, questioning me. "Come on Nina, I already said that's enough," she nearly spits out. Gertrude glares at me with her now modulated normal dose of disdain verging on pity. Lila's eyes revert to pleasingly expressive and avert back to the *kabanosy*. She closes them, and inhaling the scent, breathes out sounds of deep pleasure. Then her eyes open and turn to the ceiling as if to the heavens in a bout of thankful admiration. (The ceiling is nothing special: plain white.)

"They look and smell like the real thing," Lila says, and it seems that her adoring words are anticipating ecstasy. She is beaming. "They must be from our only Polish butcher, Kruk. No one else outside of Poland makes them as good." A few more inhales with eyes closed. (Each time, her face is truly radiant.)

Martin finishes his wine and goes to pee and wash his hands, missing Lila's ongoing abandon. Then, like a homing pigeon, he returns to the little round table for more wine. I join Lila in taking elated *kabanos* inhales. Gertrude throws us a polite smile, her eyes exuding a mildly suspicious frown.

Martin puts two wine glasses down, watching us, and between my inhalations of *kabanosy* smoky scent I watch him. A reactivated mistrust invades his body; it visibly stiffens. And a disquiet invades his eyes. Lila's nose and mine are about six to eight inches from the top of the *kabanosy* mound. A doubtful but elegantly sardonic smile appears on Gertrude's face.

I lift my head and say to Martin, "Darling, I assure you that these *kabanosy* are of the highest quality." His eyebrows furrow above the rim of his professorial style rectangular eyeglasses. "Be careful *girls*," he warns, "my wife has something up her sleeve and she has no decency."

Lila's eyes close again and her nose focuses on the *kabanosy*. Martin picks up his wine glass and his hand trembles at just a visible amplitude. "Are you going to drink your wine, Nina? I'm sure this merlot is better. Not a bad idea to drink some good wine before you go to heaven, hee, hee, hee." Fine muscles of his forearm trembling, he points to the other wine glass. "Hey, *girls*, who else wants more wine?" He is trying to loosen the uncomfortable vibe. Gertrude stares down at her silver clasp.

Interrupting my *kabanosy* smelling, I announce, "Marti, I don't need more wine — and stop trembling." I go on (to provoke him): "Are you nervous or overexcited that we *girls* will soon be in *Kabanos* Heaven and lose control? A simultaneous *Kabanos* Orgasm? But darling, I thought you might like to see us enjoying it?"

"Ha!" Gertrude has perked up. She lets loose her excitement. "So we are *girls* forever, Martin?"

He chuckles, attempting to act nonchalant and amused, before finding his footing: "Gertrude, actually patriarchs are needed in this world. Without them there would be no children and less orgasms." He follows with a double hee hee from under his covered mouth.

Gertrude fixes her neutral emotionless glare on him: "So Martin, forever a Patriarch Boy?"

"Hey, Gertrude, I don't mean to be disrespectful to you *girls*, it's just a popular American saying, that's all. So you'd prefer me to call you Women? Or Gals? And, hee, hee, hee, is kabanosee a girl or a boy?" Satisfied with himself, he takes a manly swig of merlot.

I am still six inches from the *kabanosy*. My nose lifts a little. "Whatever you want it to be, darling. Guys, boys, men, tomboys, or boy toms or boy toys — it's masculine or feminine gender."

"And some women out of desperation may prefer women — instead of idiot men," says Gertrude not too loud, looking Martin in the eye.

"So what's the problem, girls? Unfortunately, you girls often don't realize what you need." Martin almost empties his wine glass rather hurriedly in one long gulp. Gertrude, in contrast, cautiously sips her water.

Hoping that Lila and Gertrude won't hear, I hiss into Martin's left ear. "And gals or girls are needed to suck dudes' dicks?"

Lila's head lifts farther away from the *kabanosy* and she says, "In Polish slang, men are *faceci* and women are *facetki*. But believe me Marti, these *kabanosy* are from heaven and you should definitely taste one. And I'd love if you brought me another glass of chardonnay." She quickly turns toward me (our noses near) and we are eye to eye — about six inches: "But I mean it, Nina, enough is enough. I don't want to hear one word more of what you want to say. And don't contradict your older sister. She has some smart advice, and not just about real estate law."

"Hey, girls, no fighting. So, it's chardonnay for Lila. And what can I bring you, Gertrude?" Martin is in cajoling mode, practicing his stilted peace promoting manner.

Gertrude takes a sip of her water. "No thank you Martin, this girl will wait for the *Żubrówka* celebration," she says in a studiously neutral voice.

"And no more wine for me. I'll wait with Gertrude for the *Żubrówka* celebration," I say to my husband.

At the other side of the ornate oval platter, across from Lila and me, Gertrude is smelling the *kabanosy*. "Okay, Lila," I say quietly. "I'll keep my mouth shut and instead I'll report in my head. I have to express what's on my stoned mind. What can I do if I am addicted to questioning like a child that needs to know? Fortunately, a writer is allowed to dig with a stick where there is a hole, but I can excel only in monologues. Why? Because my characters avoid giving me a responsive dialogue line other than trying to shut me up. Like Martin, for example." (And you Lila, too, I said to myself.)

"Nina, but please stop saying bad things about your husband."

Gertrude continues smelling the *kabanosy* from a

reasonable distance, before suddenly lifting her nose. "You should know by now Lila that my younger sister will never understand how to discipline her mouth. Nina, why not let Lila enjoy her first *kabanos* without your complaining about your husband? Oh, and by the way, your reality is your own and no one else's. And actually no one else cares."

"I never said my reality is someone else's reality, Gertrude. And we'll see who cares."

Lila lifts her head. "And in *Rashomon*, the Kurosawa classic, everyone has a different reality of the same event."

"But I wonder, Nina," Gertrude presses on, "why you would be wasting any time on your stupid confrontations. In my opinion, it's not meaningful for anyone. So why waste your time confronting people who do not share your reality? Why not, instead of wasting our time, use your time to train your brilliant husband to better serve your needs? In my opinion, that's the role of women in our times." Triumphant, Gertrude returns to smelling *kabanosy* with an expression both victorious and satisfied, and searches Lila's eyes to assess the effect of her wit. (All this I have written down in my head.)

While I have been wishing Gertrude would go away to examine the *śledzik* again, instead of quite possibly taking another stab at me, Lila has kept her eyes closed and said nothing. Now, Gertrude gives me her casual gift of mild, dismissive disdain, and an almost imperceptible shoulder shrug (reserved for those Gertrude considers not as smart as herself and thus of not much use). Then, as if she has heard and granted my wish, Gertrude moves toward the *śledzik*, making quick tap tap taps with her fashionable patent leather boots with shiny silver clasps and overly, for my taste, pointed toes.

Our eyes closed, Lila and I resume smelling the *kabanosy*. "Nina, you can talk very quietly, but don't say anything nasty," Lila gently warns me.

"Okay. Not nasty. I wonder if our Polish Butcher Kruk who makes these heavenly *kabanosy* is cheating us because he can tell that we are Jewish. The fact is that we — you, Gertrude, and me — get cheated by him every time we shop there for kielbasa and *kabanosy*."

Gertrude is on her way back, in fast yet elongated confident steps (measured by tap tap taps of her shiny patent leather boots), but I have time to whisper in Lila's ear before she arrives, "Gertrude doesn't go to our Polish butcher Kruk anymore because his *kabanosy* are antisemitic."

Martin returns, with three filled to the brim glasses of white and red wine, a precarious load, and apparently having heard the last part of what I said, starts right in: "Girls — Lila, Gertrude — I already advised you not to take my wife seriously. The poor Polish butcher makes the greatest kielbasa and kabanosee outside of Poland. And you girls are definitely crazy for his kabanosee. And when will you finally let me witness your Kabañas Ecstasy, hee, hee, hee?"

"Butcher Kruk never cheated you — because you don't look like a Jew and you are not a girl." Gertrude proclaims as she eyes the *kabanosy* with distrust. Martin hands Lila her chardonnay and takes a casual swig from his glass.

"Girls, but his kabannossie according to my wife are the best. So why complain? Anyway, I don't mind being cheated a little. That's what country butchers do. And his kielbasie is also great . . . and these kabanossies I'm sure are great. But Gertrude, won't you have a glass of wine? Everything goes better with wine. I can get you anything you like. Would you prefer red or white?" (A glass of merlot I have not touched sits on the edge of the table.)

"No thank you, Martin," Gertrude says politely without a smile. "I've already told you, explicitly, that this girl is drinking water for now because she doesn't want to mix anything with *Żubrówka* later. But Martin, I'm wondering if you may also think that some boys drink too much wine and don't remember things?" She gives me a subtle sisterly wink and returns to her examination of the *kabanosy* platter from a closer distance than before.

"Marti wouldn't know if and when Butcher Kruk cheats him because Marti never checks what's in the greasy paper wrapper Kruk gives him!" I say, pointedly. "Butcher Kruk gives you, darling, five kielbasas but charges for six. And before I have a chance to check if he was cheated, my husband, a kind man who defends those that have less, throws out the receipt scribbled in pencil on greasy kielbasa and *kabanosy* paper wrap, and pretends he didn't throw it out on purpose. I married a fair man! But . . ." I stop myself before calling him a Trembling Darling Dupe . . . "But listen to this: Martin's reasoning for the defense of the poor Polish butcher. It's Kruk's lack of ability in the simple math required to count without cheating due to not finishing fourth grade and to the poverty of everything in the village where he grew up, like Martin, in a house with one room for the big family, and one outside shit booth. So Martin understands." I take a breath.

"Fortunately, your husband had brains for mathematics and was lucky to have a teacher who discovered him and opened up the world of education," Gertrude says surprisingly with genuine approval.

"Otherwise, Marti would not be a math professor but would be milking cows at four a.m. in the cold and dark in the village where he was born. Like his brothers. Right, darling?" I place a little kiss on his cheek.

"Nina, I probably would have escaped either to the loo or to the Loony Bin. But, what's wrong with being kind to people who have less than you?" Martin fires back, and takes a large swig of his merlot (after sniffing and swirling it beforehand, of course).

Gertrude is at the other end of the table where the herrings are and Martin is off to get more of the better merlot for himself and chardonnay for Lila. I drink a little from my almost full glass. It is a better merlot!

I bring my head closer to Lila. She moves hers an inch away. "Don't start again, Nina," she protests quietly. Both our heads are about eight inches from the *kabanosy*.

"But Lila, can I mention something subjective about our butcher?"

"Okay, if it's not too gross."

"So I was stoned of course in his store recently and I wondered if the red bulb he has on his nose grows bigger and redder like Pinocchio's when he is cheating. In Martin's opinion it's the stinky weed that fuels my nasty imagination . . ." I don't quite manage to complete the sentence because Gertrude is back from a close up examination of the herring with sliced apples and sour cream.

"Your imagination, Nina, has nothing at all to do with this subject. Or any other! My mother — "

"My mother too," I interject.

She ignores me and says, "My mother told me that real Polish antisemites have genetically specialized noses that can smell a Jew right away." An easy to miss (by anyone but me) irritated glance is followed by her steps and her heels making a more pronounced condescending click click click, as she yet again returns to the other end of the table and looks like she's about to perform a more thorough inspection of the herring in wine sauce (which is next to the herring in sour cream garnished with chives and red onion slices).

Lila, her nose now about six inches from the *kabanosy* platter, says, "Seriously, Nina, please stop saying bad things about our poor butcher." She lifts her head and widens her eyes. "Instead, just look, Nina, how neatly these beauties are laid out on this pretty platter with a gold rim, but hmmm, maybe it's too much gold for me." She lowers her head and takes a deep breath, across her face an inspired brightening smile. "Nina, these *kabanosy* are really the best on this side of the world, and I agree with Martin, let the poor uneducated Polish butcher cheat us a little if he must. It's worth it."

"Okay. Fine. The poor guy does have an incurable addiction to cheating us a little because he can tell we're Jewish. But his *kabanosy* — they are the best," I amicably agree.

Gertrude, who seems to be monitoring the situation from the other side of the table at her favorite, Matjes herring, is visibly restless. On the move again, her head held high, she tap tap taps back to our side of the table with an agitated stride. Upon arrival she states with authority, "Nina, your poor Polish Butcher has an addiction which is inherited the same way the Polish antisemitism is transmitted from generation to generation." Without waiting for a response, she spins on her heels and strides back to where she just came from: to the Matjes herring, seemingly to complete her careful inspection of it.

Martin returns with two almost full to the brim glasses of red and one white wine. "Girls, don't exaggerate, not everyone is an antisemite in Poland, and until there is objective proof — after a full congressional investigation! — against him . . . But on the other hand, there is ample proof of his making you girls happy with these kabanozeees. So, let me assure you girls — you have no reason to complain!

Hee, hee, hee." More quietly, he adds, "And it's not nice to accuse him." He puts the wine glasses down. Gertrude, at the other end of the table, has dramatically rolled her eyes when he said *girls*.

I move closer to Martin. "Maybe a *kabanos* can make you happy too, Marti. All you have to do is taste just one bite." I touch the back of my husband's hand.

Unconvinced, he gently but firmly removes my hand from his. "Nina, stop bullying me into trying something I'm not interested in. I've told you, year after year — they are not for me. Period."

I open my eyes wide. "What? Heavenly Bliss of Happiness is not for you, darling? Or is your happiness me sucking your dick?" I am whispering into his ear: "But, do I have to repeat that I suck no dude's demanding dick without foreplay? . . . But watch how Lila is holding back . . ."

"Holding back what, Nina?"

I whisper, "The *Kabanos* Ecstasy. It's too powerful to rush into. It starts inside the mouth. *Niebo w Gębie* — not an exact translation is Heaven in the Mouth — because *gęba* is not quite what we call mouth, it's a word that doesn't exist in English. In Polish there are five or more words that describe our oral cavity. And now its just foreplay, *near* the oral cavity, darling." I smile with pure charm.

Inching closer to Lila, my head lowered over the *kabanosy* platter (now just *five* inches away from my nose), I take a prolonged ecstatic breath. "Ummm," I exhale and am back at Martin's ear. "*Kabanos* foreplay activates not only my salivary glands but also my private organ, which Dr. Butterfly doesn't want me to call pussy."

I whisper near his ear just loud enough for Lila and Gertrude to hear, "So be positive, don't be afraid. Try one too Marti, it won't bite or poison you. It's cured to perfection by the *Kabanos* Hero Polish butcher with a red Pinocchio nose, and I made up this half baked joke about Pinocchio's nose, but Gertrude is seriously afraid that these *kabanosy* are not just that — they are antisemitic *kabanosy*. However, he has a wife who makes a great Polish Jewish cheesecake. Lila told me. She uses real Polish farmer cheese, not the fatty Philadelphia cream cheese Americans like. Who knows, maybe she is Jewish? It tastes just like our grandmother made when we were kids."

"I don't remember my grandmother's cheesecake," Gertrude says.

"Nina, Jesus Christ, stop this nonsense!" Lila has lost her polite patience. "I met his wife and she is definitely Polish and very friendly. So don't spoil this party for me. Stop! And I'm having one of *these*, even though no one is eating yet. So why don't we have our first bite together? Let's be positive."

"Hmmm," Gertrude throws in.

I take a look around the room. "I agree Lila — it's only me, you, Gertrude, and Martin in the dining room and I can't wait any longer either! So let's do it all together now! Like Beatles!"

Lila hasn't touched her wine yet; she is about to reach

for the top *kabanos* on the pile.

"You have my permission, Lila, I want to see how you get happy!" Martin says, suddenly jolly.

I give him a peck on the cheek and whisper, "Watch Lila bite her *kabanos* and you'll see her get happy. But do you think it's okay to eat *kabanosy* without Sylvia and Smart Alek giving us any sign to start in? Aren't you, darling, a Stiff Patriarchal Authority on decent behavior? So, tell us girls, if in your opinion is it okay for shy Lila, and not so shy Nina, and reluctant Gertrude, to start eating? Someone has to start first and Lila's delicate manners make her hesitant to be the first one to have a go at these *kabanosy* . . . of the right size, to make us *girls* happy. Darling, did you hear what I said?" Martin doesn't look at me, but he does look at Lila.

In a tone of pure cynical curiosity, Gertrude asks, "What are you whispering in Martin's ear now, Nina?"

"Hee, hee, hee, I've already mentioned that my wife doesn't understand some things about decency. And that it's not nice to laugh at an unfortunate man's nose."

"I agree, Martin," says Lila, while she removes the first *kabanos* from the top of a gloriously neat pile.

Gertrude stands there, regarding us all with what looks to me like a sizable portion of contempt, and now she is glaring at me, her lips pursed and eyes coldly blank. To Martin, she says, "I wonder if your hero Polish Butcher adds yukky chemicals and obviously antisemitic preservatives which give me diarrhea and bloat my stomach. I wouldn't trust him, Martin." She is not joking and goes back to the *kabanosy* inspecting them with heightened vigilance.

"I know something more on the subject, Gertrude," I tell her. "I think Marti would be able to taste the *kabanosy* if he had an Oxford Dictionary definition and information on the origins of the word *kabanos*. In fact, to him nothing is real unless it lives in the Oxford Dictionary! Right, Marti? And I agree with you Gertrude that it would help too if he would learn to pronounce it properly after he and I take your advice to start the necessary untranslatable Polish idiom training."

"Marti," I address my husband in a pretend sincere manner. "Gertrude has vast experience teaching meaningful Polish idioms to her husband and she thinks you'd be a good student candidate at this point, right Gertrude?" I give a little cooperative smirk to my sister.

"I agree with Nina that it would be best if Martin would try to learn a few important Polish words." She gives me a brief supportive sisterly wink, and when I look at her, she takes a quick small sip of water and says, "In fact, I *have* successfully taught a few quintessential non-translatable idioms to Douggie. And I'm sure, Martin, that if Nina applied herself to it, she could teach you as well! You actually underestimate your joint abilities in my *girly* opinion, Martin." Gertrude is pleased with herself and ends with a clipped burst of sarcastic laughter.

Lila has been tuned out. Now, she takes a few dainty sips of her chardonnay and tunes back in: "So, are we waiting for

Godot? Why is no one eating yet?" The *kabanos* in her hand has still not made it to her mouth. "I'm too shy to be first, so Gertrude, Nina, you have to join me. And Nina, please let Martin just be. Really, you don't know when to stop." Lila doesn't look at me, nor at Gertrude — only at Martin.

Gertrude's smirk is touched by a hint of indignation. "Martin, in this instance, Nina is actually right. Though your lack of brave courage to try something new can be ameliorated by a useful action of travel to new places. We *girls* agree on this, more or less. Be a brave boy!"

"Thank you Gertrude for your support," I say and take one *kabanos* from the pile. "I'll eat one as soon as Lila bites hers."

"But I want to know why our boy here feels so sorry for this jerk of a butcher?" Gertrude says with insincere earnestness.

Kabanos in hand but still a culinary virgin, Lila takes a step backward. "Why bring *that* up again, Gertrude? Even Nina has dropped it."

Martin is back from another trip to the round table. "Gertrude, I think you've had enough water. Maybe you need something stronger after all." Without waiting for her response, he hands me a glass of red wine without looking at me. "And Lila, you probably want more of that good chardonnay. But girls, can you please convince my wife that wine is better for her than that illegal stuff she smokes? She doesn't know that it distorts her reality, and I wouldn't put it past her to write it up, make that write it down, pretending it is fiction, hee, hee, hee."

"I agree with Martin, Nina — you should not gossip or create gossip stories that harm . . . on any subject." Lila reaches for her new glass of chardonnay.

Finally Gertrude accepts the glass of red wine from Martin, thanking him, and ignoring Lila's plea to drop the subject, she returns to the scene of the conversational crime: "And Nina is probably correct that the Polish Butcher is cheating us. But no need, Nina, to bore us with your half baked Pinocchio joke." Gertrude winks at me, in a sisterly conspiracy.

Then she continues in Polish: "Nina — get it straight. This Polish crook of a butcher cheats because just as a great majority of Poles are, he is an antisemite. So don't waste your time, Nina, making stupid jokes about this primitive idiot."

Lila removes herself one more step away (and says in Polish): "For God's sake, I'm going to lose my appetite — and before I even taste this *kabanos*! This butcher talk is truly disgusting. Could we not talk about it ever again?" Her disapproval approaches the volcanic. "Gertrude, do you think you can stop your sister?" With the unbitten *kabanos* still in her hand, near the controversial platter, Lila looks like she has been attempting, and failing completely, to control her fuming anger. She addresses me sharply: "Nina, stop this right now! Or I may never want another *kabanos* again! I mean it! I'm going to throw up!!"

Trying to confine her agitated state, she places her glass

on the table and puts her hand over her mouth, and with her virgin perfectly smoked *kabanos* in the other hand with its slender fingers and pretty red nails, Lila retreats to the opposite side in decidedly less dainty than usual steps on her high heel sandals that display to full advantage her toenails lacquered red.

"Hee, hee, hee, so what was this animated scene in Polish all about?" Martin asks, taking a sip of white wine (how many has he had?), after giving it a few of his always the same assessing sniffs. "Not too bad," he says, and twirls the stem of the glass a few times.

No one else is in the vicinity and Gertrude jumps in, trying to beat a dead horse back to life. "Anyway, in my opinion it is idiotic of you, Martin, to be wasting any time defending this butcher. And don't complain later that I didn't warn you that these *kabanosy* are likely laden with highly toxic Polish antisemitic preservatives," she explains with a haughty blank stare, angled slightly off to the side, so I won't notice, but I do.

Following this performance, Gertrude click click clicks away, clutching her glass of red wine, her indignation center stage all the way back to her spot by the Matjes herring.

Lila, an untasted *kabanos* languishing in her hand, seems to regain at least her external veneer of calm. She is now next to Gertrude. The two of them proceed to examine the three different varieties of herring on three simpler white platters with silver rims.

Martin quietly sips his white wine. Suddenly, Gertrude lowers her head almost all the way down to the floor, and her attention focuses on my safety pin securing the ankle strap of my right worn leather flamenco style BeautiFeel dancing shoe. "So, it seems, Nina, you like safety pins on everything these days?" A diffused scorn permeates her voice. "Could it be your new fashion statement Nina, or is it just an attention getting device? Or do you think it's some kind of art?" Whatever was in her voice spills over to invade her facial features.

My loyal husband piles on: "In fact, Gertrude, I've told Nina many times that she looks like a homeless person with that safety pin. But of course she doesn't listen to me. Maybe she'll listen to you."

I take a hesitant sip of merlot from an extra glass Martin left on the edge of the table and look at Gertrude. She doesn't look at me — as usual.

"Gertrude, my husband listens to you, but not to me so maybe you can elucidate even better for him about Polish butchers? You have a rational brain, while I have the brain of an irrational wife — a wife whose reality is colonized by an illicit imagination caused by stinky weed." I wink. "So Marti does not believe me."

Gertrude doesn't wink back, but obliges Martin: "Well, I might as well tell you, Martin, because Nina takes too long to tell her jokes, that in general I support her view on the subject of tasting something new. But let's be considerate. It looks like Lila is very hungry and wants her *kabanos*, and can't eat it in the present circumstances, so Nina, in my opinion, should save us the Pinocchio details of a nose growing bigger when it cheats us from behind his counter. Oh, and may I repeat the fact that a Polish Butcher can smell that we're Jewish, which was confirmed by my mother, who survived the Holocaust. In addition, as you well know, the majority of the population of Poland is antisemitic, and that's why we are here, out of Poland, fortunately. Martin."

"Your mother was a real hero," Martin says.

"*Our* mother," I say. "But Gertrude, why do you never say our mother I wonder?" But Gertrude ignores me and turns her attention to Lila who is back drinking her wine. The *kabanos* hidden in Lila's hand is still unbitten.

Lila attempts to appear calm but can't disguise that she's pissed. "Hey Nina, please let's not spoil this very nice party occasion by talking about unpleasant things!" Her tone is pleading, but firm.

Gertrude's eyes narrow. Her coup de grâce comes in a flood of condescension: "Lila is right, let's not allow Nina to spoil Sylvia's happy occasion. Martin, why don't you take it upon yourself and finally make your wife stop this farce. Her sense of timing is typically terrible. And it looks like Lila may faint if she doesn't eat the *kabanos* right away."

"But will you listen to me, Gertrude," I insist. "I want to say something important which is on my mind."

"As long as it's not your dirty laundry, Nina."

"What's private to one is not private to the other. And

some prefer not to know and not to say anything. Which is why I — imagining I'm a real writer — write straight from my head, daydreaming with a pen in my hand."

"So you need to say everything on your mind, Nina? Even though no one asked you? Is that necessary to be a writer?" Gertrude's mock gently inquires.

"True enough, Nina, no one asked you to tell us why and what you write," Lila adds.

"It's why I read my nonsense only in my fiction class, stuff you wouldn't want to hear. You'd kill me if you did, Gertrude. And my characters are exaggerated products of my imagination. They are just characters, not real people. And Lila, I'm sure you wouldn't want to hear all the uncensored stuff."

Martin seems amused. "Hee, hee, hee, Nina, why don't you write a food column instead in a travelogue?"

"Martin, Nina may bring up private dirty laundry things even in a food travelogue. A hard to digest habit. My opinion." Gertrude, having spat out her little mean joke, makes no eye contact with me at all.

"But you two sisters shouldn't talk like that. Take, for example, Lila . . ." Martin says, his attention now on the far end of the table where Lila, probably to avoid the crossfire between Gertrude and me, has taken refuge. From the table length distance, Martin again surreptitiously surveys Lila's petite figure in her high heel sandals, on her tiptoes as she bends gracefully over a white porcelain gold rimmed plate with chicken liver pate surrounded by cornichons. She has an elated expression on her face. Meanwhile, Martin's discreet gaze behind his professorial rectangular bifocal lenses lingers at the fine black lace of Lila's décolletage. I think Gertrude also noticed that.

Then, Martin doubles back and doubles down on his advice to Gertrude and me: "You girls shouldn't be talking badly about that Poor Butcher. So what if he has an unattractive nose and cheats a little? Great kibanosees are an offspring of an authentic Polish Butcher, a creation worth turning a blind eye to small transgressions and paying a little extra for," Martin counsels. "So you girls should just enjoy these kabanossii, though they're not for me, hee, hee, hee."

"Ha Ha Ha!" Three crisp bursts of undiluted sarcasm have managed to escape from Gertrude's mouth. "So Martin, will we always be *girls* till we die? I am asking you yet again, because you will not give me an answer. And you will be an Old Boy? Is that correct?"

I face Gertrude, who is examining the tip of her boot. "Shit, there is a scratch" — confirming her suspicion.

"Gertrude," I say pleasantly enough, "patriarchs call women girls. We can't change that. But change, when it happens, starts at primary roots, according to Dr. Butterfly."

Gertrude is fixated on her footwear, trying to scrape off the whitish spot (maybe a bird shat on her boot?). "Oh, and what else did this Madame Butterfly have to say?" she asks disinterestedly.

I pretend not to have heard her and walk away.

Martin downs his new glass of white wine, after several glasses of different red. "Girls, there is nothing wrong with patriarchs. In fact they are very much needed. Without us, how would you girls make kids? And some of us even cook the dinner." (He doesn't say that girls should suck boys' dicks for that.) "And when Nina is stoned, she definitely needs someone to control her. And someone to be responsible to." His hee, hee duplet (where did the third hee go?) is delivered through fully covered teeth behind his squeezed lips.

A fresh wave of animation appears in Gertrude's cautiously calculating eyes. "So Nina, why not finally write your book and ponder on all that. And it is fiction, right? Will anyone publish it?" (She is taunting me. The gloves are off.) "But you won't put our real names in it, I hope."

"No, of course not. My book may be a polemic on why some Patriarchs are Idiots, and why some Matriarchs are smarter. But fiction."

This time Gertrude looks at me, with an expression I can't decipher. "That's what I meant, Nina. So it's a good thing you have so many years of experience with your Patriarch Husband. Oh, and Nina, count on me, you can interview me. If you want more material on the subject. I have a husband too. And anyway, Nina, you should realize that you're very lucky that your Patriarch Husband brings you coffee in bed, cooks for you, pays your bills, throws out your garbage, and hangs out your clean laundry and your coat. For a patriarch, that's some real service! My Douggie needs some further training, in fact. But you Nina, with all your experience, should be able to teach Martin to restrain himself from giving unasked for advice to us mere girls." She takes a sip of red wine — her first sip. "Not too sour, Martin, pretty decent, actually," she says. "But I hope it doesn't give me an outbreak of rosacea on my face."

"Marti, don't worry," I say loud enough for Lila (she is again at the other end of the table) to hear, "Us girls and boys will be under fictitious names." I bestow a little peck on Martin's cheek.

"Hee, hee" — has he permanently misplaced his third hee? — "in America, *girls* is just a commonly used expression," he insists. "But Lila must be starved," he says as he watches her hover at the other end of the table, *kabanos* still hidden in her hand.

I sense that Martin wants to put a definitive end to the protracted noxious vibe between me and my sister which must be unpleasant to watch and hear. He is trying to change the subject, and cajoles us in the tones of a wise parent (which I detest, as I am neither his student to be advised nor his child to be corrected).

"Girls," Martin continues. "I want to see how you finally enjoy these kabanosees. And of course since there are three of you — a multiple orgasm, hee, hee, hee. And I want to see and hear it in triple time, finally, as a matter of *fact*, not opinion."

Gertrude's just about always suspicious eyes open

wider, her shoulder executing a tiny shrug, and from above the *kabanosy*, she tells Martin, "But don't let Nina start on another one of her half baked jokes, because Lila wants no part of this debate. And she is starving!" With a motion of her pretty head, Gertrude indicates Lila, who is now next to the chicken liver paté (*pasztecik*) with cornichons, with her still virgin *kabanos* in her hand. And unexpectedly, Gertrude looks at me with a conspiratorial affectionate sisterly gaze that conjures up unspoken understandings between us.

But I am still smarting from her latest remark about my half baked joke and say, "Gertrude, but why don't *you* tell a joke? You're much better at jokes than me."

"Maybe later. But where is Sew? He could improve on your joke even better, Nina," Gertrude advises.

"He is late but of course he will not tell us why. That's Sew," I say.

"We need him, especially for later," says Gertrude.

"I agree. But for now what can I do to get my husband to taste a *kabanos*? He is still afraid to experience a new taste. And what about Heaven in the Mouth, Marti?"

"Don't be silly, Nina, your Heaven in the Mouth is not my Heaven in the Mouth. I'm just not interested in kabenosee! But we both like good pasta, and if properly al dente, pasta is a truly Italian Orgasm. Hee, hee."

"An operatic event, the Libiamo aria from *La Traviata* — a doubly joyous operatic orgasmic event, especially if the pasta is rigid enough, which happens under the sophisticated supervision of your wife, right darling?" I give him a quick kiss.

"A twice repeated Italian operatic pasta al dente orgasm is even better! No need to complain about *that*." He kisses me on the cheek.

At the other end of the table Lila inspects the *mizeria*. She doesn't seem interested in our conversation.

Martin offers me a compliment: "The problem is that Nina does have *too* great of an imagination."

"Thank you Marti," I say affectionately and give him a sweet smile, a prelude to a kiss my lips do when I call him Marti instead of Martin, and he notices and smiles ever so slightly, and his eyes throw a tender fleeting look into mine and he kisses me on the cheek. Gertrude watches us.

"Well Nina, are you or are you not going to reveal to us your wisdom before Lila will die of starvation!?" Gertrude is growing impatient.

Meanwhile, a cold breeze and somehow unnatural muffled sounds emanate from the open door in the foyer. There are too many voices and I can't distinguish words. "Well, are you going to tell us something important and not too private, or not?" Gertrude reminds me.

"I'll not bore you at the present moment, Gertrude, but I'll put it in my book." I look at Lila who seems distracted by the noises from the foyer.

Gertrude seethes. "Well, Nina, as I've explained to you ad nauseam, it's your reality and I wonder if you'll be objective enough to write an accurate account of your own shadowy motivations." She produces one doubting not too well intended bark of a laugh and walks back to her favorite *śledzik* (Matjes of course), her heels making what sounds to me like a disdainful staccato rhythm.

Lila is back by the *kabanosy* with her unbitten *kabanos* in the same position in her left hand and a glass of chardonnay in her right. Now she *is* listening, and looking me straight in the eyes. She says sharply, "And don't you dare, and I mean it Nina, say anything private about me in your book."

"Lila, I create characters, so aren't they my literary property to do with them whatever I want? Like the beautiful Equations Martin creates — aren't these our intellectual properties?"

"Unfortunately, Nina does not understand being polite to her friends," Martin says after a thoughtful sip.

"And Martin, what did you advise her, I wonder?" Gertrude's scornful interest is activated.

"Hee, hee, hee. I advised her *no salacious details*. Nina doesn't need to assassinate her husband's character. The character that happens to look and talk and laugh like me hee, hee, hee. In my opinion, Nina needs to curb herself. What if her book is available for public consumption? It will for sure ruin my reputation, but she doesn't care. And I advised her not to make bad jokes about the poor butcher." Martin doesn't look at me at all.

Gertrude ignores me. She is eyeing from the distance,

on the opposite side of the table, what looks like another version of chopped chicken liver (*pasztecik*) on a bed of arugula. Then she walks over there with a studied, silent calm and Lila (the unbitten *kabanos* still in her hand) joins her at another choice spot: the Majtes *śledzik* plate.

Martin looks around the room and suddenly places a marital peck, no, actually a quick kiss, on my lips, drawing me toward him with an unusually passionate energy as if he has been unleashed from his usual restraint. He even musters a close up direct Eye Contact and proceeds to whisper in my ear, "Nina, by the way, the French country butcher in Pagnol's silent films fucks his own wife in his own butcher shop, on a huge butcher block table. And I'm sure that first she sucks his dick. That's what I like."

At the other end of the table, Lila and Gertrude are studiously examining the various other delicacies.

"And the Russian butchers, what do they do in their butcher shops with their wives, darling?" I ask Martin sweetly.

Gertrude is back, perked up, and for a change she faces me with her blank mildly amused look. "I vote that Nina poses this question directly to the Russians when they arrive." She looks toward the open door in the foyer. "I think the Russian Jews are at the door, in fact. Russian is being spoken at the door," Gertrude announces.

I say nothing but lower my head over the pile of *kabanosy*, inhaling their smoky scent with a demonstrative gusto. Martin observes me with a shy smirk. "And I vote that you girls finally taste these kabanosees, courtesy of the Polish butcher whose idea of heaven I believe is ideally executed, hee, hee, hee."

"But darling, I thought you stopped believing in heaven when you were sixteen. And now you believe only in the University, the Equation, and Irish Whiskey, Amen. And you refuse to savor Heaven in the Mouth. *Niebo w Gębie* — can you say it properly darling?"

Martin looks at me stupefied as if he hasn't heard. Or maybe he is readying himself to get another glass of wine. Or looking for Lila, who is no longer by the long rectangular table.

I say to him a little too loudly, "Marti! please don't escape!" and more quietly, "Marti, try a *kabanos*, it may return to you your faith in heaven, so for heaven's sake, darling, try something new before you die, besides the not quite the same unknown in your always to be improved Elegant Equation — the one that lives 24/7 in your head." I take a few exalted inhalations over the *kabanosy* platter, lowering my head another inch or more and exhaling to the side.

Gertrude is speechless, her blank stare seemingly meant to paralyze me. Martin, for his part, assumes a concerned expression: "What are you doing, Nina? It's not hygienic, you shouldn't sniff those kabanosees like that!"

"But I'm not exhaling onto the *kabanosy*, darling, I'm only *inhaling*. Remember the magic six inch intimate distance? Erotic can be small, it doesn't have to be big. And sniffing the sanctus spiritus of *kabanosy* is a prelude to the *Kabanos* Kiss. And to Heaven in the Mouth."

"Not a bad joke Nina, hee, hee, hee."

Gertrude seems mildly disgusted.

Lila materializes from I'm not sure where and joins me with her nose near mine over the *kabanosy*. "They do smell heavenly, smoky, and garlicky. Divine!" she says and inhales with her eyes closed and turns her head toward the ceiling, exhaling slowly. Once again a spontaneous beatific smile brightens her face.

Gertrude watches the scene. "Martin, *Niebo w Gębie* — can you repeat that?" She encourages him in a pleasant way. "And if Nina helps you practice Polish pronunciation enough, I bet that soon you'll be saying things in Polish as well as my talented husbie can!" Then her tone changes to a bit spiteful. "So Nina, there is no reason why you shouldn't teach Martin as soon as you can." She reaches for the *kabanos*. "I hope that that Polish Butcher didn't poison it." She brings her suspicious eyes closer to the *kabanos* she is holding in her hand.

I pick from the pile my first *kabanos* of the evening.

"Hey, let's eat," Lila says and gives me a wink. Her *kabanos* is now in open sight. "No one is watching so we can devour them. Nina, you go first."

With the *kabanos* between two of my palms in front of my nose, I close my eyes and pray in my head: Inhale the heavenly abandon of our communal ecstasy!

"And Martin, please join us for our first bite," Lila pleads.

"Darling, to the *Kabanos* Heaven just say Amen."

Gertrude looks at me coldly. "Are you done confabulating on your antisemitic *kabanos* yet, Nina? Is that your half baked joke that you wanted to crack us up with? And for your information, Nina, I think the problem here has nothing to do with the kaba or any other nose, which Martin can check on in the Oxford Dictionary."

"My half baked joke I stole from Pinocchio as you know." I say that knowing she will come up with a new insult.

"So can't you come up with an uncopied version, Nina? If you want to get any attention, be original." A triumphant grimace appears on my older sister's mouth.

"Gertrude, didn't you say that reality depends on whose original version it is?" I breathe deeply in and out through my nose to infuse calm into my being. I stop smelling the *kabanos* and am speechless, feeling a hit of burning acid swirling in my gut.

Martin throws a disturbed glance my way and puts his hand carefully on Gertrude's shoulder.

Lila looks like she will lose it if she doesn't bite into her *kabanos* soon.

DR. ANGELA BUTTERFLY, MSW, PH.D.
INTIMACY SPECIALIST
(5th Session)
7/13/05

I initiated a discussion of progress on communication, which along with eye contact, both inside and outside the bedroom, is key for sexual expression to thrive.

Today I emphasized how ruinous revenge can be to intimacy. Nina was emotional talking about her older sister who in private had told her that she feels for her nothing but pity. However, in their youth they had been close, especially when they were pregnant with their first babies and wore the same Laura Ashley flowery dresses.

Between sessions, N had left a phone message for me complaining about M's "demand" for oral sex twice a week. In session, I informed her that she has nothing to lose, only to gain, by helping M transform his "demands" into "overtures." She responded defensively that her inability to open up to express affection and sexual intimacy is exacerbated by M's undermining "the very essence of my being, as an artist and a writer." I responded by asking if withholding oral sex was her revenge.

M suddenly became very present, and asked her the same question. She didn't say anything – unusual for her.

We took a five minute break.

Regrouping, I suggested that they experiment with role-playing: Teacher(adult) / Pupil. N quipped, "Only if I can play the teacher!" Then giggled stiffly.

Just then N's phone rang. Their older son was on the line, and I overheard him loudly and breathlessly reporting that their younger son had been injured playing basketball.

Session aborted. N and M rushing off to Kaiser ER.

(N called later to say that the boy is fine.)

Plan: Explore the nature of revenge destroying relationships between people.

———————

TRIPLE KABANOS ORGASM

"Taste my Heaven in the Mouth before you die, darling!"

Bolero — Ravel (continues)

In unison we take our first bites. "*Niam, niam!*" In a spontaneous collective threesome, we smack our lips, looking at each other, then even more affectionately at our *kabanosy*, still more or less six inches in length and a quarter inch in diameter, just the right size for a handheld snack. The young couple is at the wine table, watching.

Martin, his kindly amused grin stuck on his closed lips, does his hee, hee, hee triplet. "So, girls, it is moist to perfection? Not too dry? Shall I bring you Wyborowa vodka to go with it?"

"Not too dry, darling, not like a nun's pussy!" I whisper in his ear, and when he lets out an amused hee, hee, for his benefit I demonstratively smell my half eaten *kabanos*. "Marti, trust me, this is a Perfect *Kabanos*, not yet shriveled at all. Oh no, don't go away, Marti. At the least, aren't you interested in sensory coordinates of heaven? Darling?"

Lila daintily bites off a piece of her *kabanos*, chewing it with her eyes closed and turning her face up (in the direction of heaven). Her facial features smooth in this pleasure soaking act. "This is bliss," she says stretching out all the letters of *kabanos* blissfulness.

I close my eyes and chew with exultant abandon, then look my husband straight in the eye with an exultant expression produced by what is in my mouth — which I want him to share with me.

Martin gently moves me a step away. "So how is this

171

heaven in the oral cavity, hee, hee, hee."

Gertrude is chewing with cautiously restrained enthusiasm and watching us. "Nina, it seems that Martin is seriously ready to know the meaning of *Niebo w Gębie* before he can try it. So why not start your training now?"

My husband continues to show zero desire to taste the *kabanos*, telegraphing his disinterest by folding his forearms in a protective self embrace, his back arched to increase the distance between his nose and the *kabanos* I hold in my hand. A charming provocative smile spreads from my lips up into my eyes, as with a studiously refined restraint I keep presenting the *kabanos* to him. It is too close; he bends his torso a little farther back.

"Hey, darling it's not a dangerous object!" I'm teasing him.

He bends farther still away from me. "Hey, Nina, actually I am not that hungry, but the three of you girls really look like you're entering the real heavens, hee, hee."

We stop chewing, all six of our eyes on Martin. The *kabanos* I want him to bite is a tiny bit nearer his nose and I am daring him. "Darling, if you taste it, like Gertrude says, you will be able to understand *Niebo w Gębie* accurately and say it with a good accent. And it would be a proper scientific experiment leading to an empirical conclusion. I read it in the *Times,* in the science section, that fear of experience may lead to impoverished auditory tactile olfactory inputs, which are all interconnected with the hippocampus and mixed up with limbic emotions and memories and even libido . . . Therefore, Marti, you should taste it!" I bring the *kabanos* a tiny bit closer to his nose (remembering from a psychology lecture years ago that you can overcome a phobia of most things by successive step by step approximations). "And maybe then and only then you'll know what a *Kabanos* Orgasm is, darling: an experience, which is not a word in the Oxford Dictionary . . . Gertrude, do you agree with me?"

"Hee, hee, hee." Martin takes hold of my wrist, looks at the *kabanos* and I can feel his fingertips trembling.

"Anyway, Nina, it could be that your ambition is too great after all," Gertrude says, watching Martin closely. He moves his torso and head even farther from the *kabanos*. I bite a little tip off of it to taunt him and he arches his back while his eyes fill with distrust and fix on the long finger sized *kabanos* in my hand, as if it were a truly dangerous object. I touch the top of his hand. It is tense and sweaty, almost twitching at threshold level, and he takes a stronger hold of my wrist, keeping the *kabanos* from getting closer to his nose and mouth, and in this position he laughs tensely, hee, hee, through his tightly compressed lips.

"Hey, Nina, since you say you're a writer, couldn't you just describe the flavor of this kabanosee to me and maybe then I could taste it fictionally, hee, hee, hee." His hold on my wrist grows firmer.

"Darling," I coax him in a soft tone. "Dr. Butterfly would applaud you. A six inch distance for viewing the object of your fear, and of my desire, is courageous. And a good practice for the eye to eye distance of six inches, optimal for a Happening between long term partners like us chained to each other in their domestic prison of habit. And by the way, Madame Butterfly (I say this for Gertrude's benefit) said that sex between four eyes needs to happen first before a stiff dick takes over." Gertrude and Lila look at me and say nothing. I look into Martin's eyes, then sniff Martin's *kabanos* in my hand. My wrist is still in his strong hold.

Ever watchful, Gertrude is chewing her *kabanos* steadily with measured non-enthusiasm. "I'm afraid it'll upset my stomach. Who knows what this butcher puts in it? So if I were you, Martin, I wouldn't let Nina force you. Fight for your rights, Martin! You're not used to preservative laden antisemitic sausage, so it will likely upset your stomach. Be careful!" Per usual, Gertrude seems satisfied with her admonishment.

My husband makes a face of apologetic resignation. "My wife thinks she can make everyone abide by her rules." His hold on my wrist remains firm.

"And you abide, Martin? Even if the rules are stupid?" Gertrude regards him with mild indignation and bites into her *kabanos*.

"Martin has strong opinions on many things that are not his business — like my shoe with the ankle strap hanging on the safety pin making me look like a homeless person. Right, Marti? But today he didn't notice my shoes! Only my black nylons. And he always says that my hair is a mess and wants me to get a decent haircut. But I don't trust haircutters."

"I can cut your hair Nina," Gertrude offers with surprising affection.

"Nina, I also think your hair is too chaotic, but you are getting off the subject," Lila says, and bites her *kabanos,* but without elated expression and without closing her eyes.

"Well, I cut my hair, my husband's hair, and my boys' hair. I'll cut your hair too, Nina, if you want." Gertrude sounds genuine. "You don't need more chaos, Nina. I thought you said that you had enough of it inside your head?" She happily giggles.

"Marti practices static chaos in his Dynamic Chaos Equation Studio and I don't complain because it's not my business," I say to Gertrude. "And I like my messed up hair to cover my irrational head plus my unshapely chin, and the safety pin is a life saver where and when needed — and it is also an original fashion statement."

"Nina, a safety pin isn't exactly art to me." Gertrude's conclusion is accompanied by a left shoulder shrug and visual inspection of her perfectly polished black boots with the pointy toes and shiny silver clasps. "I think you just want to bring attention to yourself, Nina, but why destroy things and rip them on purpose?" She points to her boots. "I bought these on sale twenty years ago but I take care of them so they look like new. You could do it too, if you wanted too. And in my opinion, Nina, if you worked full time like I do, you could even afford an elegant Armani suit."

"But Gertrude, first it's not my style, and second I prefer to work half time so I have the other half to do nothing. Third, I don't like shopping."

In the meantime, Martin returns to a fully upright uptight defensive mode. I move toward Lila, who is now enmeshed in focused and elated concentration, lingering over chews of the *kabanos*. She interrupts for a moment. "Martin, it's Heaven in the Mouth, this time Nina is right, you should try it!" She resumes chewing with her eyes closed.

I bite into Martin's *kabanos*. "Darling," I say to him, making sure Gertrude is listening, "What if I check it for you again to make sure it isn't poisoned?" My eyes show earnestness as I take another bite of Martin's *kabanos*.

"*Kabanos Perfekcja*," I proclaim, after three methodical chews with my eyes closed. Then, with eyes open.

Lila stops chewing. "Nina, don't torture poor Martin, for God's sake. But trust me, Marti, it is just right today: in terms of maturity and smokiness, it's perfect." She closes her eyes and finishes chewing what she had in her mouth, then swallows.

"But Lila," Martin says, "can you spell this Kabanosiie Perfekceyja for me? Is it the translation for heavens?"

Gertrude, who is watching and chewing cautiously, doesn't miss her chance: "Nina, I'm advising you again that you should seriously start the teaching sessions with your husband right away. And I confirm that he is displaying a significant readiness, in fact!"

Lila touches Martin's hand and is slowly spelling the *Kabanos Perfekcja* for him. After several patient tries, he still mispronounces it, and Lila, as if to enjoy the end of her first *kabanos* in peace, steps away. Gertrude is chewing her *kabanos* more cautiously.

I chew on my Heaven in the Mouth enthusiastically and ignore Gertrude. Martin's *kabanos* is still in my hand and still about six inches from his nose; his torso is bent back, but not as far as before.

Very quietly, so Martin won't be scared that someone else might hear, I whisper: "Darling, you can flex quite far in order to not face the fear of the unknown . . . Okay! Fuck you, don't taste it! Don't taste it unless you desire to know!" I put his *kabanos* in my mouth as far down as I can and look him straight in the eyes and confide in his ear, "That is why we don't have intimate together sex, darling! Spontaneous foreplay with the unknown is missing. And the French butcher you so worship in the Pagnol films fucks his wife on his big butcher block, wham bam thank you ma'am! Less than thirty seconds. Not enough for any woman, rational or irrational, darrrling." I roll the "r" in Polish for emphasis.

I take my mouth away from his ear and for a moment he tolerates my eyes looking into his while, defiantly, I put more of his *kabanos* into my mouth.

"Hey Nina, you know what? I wouldn't mind if you put my dick all the way like that in your mouth from time to time, as a matter of a fact." Resentment courses through his whisper. He looks around the dining room.

"Martin advises me to write a discreet food travel book," I inform Gertrude and Lila.

"Sure Nina," Gertrude delivers in a tone of straight-forward practical advice, "You should force your husband to go on a trip together and see the world. In my opinion it would be even more useful."

"But why are you insulting your husband, Nina?" Lila says quietly.

"Because Martin rather than travel with me advises me to chisel my writing skills and describe the taste of the *kabanos* for him in a travelogue restaurant book, and if the book is good enough, he won't have to go anywhere and not taste the *kabanos*. *Why* experience the new thing together? And so he thinks the role of a writer is to save people from having to travel even if they can afford it but are afraid to experience the new. Right, darling?"

"You're right, Nina. In fact, I'd rather be home right now."

"And darling, didn't you also say that such a travelogue book might sell, so we wouldn't have to go on a trip paid for from your salary, especially if it's somewhere you do not want to go? Where plaques and statues of wise men of the past are missing?"

"Hey Gertrude, maybe you can help Nina edit a nice food travelogue?" Martin suggests.

Almost Finale!

In a simultaneous symphonic harmony of appreciative sounds, Lila, Gertrude, and I chew with dramatic abandon, our thankful eyes directed to the skies in a collective gratitude of significant magnitude. The *kabanos* flavor is bursting in waves and I can feel it spreading all over my being. *This* is a Triple *Kabanos* Orgasm, I comment in my head so as to not offend Lila. Gertrude trains on me her kind and longer than usual filled with *forgiving* tolerance Eye Contact.

I return my attention to Martin, with renewed hope of arousing his courage to *together* taste the unknown, and of reaching the deeper sensual layer in his blue eyes behind his rectangular glasses. He bends a little backward again (his attitude of preemptive defense). I start to gently taunt him: "Marti, don't be afraid." I am enjoying holding the *kabanos* in front of his nose. "So darling, you're inflexibly serious about not being interested in knowing what you're missing, yet your torso is amazingly flexible! Your torso flexibility paradoxically serves you to not taste that very thing you're missing. Isn't that an existential paradox? Darling, you conquer the fear of the unknown when you meet her face to face, not rigidly bent away from facing her." I'm proud to have expressed myself so eloquently.

Martin straightens up and looks as if I am making no sense (a state of mind he habitually assigns to me). Gertrude stops chewing, maybe preparing to unleash a superior burst of indignation. "Nina, you're lucky to have such a flexible husband. But too bad that it is not when it's needed. Ha!" Her laughter rings unpleasantly in my ear.

"But ask Marti about a Perfectly Balanced Equation," I say with a straight face.

Gertrude contributes: "And Nina, you shouldn't complain. Douggie sometimes is so rigid that he hits me by accident in his sleep. But Martin, for now, could you get my sister to shut up and save us from her circus? I think Nina wants to manipulate us like puppet actors on her imaginary *Kabanos* Orgasm stage, and in my opinion, Martin, if you gather enough courage and taste this Polish antisemitic sausage, maybe Nina will stop herself from torturing all of us. It may not kill you, Martin, but it may shut Nina up!" Gertrude is pleased with her wit.

"I still think the best solution for Nina is to describe the taste of this kabanosee for me in her travel diary in Poland: In Search of the Perfect Kabanosee Orgasm. That would also sell, I think. And I don't have to taste it. But my wife doesn't find that logical."

Lila, onto her second *kabanos*, stops chewing. "My friends, enough of this!" she says, obviously fuming. In controlled yet peeved dainty steps, she escapes to the other side of the dining table and stops by a large platter with a silver rim, where the Swedish Matjes herring is proudly laid to rest, with half circles of red onions around it.

Gertrude finishes the cautious chewing of her *kabanos* and throws me a dismissive glance, then follows Lila to the Matjes, her favorite herring.

I stay put, and turn the *kabanos* in my hand: "Darling, this is your last chance in this overly lingering scene now without any witnesses! Darling, taste Heaven in the Mouth before you die!"

Finale!

Martin — free of the *kabanos* in front of his nose — is amused as he watches Lila, Gertrude, and me hovering over the platter in dramatic camaraderie, inhaling the scent, before selecting the next one from the top of the pile and putting it in our mouths.

"I am in heaven," I say looking upwards. And it seems that Gertrude, in spite of her reservations, is in heaven too. And so is Lila. But suddenly Gertrude stops chewing.

"I better not eat any more, I don't want to get fat," Gertrude announces after her third *kabanos*.

"I can't stop," Lila says without lifting her head, her eyes fixed on the pile of *kabanosy*.

"I can't stop either." I take a new *kabanos* and bite a piece of it and with my mouth full, look at Martin, who is now unamused. "But I couldn't get Marti to taste the unknown. He is fearful and suspicious and distrusts whatever he doesn't know." I resume chewing meticulously.

Lila places her hand on top of Martin's with tender reassurance: "Marti, please do not run away for the wine again. Nina is right, do try the *kabanos,* please! For me?"

"Martin, I agree with Lila and for once with your wife." Gertrude says. "Anyway, on a fortunate note, you must have a strong Irish stomach, since you can stomach my sister marketing herself as an artist of manipulating any moment. So I'm quite sure you can also handle our Polish Butcher's authentic antisemitic *kabanos*. But I'd also like to know why you can't understand that neither Nina nor anyone else can fully describe for you the taste of *kabanos*. In my opinion, the best solution is to taste the *kabanos* and put an end to this boring suspense. And while you're at it, I already advised you on that — why don't you go with Nina on a trip to somewhere you've never been before," Gertrude suggests without cynicism.

Between meticulous chewings of my *kabanos* I say to Martin, "Gertrude has a great idea." Then I say to my sister, "But Gertrude, wouldn't you agree that the first step for Martin is a tiny baby step to taste this authentic antisemitic *kabanos*, and shut me up?" I look straight into her eyes, and she turns them away.

"You can think whatever you want to think, Nina," Gertrude says with her older sister's studied cold calm; her *kabanos* finished, she retreats to the other end of the table. Lila is already there, by the chicken liver pate (*pasztecik*) with cornichons.

Lila and Gertrude have returned, and with a bemused smirk Gertrude reaches for her fourth *kabanos* and says, "Actually I can't control myself today, antisemitic butcher, preservatives, or not. I'm going to have another one. But I hope I don't get fat. And no need to be afraid, Martin."

I bring the *kabanos* an inch closer to my husband's nose. He is leaning back from it just a little bit. He gives it another appraisal. "Well, I just don't like the look of this one," he sniffs it. "How do you girls know they're still fresh?" He holds my wrist tensely.

Gertrude is quick to respond: "So you think girls are more trustworthy in matters of freshness but not of worldly stiff assessments?"

Lila stops chewing. "Gertrude, Nina, stop this. It's silly."

"Hey Lila, why don't you explain to Martin that trying new things is worth it. He trusts you more than us," Gertrude says while giving me a sisterly wink. Lila gets a meaningful look from her too.

"Actually, *kabanosy* are smoked and dried without chemical preservatives so they don't spoil," Lila assures Martin.

"So for blue heaven's sake, Marti, I beg you please try it so we can be done with this prolonged scene and not bore Gertrude and Lila to death. Hey Marti, what if I bite this particular *kabanos* meant for you, since you don't trust it? And maybe after I check it out for you, you will believe me that it is not poisoned!" I look at my husband, free my wrist, and take a demonstrative bite of his *kabanos*.

"But didn't Gertrude say that it could give me a stomachache?" Again he is firmly holding onto my wrist attached to the hand with the *kabanos*. He looks at me with serious concern.

"Oh Maartin, some boys should realize that sometimes the benefits outweigh the risk of a new experience!" Gertrude says emphatically giving me a supportive sisterly wink.

Martin bends back his torso, just a little further away from me, and as if he were about to risk something potentially disastrous, inhales tentatively. He cautiously brings my hand with the *kabanos* closer to his mouth.

"Okay, fine, I'll taste it," he blurts out anxiously with quietly pissed off resignation, and, without further sniffing it, he takes a tiny bite. He is chewing it with extreme caution. The three of us are watching him with hopeful anticipation in our eyes.

Unable to restrain herself, Gertrude interrupts Martin's prolonged pedantically distrustful chewing action:

"And? What's the verdict?"

I take a big sniff of his *kabanos*, look into his eyes, then take a big bite, as I catch my husband sending secret glances toward Lila's pretty décolletage.

N reports that she followed my advice by placing I LOVE YOU stickers on the fridge, as a "spontaneous loving action." M, she said, did not notice. He responded that he did, but was either busy making dinner or drinking whiskey after long days at work. "Weekends?" I asked. "I'm busy with the kid's soccer games," he replied.

I asked N to read from her journal, which she always carries. She did so, seemingly without thinking, from a random page:

"The sun came out and I was alone in bed, the kids were still asleep, and like every day, Martin was down in the kitchen grinding fresh coffee beans, feeding Alexis in her special bowl and toasting sourdough bread for toast with cheese for our breakfast in bed (we share the cheese with Alexis). The divine smell of freshly ground coffee – every morning – is wafting up the four stairs from the kitchen to my nostrils and I'm dozing back to a half dreamy state. I play with myself under the covers, leisurely giving myself an orgasm (it takes about 20 minutes while he is down in the kitchen), fantasizing about a handsome muscular neighbor friend who, when I go for my walk, runs in his shorts with his penis sticking slightly out. (I told Martin about this later and he was not jealous, but

actually aroused and "glad" I "had a good time.") I think my neighbor pretends he doesn't know that his dick sticks out."

I motioned for N to stop reading, but M said, "No, let her go on." She did.

"I finish myself off just as Martin enters the room with an oval tray covered with a round hand-embroidered Polish linen napkin (one of very few treasures I still have from my early life in Poland) stained with coffee. Since the kids are still asleep, he is wearing my old quite torn Indian silk flowery robe. He walks in proudly presenting the tray and I watch his calves and his muscular thighs through the tears of my silk robe. They are still very shapely and his ass is still tight and young. I feel a sudden surge of desire. I don't tell him. Why don't I tell him? So why can't we just fuck like other people do? Or do they??? After twenty some years together, sharing and fighting about where is the TV remote in our old queen bed...?"

M: "That's my wife – but I'm okay with whatever makes her happy as long as she doesn't bring it home."

Unproductive session, with glimmers of hope.

———

DANCING IN THE LIVING ROOM

"Who is that creep?"

Soulless Elevator Muzak,
fortunately not too loud
(and in her head, a slow samba
— The Girl from Ipanema)

Not used to high heels anymore, just a bit off balance, her awareness sharpened thanks to the cannabis, Nina stepped over the small threshold to the living room, trying to appear confident. She placed her right hand on her right hip to feel the silky velvet of her very special — not at all on sale — black dress. Actually, she felt almost grounded in her sexy medium high black BeautiFeel flamenco style shoes. Luckily, the broken ankle strap was securely fastened with a safety pin — good thing Martin did not notice!

She felt an erotic pressure on both of her inner thighs, from the elastic bands holding her black nylon stockings in place. They were the old fashioned transparent ones with a seam. The ones Martin chose for her at Victoria's Secret. She remembered how during the drive Martin had stroked her stockings, placing her hand on his crotch without opening the zipper, to feel his hard on, a breach of his usual protocol, an abrogation of his standard of decency.

Without a doubt, her dress flattered her shape and made her waist look smaller. Earlier, in her dressing mirror, she'd studied herself carefully from each side and from the back, and when Martin wasn't looking she'd ripped a bit more the side slit of this expensive dress he'd bought for her — which of course he wouldn't approve of — not just to show more leg, to about midthigh, but also to allow her full freedom of motion when dancing. All her skirts and shirts in fact were more than slightly ripped or altered with scissors and finished with safety pins, so that the hem was rounded and jagged in an unpredictable manner. (Martin constantly worried that she would wear faded black clothes with various sized rips and random holes to his office party or the theatre and embarass him.)

She luxuriated in the feel of the silk velvet dress flowing over her body. It fit her like the softest glove, yet hid her major imperfections; the peplum highlighted her slender waist and voluptuous breasts, and emphasized the roundness of her hips after two kids. And her stomach looked almost flat when she sucked it in.

Which she did, and entered the parquet floor of the living room. Two non-Polish speaking couples were dancing . . . or rather swaying monotonously to no soul bland American muzak; not too loud fortunately, so she was able to hear their dull small talk about real estate and their kids choosing the right college.

Like a feline atop her BeautiFeel medium heels, Nina silently angled around the dancing couples (her right ankle strap thank God still attached with the safety pin). To look like she had a purpose, she stopped to examine a large geometric abstract painting above the overstuffed with big pillows matching the dark gray couch, and was relieved that she'd found a refuge from looking like a girl without a boy to pair off with at the school dance. She planted herself in front of this large over the couch painting (perhaps still looking stupefied despite her attempts not to). The painting's colors were muted neutrals and the lines on it didn't do anything for her; the boring thank God not too loud elevator style muzak was ornamented with more equally boring soulless chit chat.

Standing by the dark gray couch, she was writing in her head: "The muzak — easy listening like on the bad local AM radio station — shit, I should leave this dead living room, it's fucking cold and stiff, no vibrant colors, and even the air here lacks soul, just like the muzak . . . numbing at best." She was on the verge of soul suffocation, and to save herself started to inaudibly hum the slow and sensual "Girl from Ipanema." She closed her eyes, the samba comforting her, and began talking to herself in her head: It would look weird to walk out just after I walked in, but . . . no one is watching. (She took a deep yoga breath.) They've all noticed me! On the edge of dance floor, not knowing what to do.

The two couples continued swaying to their banal exchange about expensive cars and houses on the market, then the Ipanema Girl screeched to a halt, like a needle racing across an LP . . . And again I am assaulted by the third rate elevator muzak and the painting without soul embellishing the ambiance of this dead living room, she summarized in her head.

If I stay here, she thought, I'll just get lethargic. In dire need of a more stimulating environment and something to do, with her right hand she examined the fabric and texture of the opulently plush darker shade of gray pillows on the couch. Maybe five minutes passed in this stuporous way, before she tentatively sat on the couch, intending to look through the book on *Obscure Jewish Abstracts* on the table made of cold, thick. smoky black glass.

Everything in this room seemed ridiculously opulent and oversized. Especially the abstract painting above the oversized overstuffed plush dark gray cold to touch leather couch with the matching large pillows. She felt like she had taken acid or magic mushrooms in the wrong place, like Alice in Wonderland. She stood up without looking at the book on *Obscure Jewish Abstracts* and took a step back to try to get a better understanding of the abstract painting. Despite trying, she had no definite feeling about it after all; maybe it has a meaning I do not get, she pondered, and made another attempt to discern its possible abstract meaning. What the fuck is it that the painter felt? Shouldn't I feel something if it is art? The colors are cold and neutral. They fit the couch. Maybe I just don't get this kind of abstract couch art? She focused from different head angles to make sure she wasn't missing an essential element among the straight edged shapes intersecting in a confusion of lines. Doesn't the painter want the audience to feel something??? Anything??? She repeated this question in her head while looking at the painting more intently still. But she experienced nothing that stirred her.

Is it art if it makes you feel nothing? Picasso said if it is not erotic it is not art, she ruminated. Maybe if I half close my eyes. She did so, then opened them slowly. A blur became a dark gray *aha* of an impression, no preconception. Abstract has no preconception. No judgement. Hmmm — could this art be an abstract symbol of suburban taste?

She wondered where Sew was. Why was he late? His paintings of people attempting to look happy were always without a smile. But when Sew himself laughed, he laughed with wild gusto, till tears came to his eyes. Was he trying to kill his sadness? The melody of "Girl from Ipanema" was in her head again. Sew. A melancholy portraitist with a sad smile. An artist of the bittersweet. There is no bitter without sweet and no sweet without bitter . . . Sew, she thought, ought to make a self portrait looking deeply into his own eyes in the mirror. What if I close my eyes more than halfway . . . this soulless abstract here will become more blurred, and maybe . . . I will imagine feeling something. She closed her eyes fully and in her head she heard the samba and began to remember scenes from *A Man and A Woman.*

"*Zatańczysz?* Will you dance?" A man's voice suddenly interrupts her in Polish and in English.

"*Tak.*" Instinctively, without opening her eyes, she responds, eager not to have to keep pretending to appreciate Sylvia's taste in dead living room abstract art.

She opens her eyes to a short glimpse of his face. He seems to be avoiding her eyes. His face is neither attractive nor ugly. The nose too broad. A bit red. Head completely bald.

In the Polish gallant style, he boldly leads her to the shiny parquet dance floor, his hand casually on her shoulder, while his other hand encircles her waist with pleasantly light pressure. She closes her eyes and focuses on the feel of his hand on her waist, as if anticipating that the pleasure of it could be spoiled by focusing excessively on the muzak void of character. They start dancing and she tries to ignore that they aren't dancing in sync with the rhythm, which without exaggeration is undanceable. To distract herself from the unsatisfying feeling that their steps are not synchronized, she closes her eyes, this time hoping it will somehow lessen the undesirable aspects and make it possible for her to dive into the experience. And maybe the muzak will magically transform into something inspiring, the kind that moves the soul.

Suddenly on her cheek she feels a hair moving imperceptibly. Or did she imagine it? No, she is sure that the hair on her right cheek definitely is moving ever so slightly with a pleasing warmth around it.

Under the influence of this sensory delight, she vaguely tolerates the soulless muzak with a sensation of sedation, not unlike being in a dental chair, under nitrous oxide gas and oblivious to the scraping and pulling invasion of her mouth in the quiet office, muzak piped in from the ceiling. ("This is a dance floor, not a dentist's office," she would write later in her diary.)

The next warm breath on her cheek is delivered with great accuracy, as if aimed at another hair on her cheek. She is sure she did not imagine it this time, very sure, and as if entranced she anticipates it moving closer to her right ear.

From the dining room she hears the quiet voice of Lila and Gertrude's louder self righteous laugh. Soon, there follows vague anemic collective ha ha ha's of the unconvincing laughter. She opens her eyes. Lila and Gertrude are at the table with appetizers, and Martin is leaning against the wall near the round table with the wine and a large crystal decanter. A full whiskey glass is in his hand and his other hand is tugging anxiously on his beard — and with the intensity of imminent danger he is watching her dancing with the Bald Bold Man.

She closes her eyes, not wanting her pleasure destroyed by the image of her husband with desperation in his eyes, leaning tensely against the wall. Dancing to soulless music can be calming, she says to herself as she observes with surprise that the muzak does not irritate her anymore. And she and the Bald Bold Man are actually moving together . . . the rhythm easier to follow. (Or was she, she pondered later, twisting reality for a hedonistic purpose so she could go with the flow and get out of it what she could? For doesn't a moment only happen once?)

When she opens her eyes, Martin is watching them straight on, and his whiskey glass is nearly empty. There are two ice cubes in it but she can't hear the clink clinks nor see the ice cubes maybe trembling.

She positions her head so Martin can't see her eyes and she can't see his either. Now the rhythm is quite danceable. She closes her eyes again. The hand of the Bald Bold Man encircles her waist with increased confidence that makes her heart skip a beat and causes a contraction between her inner thighs. His breath on her cheek feels warmer. The slow dance music is truly calming now. She opens her eyes to take a fleeting glance at Martin. There are only unmelted ice cubes in his whiskey glass. She closes her eyes and lets the numbing muzak invade her ears, till a gentle puff of hot air is delivered near her right ear, and soon after, another one, close to her other ear. More breaths . . . She has to stop herself from audibly gasping in rhythm with her body's anticipation. More breaths still.

If I open my eyes it'll be ruined, she ruminates . . . But the no hurry, neutral tempo soothes her into an effortless synchronized swaying together — like a lullaby before falling asleep. Hoping for this not to end, she is no longer wishing for the music to be more inspiring. The Bald Bold Man's breath gets hotter and lingers.

"Would you like to have an affair?" A sudden whisper, a dare, is delivered directly in her ear, each word distinct and clear like a hiss with a sinister quality. It interrupts her dreamlike state. Like a flash attack — a surprise of forceful magnitude — his words immobilize her and she opens her eyes. Three more hot breaths near her ear, and then the other ear. He is awaiting her response. She takes three calming yoga breaths while the Bald Bold Man is breathing on her neck, moving the delicate hairs on it. Her heart is pounding, excited, dismayed, maybe terrified; again she makes herself take three calming yoga breaths. But she is not calmed. The muzak becomes harshly disharmonious and invasive, and her mind becomes unfocused and she knows she is incapable of devising any rational plan of action. She needs to see his eyes, the windows to his soul. But his mouth is near her neck and Eye Contact is not possible.

Nervously they sway in a muzak blur, his cheek making her cheek sweaty. A new spurt of intrusive heat is delivered inside her left ear. His hand around her waist gains firmness and in one confident motion causes her to lose her will to oppose. Forces her to remain where she is. In his tight hold around her waist. She pulls her stomach in.

"I don't know." She hears herself as if it is not her own halting whisper. His cheek presses hers tighter. The muzak has become stupefying. She has a fleeting sobering thought, vaguely about the need for a more careful examination of the Bald Bold Man's proposal. She mulls it over unproductively for a few back and forth sways to the dreadful muzak, but soon his unrelenting breaths in her ear assert their power and she instructs herself to stop thinking. To let herself feel a surge of excitement.

"Be careful," she whispers near his ear. "My husband is watching." She looks in Martin's direction. An unsettling despair is in his eyes. To escape from feeling guilty, she turns so that Martin can't see the expression on her face, concentrating her distracted focus on the Bald Bold Man's hot cheek touching hers with stubbornly pressing insistence and persistence.

From time to time she surreptitiously watches Martin, while avoiding his disturbed gaze. She sees him pour red wine into a crystal glass and carry it to the threshold of the living room (to see them better). In a tense controlled manner he swirls the stem of his crystal stem wine glass without spilling a drop on the shiny parquet floor. He leans against the wall closer to the living room threshold, watching them dance. His stiffened body and face seem to be a house for his fear, fear of another man breathing in his wife's ear. With the subtle movement of her head, Nina indicates her husband to the Bald Bold Man.

"Is that him?" he insolently hisses into her ear as his head angles sideways to regard the figure of Martin, her husband, in the pose of watchful suspicion, cornered by the wall. They both regard her husband, whose eyes are fixed on her, his wife, and in her head she comments that he is ready to claim her as his property. She closes her eyes again. Their swaying together to the muzak becomes constricted. She opens her eyes from time to time and watches the crystal stem of Martin's half full wine glass being subjected to repetitive motion; still nothing spills. He is ingesting the wine in long sips, and after each sip he swirls the stem of his wine glass. The Bald Bold Man shoots a knowing glance at Martin, who accelerates his swirling of the stem of his almost empty glass.

"He is no one." His cocksure convinced beyond doubt hissing in her ear is louder than before. The sinister hiss repeats its pronouncement. He positions his bald head slightly to the side and continues studying the figure of her husband, who now seems to be an embodiment of readiness to fight for her, while the man hissing in her ear is ready to do battle with her husband leaning against the wall, twirling the stem of the now empty wine glass.

The Bald Bold Man lets her meet his smallish and bluish gray eyes for a moment and continues to study her husband.

"*On nikim jest*! He is no one!" He delivers his final conclusion with a louder and more sinister hiss into her ear. "*On nikim jest*!" his arrogant hiss reiterates and he deliberately slowly releases hot air into her left earlobe, near the cubic zirconia stud (a present from Martin for her last birthday).

During the next track of the CD, the Bald Bold Man's breath grew hotter. Eyes closed, she let herself fall into a half conscious trance, but nevertheless was thinking: Should I walk away from this guy right now? Shouldn't I be outraged? This fleeting burst of rational morality was erased (which happens when strong sexual desire hits, she'll think later). Her "should I" did not last long. Their bodies were in lustful sync and the soulless muzak was tolerable again. In fact, she found herself wishing that the CD track would last longer; despite its soullessness, she found it soothing and fell headlong into a daze, till a question in her head shook her awake: How can this guy say Martin is *no one*?

"How can you tell my husband is no one? You do not know him at all," she whispered, her head next to his chest. His heart beat fast and that took away her reasonable thought process yet again. After a few more hot breaths she didn't want to stop anything.

They swayed to the unremarkable muzak for the duration of the third CD track, while his insistent hot puffs excited the inside of her other earlobe, and the corner of his mouth was almost touching the cubic zirconia birthday present.

Undeterred, his whisper hisses in distinct Polish and English: "*On. Nikim. Jest!* He. Is. No. One!"

"But how can you tell? You've never met him." She is angry at the Bald Bold Man, rising to defend her husband and the father of her sons.

He throws a quick derisive peek at Martin. "*Bo wiem,* I can tell." His bilingual whisper sounds perversely mean — and yet she doesn't walk away, but on the contrary is entranced by it and at his breathing directly on the cubic zirconia earring on her left earlobe. (Why, she would wonder later. Was it the sound of Polish in her ear with the cubic zirconia earring, a gift from Martin? Had a mean paradox mesmerized her into this stupor, this submission?) The pressure and temperature of his hand on her waist grows and once more he pulls her closer with confidence, which gives her a new thrill deep between her thighs, where eager and spontaneous contractions are happening, and the deadly boring muzak seems to spring to life — or is it enhanced by the rhythm of his relentless puffs of hot breath, now into her left, and now into her right ear, moving the imperceptibly tiny hairs inside, terribly close to the cubic zirconia earrings.

Suddenly the hold encircling her waist tightens in

one quick motion and she gasps inaudibly and closes her eyes, to not see Martin, to escape the guilt, as the cubic zirconia is desecrated by the Bald Bold Man's disregarding hot breaths. She surrenders fully to the swaying and the rhythm of his breaths. But from time to time she still has a fleeting thought that the muzak is less than inspiring.

The next track of the elevator muzak began and the Bald Bold Man did not release his hold of her. Martin continued to watch them. The new track featured the same lack of that something that moved her soul (which she'd imagined or sensed at the level of her solar plexus), so she closed her eyes and allowed herself to succumb to the even rise and fall of the Bald Bold Man's breath into her earlobe (right next to the zirconia stud). A transient thought passed through her consciousness, that the bald man's audacious boldness should outrage her. . . . She should walk away. Now! Her mind was visited with conflicting wants and shoulds, till the track ended and the Bald Bold Man took his hand off her waist and without a smile, not even looking at her, said: "*Dziękuje*. Thank you." In a seemingly premeditated manner, he immediately turned away and strode slowly and deliberately to the dark opulently oversized gray couch. He sat on it; he nonchalantly crossed one leg over the other, fixed his eyes on his shoes, first one, than the other, and began paging through the art book on Jewish Abstracts on Sylvia's black, smoky, glass coffee table.

Nina returns to the dining room where Martin, his posture stiffened by suspicious watchfulness, is leaning against the wall close to the round wine table, waiting for her, twirling the crystal stem of his wine glass — full again — in his right hand. He puts his left palm on the table. His jaw is twitching lightly, his lips are firmly closed, and he seems to be attempting to control his tongue inside his mouth.

She says, "Darling, you look like you're ready to protect your real property! Me! Your lawful wife!" She feels guilty but her eyes are half joking and she puts both her hands around her husband's neck. Stiff necked, he doesn't respond. Looks at her sternly. To mellow him out, she bestows a brief marital peck on his lips. He doesn't look at her. He looks at the Bald Bold Man, lounging on the couch, inspecting the art book.

"Who is that creep?" Martin whispers and shoots a guarded yet threatening glance toward the Bald Bold Man self importantly occupying the dark gray couch. As is Martin's well established habit, he scans the room in several short jerky eye movements to make sure no one can see his potential disgrace.

"Darling," Nina says quietly, "why do you think he is a creep? But fuck!! Look who seems to be gravitating toward that creep!"

The Bald Bold Man is still on the couch, his legs negligently crossed. Lila is examining the abstract painting over it, and being petite, to seem taller she is standing on tiptoe in her high heel open toe sandals, fresh red lacquer on her shapely toenails, while the Bold Bald One continues contentedly flipping the pages of the *Jewish Obscure Abstracts* book; between the page flipping, he takes a few glances at Lila. Nina notes that his nose is not attractive. Actually, in profile, it is slightly bulbous.

"He is a creep and he is ugly. What do you girls see in him?" Martin says and takes a determined gulp of his wine.

"Darling, how do you know he's a creep?" Nina repeats more emphatically than before. "You don't know him at all!"

"Hey Nina, I'm not an idiot. I can tell." Martin takes an energized sip which signifies his definite knowledge. More stem twirling.

"Ha ha, Marti, creep or not, all you men think the same when it comes to winning a female or defending a female, as if she is your own real estate property!!! I see that you're also afraid that the ugly creep is going to put the make on Lila. And by the way, darling, paradoxically that creep said he could tell that you are no one. In fact, darling, it's unbelievable that you and the creep came to almost the same conclusion about each other! By the way, you will not believe me, but I almost walked away when he said that you were no one. Hmmm . . . are both of you right or both wrong?"

Martin's chin stops trembling. "Right or wrong about what?" He takes a perplexed sip.

"Obviously, darling, about being able — on first contact and from a distance — to tell that you are no one and he is a creep! How civilized, Marti. But darling, this would not have happened if you, instead of him, would dance with me."

"I couldn't dance to this noise, Nina, but I'll dance with you at home, to Cesaria Evora."

"But Marti, you don't! And when I dance alone in the living room, you act as if you don't notice me."

"That's not true. I do dance with you sometimes when the kids are not home. And on your birthday and on New Year's Eve." Martin is glaring in the direction of the Bald Bold Man, who is throwing more frequent not too secret glances at Lila.

"Darling, do you realize you look like a property owner ready to protect your property! Not just me, your rightful wife, but also our friend Lila!"

"Nina, I didn't like the way that creep looked at me when he was dancing with you." He darts a suspicious glance toward the living room couch.

"Look, that creep is still on the prowl, this time for Lila, darling!"

"You got that right, Nina."

"Wow, but I'm hardly ever right, darling! This deserves a note, this is a significant developmental step in your personal growth!" She kisses him briefly but affectionately on the lips.

He returns a marital peck on her cheek and takes a sip of his wine. "Let me pour you a glass of red, Nina. You need it after this creep."

"Marti, how about you write a story? Who Is That Creep Poaching On Professor Martin's Wife?"

"Hee, hee, hee. And since when does real estate interest you, Nina? But are you sure that a nice Bordeaux would not interest you? I did see a nice Bordeaux you may like."

"I don't want a nice Bordeaux, Marti. But the title of the story you should write is inspired by real events."

They were at the round table, just the two of them. "Hee, hee, but Nina, first give me a two sentence summary, but don't speak loud," he whispered and took a long sip till not much was left in the glass with the crystal stem. His hand didn't tremble anymore but his eyebrows knitted as he scanned the immediate environment.

"But darling, first don't I need to check if some weird words I may use exist in the Oxford Dictionary? Didn't you say that if it doesn't live in the Oxford Dictionary, it doesn't exist? But don't interrupt me if you want me to summarize on the spot. So listen: At a lavender scented distinguished suburban party, Professor Martin Didn't Notice does notice a shamelessly baldheaded ugly insolently bold creep on the prowl for Professor Martin's double real estate property: his wife and her girlfriend."

"Hey Nina, look, the creep is asking Lila to dance!" Martin whispered in a rare for him emotive manner. Then in a rapid motion he downed the last sip and put down his wine glass on the round table and removed and replaced his eyeglasses on his nose.

"Marti, the creep is asking Lila to dance because Lila is the only woman without a partner in this dead living room and the creep is the only man. But if you dance with me maybe we could fuck — because two people dancing close together to soulful music is an erotic foreplay act and for this reason it is prohibited by the Jewish Religion, since it may lead to sex on unassigned days, while lying down routine sex on proper days is okay and in fact prescribed. How exciting. But this unfortunate wife must dance every day. While her husband ignores her need and walks by quickly so she doesn't see his uncomfortable expression when she is dancing in pure joy alone in their living room. But when the kids are asleep he wants her to suck his dick . . . wow isn't it romantic!" She kept her voice discreet.

"Nina, stop ranting and raving. Just give me your summary of that creep. And don't expect me to dance to that awful muzak." Obviously agitated but in control, if barely, Martin reached over to read the label of an unopened bottle of Bordeaux.

"Marti, look at me instead of the wine bottle! Or maybe you are afraid to hear the end of 'Who Is That Creep' Darling? . . . Hey, look!"

"That creep is really pissing me off!"

The Bold Bald Man was dancing with Lila.

DR. ANGELA BUTTERFLY, MSW, PH.D.
INTIMACY SPECIALIST
(7th Session)
8/10/05

Theme of Session: How to keep romance alive in a long term marriage.

Discussed:

– different kinds of talking (not just about grocery lists, etc.)

– no two people in the world can share everything

– partnership is about accepting what cannot be changed (and not complaining – per M)

– sharing in a spiritual sense what can or cannot be said – per N

– sharing a good lubricant: a couple's trip to Good Vibrations store recommended.

For future discussion: Is falling in love a very sexy illusion? Or is it an intense infatuation from unknown causes which can last or not last. Per N, it can be ruined by or not ruined by Marriage. Per M, it is about accepting and not complaining about what we cannot change.

M was quiet when N (with a glimmer of humor in her eyes) said that he is dependent on her foot to fall asleep. "Is it a sign of love or of a weird dependence that he needs to hold my foot?" She further philosophized, admitting that she focuses excessively on domestic quibbling with M unjustly, but that generally she has to keep her brain active, which she implied was cultural in her Polish-Jewish upbringing – to express anger by yelling, in opposition to the silent reserve in M's upbringing, where self-pride is the most important thing.

Despite what N thinks – that M is stingy with emotion – I do not agree. He misses County Kilkenny, where he grew up, with its "gentle hills always green except gold during the harvest," and he misses the ruins of a monastery where as a boy he used to hide and smoke cigarettes. He said that with tears in his eyes.

I pointed out to N that she tends to present only irritating sides of M, while ignoring his intimate pleas for her affection.

Productive session.

———————————

IN SYLVIA'S GUEST WC

*"By the way, is the bottom
of the toilet lavender?"*

*Polish and Jewish Folk Music
(wafting from the living room)*

"**B**ut let me go first, Nina!" Lila and I are in the Guest WC. We practically raced to get here. She is at the toilet bowl, which is not white but pale lavender. I lay on the Italian marble checkerboard tiled floor, flat on my back, trying to slow breathe, looking at the ceiling; it is plain white. The cool marble tiles are soothing. My head is spinning. Lila kneels, trying to open the lavender lid.

I begin a monotonous monologue toward the ceiling: "Lila, Sylvia told me there is a hidden button at the back of the toilet seat which opens the cover. I hope you find it soon. But by the way, isn't it good to expel what needs to go? We were expelled from Poland and here we go, expelling what? *Żubrówka* infused sorrow into such a pretty lavender toilet bowl." My words get progressively slurred. "By the way, Sylvia said that this button controls the lavender lid and works very well because it is Swiss magic precision made. Lila?"

Lila is fully preoccupied with looking for the button, so I lift my head off the floor. "But Lila, when I'm close to the end . . ." She is down on her knees, her red nailed fingertips touching the toilet lid not at all frantically, but with patient focused concentration. And she is wearing an admiring expression. As if interrupted in her own reverie, she says, "Hey, but what end are you talking about, Nina?"

"I'm telling you, this lavender toilet seat is for sure the highest end — designed especially for Sylvia, and because of the custom color tint it's many times the price of a regular white toilet. But Lila, existentially speaking, I'm thinking that at the end it doesn't matter . . . if we throw up or cry or . . . you know what, into an ordinary or into a designer toilet," I finish in a languid manner, continuing to watch Lila's perfectly shaped red lacquered fingernails probing around and under the lid, a determined expression on her face.

"How do I open this, Nina?" She still isn't frantic.

"If we can't figure it out, I can go get Marti while I still can," I offer.

"Don't call him!!! I don't want him to see me like this! Hey, I found the button!"

The lid pops open. But almost as quickly, it shuts itself. Silence.

"Lila, you're lucky to have a rationally scientific head, no way I could figure out how this Sesame Open button works. Do you know why Martin respects his female students who are good at math? Because they have rational heads, despite being women. His words."

This goes on for a good five tormented minutes, a kind of comedy routine with tragedy mixed in, then comedy again. We just want to throw up, but can't.

I hear Polish folk dance music through the closed door and think, this isn't fair, others are having a good time. And I'm missing the folk dances I love. I lift my head. "Hey, Lila, can you hear? They are playing *"Poszła Karolinka do Gogolina.* . . . Maybe *Karolinka* went to *Gogolinka* to throw up, Lila?"

Lila erupts with a wave of irritation. "Jesus, shut up,

Nina, I need to focus. What's with this button?"

Meanwhile, a monologue directed to Sylvia's Guest WC ceiling continues in my head, more or less about *Żubrówka* inducing laughing and crying and wild dancing. *Krakowiak* and *Kujawiak* . . . and the waltzes and polkas, barefoot with Gertrude in pure abandon — as if we forgot we didn't like each other. Or maybe we like each other somehow. And about Polish folk music being a balm to our collective Polish Jewish rooted limbic endorphins, causing a mix of the joyous and the melancholic? But then there are consequences for some of us, like what we are immersed in right now.

The lid is still not opening, and Lila becomes frantic. I'm quietly talking as if to myself, "Hey Lila, I'm about to throw up on the floor! Should I pray in Polish that you open this lid very soon?" I open my eyes and lift my head in her direction. Searching for the secret of the Sesame Open button, she doesn't respond.

Then she abruptly stops her tense exploration of the button and takes three deep breaths. Just then the lid pops open. Her head is invisible inside the toilet bowl. Her voice verges on ecstasy: "Thank God — just in time!"

"Is the Bliss about to come?" I ask.

"Nothing yet," Lila says, her voice rising out of the toilet bowl.

I close my eyes, feeling dizzy but not too nauseous. I am still flat on my back, hands on the cool pink gray marble. I open my eyes to examine the checkerboard tiles, then slide closer to Lila. She is kneeling in a prayer pose, her head inside the toilet bowl.

"Hey Lila, actually what could be a more intimate communication than sharing such an exquisite toilette experience like this? Despite the revolt in our *kishkes*?" I pose this as another question with no answer and observe the ceiling, which, I'm obsessively thinking, unlike everything else in the Guest WC, is not remarkable at all. In fact it is plain vanilla . . . or, as Gertrude explained, the fashionable Swiss coffee vanilla currently all the rage with realtors, basically a shade of off white.

Lila completes an anemic retch followed by an unproductive belch. It's only a meager down payment. She flushes quickly but her head is still inside. "What do you mean, Nina, to communicate better?" comes out, muffled.

"I mean, Lila, the ironic charm in our intimate unpolished intoxicated expression of togetherness in this opulent Guest WC. Well, except for the ceiling."

She doesn't respond. "Okay Lila, concentrate. Let it all out. I'll be quiet. By the way, I'm still holding it in, but it's churning in my *kishkes*. Have mercy on me, Lila. Can we switch places? Or not yet?"

Lila sticks her head out: "Just be quiet Nina and I'll be done sooner."

So I close my eyes and continue in my head: *Żubrówka* cleanses our souls of the pain from being thrown out of the place we considered ours. Now we are here in Sylvia's Guest WC . . . and . . . I'm trying not to look at an unfortunately entirely unremarkable off white ceiling which if it had been painted during the Renaissance would be a symbol of the sky blue heavens. I don't pray, but who would pray to a heaven represented by a pale vanilla ceiling? But on the positive side, the modern composite lavender toilet that Sylvia chose has a magic Sesame Open button that works. And the floor is a checkerboard of marble squares. Just add checkers . . . I open my eyes.

Lila's head is out. Both her hands are on her chest, protecting the delicate black lace border of her décolletage, and she says "Nina, why do you talk like that about Sylvia? She earned it all herself."

"Because she is focused unlike us and has a great business sense, which maybe we don't have," I say.

"Speak for yourself, Nina. My focus is just fine." Lila's head goes back in and she produces just a minor belch.

I lift my head to look at Lila. "So it's okay if I just report subjectively of course, what I see and hear? The first thought that comes to my head is that with your head bowed inside the toilet bowl, on your knees, Lila, you look like you're at a private church pew discarding troubling thoughts. There is a certain sense of stability in this scene." I complete the sentence in an uplifted monotone. "A stable state of throwing up, in other words."

Lila's head comes out but her eyes are closed. "Hmmm, Nina, I wish I could be getting rid of all my sins. But I'm not sure if I agree with your wordy explanation of something to do with stability. I think stability in itself is a good thing."

"Even if it is a stable state of hopelessly unfocused confusion? As opposed to a predictable repertoire of unpredictability? Which by the way is my thing . . . But can stability be unfocused? Isn't that a contradiction? For example a table is not a table if it is not stable. So maybe to be stable you have to be a table."

Lila doesn't laugh. "Nina, why don't you focus instead on the fact that you are lucky to have a stable Martin." She returns her head back to the toilet bowl.

I spread out my arms on the cool tiled floor. My eyes are closed and I quietly say to the unimpressive ceiling, "Poor Martin is not so lucky to have me. And by the way Lila, do you think the soul is a focused or unfocused stable entity . . . and what use is the stability without a quest for an unexpected solution? Doesn't it lead to a stable focused stagnation with total inability to make decisions in our stable, uneventful life?"

"Quit talking, Nina! And speak for yourself!"

I do, but only after saying that Martin calls me a fuzzy philosopher; most often he thinks I'm just weird. Observing the undistinguished ceiling, I continue very quietly speaking in a drunken monotone: "I wish this ceiling had soul . . . blue like in a poetic Polish sky with feathery white clouds instead of this pukey Plain Swiss Vanilla . . . as opposed to the Sainte Chapelle's celestial ceiling, which was so inspiring that my Polish Jewish atheist nostalgic soul actually had a spiritual orgasm with real physical consequences."

Lila pulls her head out of the toilet bowl and looks at me with bleary eyes. "You and your spiritual orgasm, Nina. But I don't follow your thinking." (So I must have been talking louder than I intended.) "But I must say, Nina, that you look almost angelic on this marble checkerboard. It would make a nice photograph, in fact." Lila's head is back in the bowl.

All ten of my fingertips are feeling the cool marble tiles. "And while waiting for my turn, Lila, it would be even nicer here if there were marble checkers to make simple moves with. Hey, we could benefit from some simple move, to practice in our uneventful nothing new lives, while we wait for something to happen while looking at the bottom of this fancy toilet and an uninspiring ceiling . . . By the way, Lila, is the bottom of the toilet lavender?"

Lila's just belches from inside the bowl. Suddenly I remember the Bald Bold Man. "Lila, actually I'm thinking about confessing a future sin to you."

"Oh, please Nina, maybe I do not want to hear or know about your future sin!"

"You're right, it's not the future, but the present moment that counts, and I must say that now as I lie here flat on my back on this cool marble floor, that if I didn't have to throw up I'd be quite happy on these checkerboard tiles. In fact, my wretched back feels luxurious, but on the other hand, as I'm looking up at the ceiling, I must repeat that it is really remarkably not inspiring. Off white elegance is what I despise. Did I tell you that already?"

"Yes. More than once."

I take three breaths. "Lila, do you remember the bald guy you and I danced with before the *Żubrówka* Melancholia started?"

"What *Żubrówka* Melancholy? I don't remember this Melancholy. But why are you asking? Are you interested in the bald guy or what?" Her voice has taken on a sharp edge.

"I think he is looking for a woman to have an affair with. Just fucking."

"Oh? But please don't say such crude words, Nina. And how do you know that he only wants sex?" Her incensed voice is amplified from the inside of the bowl. She takes a peek just from above the rim of it, long enough to say, "Nina, stop it, I'm not interested at all."

I sit up on the cool tile floor, my legs extended all the way. "But do you want to know what Sew told me? He knows the bald guy a bit and . . ."

Lila's muffled voice perks up. "Oh, and what did Sew say? So he did make it to the party? I didn't see him come in."

She is taking forever. I drift off, remembering the bald man's sinister hissing whisper in my ear. I don't say anything about *that* to Lila. And I haven't told her that Sew told me the bald man's wife died a year ago and her ashes are still in his bedroom. I also didn't say what he told Sew, that Lila was too delicate of a bird for him. I close my eyes so as not to be bothered by the ceiling, my fingertips again feeling the soothing cool of the marble floor. I open my eyes; it helps with the nausea. Lila's head is out of the toilet bowl, all the way out, in the open finally.

"Hey Lila, I can't wait any longer, so can I have my turn soon? Is phase one over?"

But Lila's head goes back inside the bowl. "I'm not done yet, Nina."

I am tempted to tell her, but don't, that Sew also told me he himself likes Lila but that she is too delicate of a bird, too delicate for him as well.

I lie down again and close my eyes (so as not to be irked by the starkly off white ceiling) and wonder if the bald man also blew hot Polish Jewish breaths into Lila's ear. She seemed to enjoy dancing with him. But she wouldn't be interested in an overconfident guy who only wants sex and doesn't look her in the eye. So why am I interested?

"I would never call a guy first," Lila asserts from inside of the toilet bowl.

"Why, Lila? If I were interested in a guy, I would call him first."

"Hey, seriously Nina, don't you dare give him my phone number if that's what you have in mind!! So, you're going to call him yourself? Right?" Suddenly Lila sticks her agitated head up into the open air. "Or what are you really plotting now?" Lila's head disappears.

"Lila, if I do call him — since you're not interested right? — I'll tell him explicitly that you're not available." Hmmm, I say to myself, he is bald which means he is full of testosterone and he may be a good lover . . . But how can

I get his phone number?

"I think my problem Lila is that I need a real good fuck."

A muffled monotone from the bowl: "I've already told you that word is too crude for me, Nina. I'd rather not hear anything more, please. Call him if you want. I said I was not interested and I mean it." And immediately her offended head is out of the bowl, and she says, "I told you that I always want the guy to call me first to let me know he wants me. But can you stop talking, Nina, or I'll never throw up and you'll have to wait forever." Her pissed off head goes back inside the bowl. So, is it lavender inside or not?

In silence I'm pondering how I can get the Bald Bold One's number from Sylvia . . . by lying that I want it for Lila? Wisely, this does not spill out of my mouth.

Lila's head is coming out and bobs upward in a rapid move. "What are you still plotting, Nina? Don't you dare, Nina!!"

"Don't I dare what, Lila?"

"Don't you dare tell anyone that I'm interested at all! I'm not interested!" And her unhinged head falls back into the toilet bowl.

I'd nodded off, I realize when I wake up. I resume looking at the ceiling. "Lila, have pity on me, so far you are just belching from time to time and I feel like I'm waiting for Godot... But is there a God of Puking?"

"Unfortunately Nina, I'm not done." The voice from the inside sounds pleasantly calm. "But I'll try harder."

"Lila, this is torture." I take deep breaths to control the nausea. "But can I ask you about something?"

"So what is exactly on your mind, Nina?" she asks suspiciously from the bowl.

"Why some of us, unlike Sylvia, can't make it in business and in love. And she can. Plus good facelifts, a beautiful house, and a jovial handsome husband to be who laughs with her at idiomatic Polish jokes. And us? You don't make enough for a car that won't break on the highway. I'm lucky that Martin has a decent salary, but not enough for a marble floor like this, which by the way is soothing as it is cooling my wretched body right now. Just imagine, to be with a sexy smart man who speaks your childhood language . . . would we be happy? What if we wouldn't be happy even if we ought to be happy?"

A short silence. "Maybe we don't know how?" comes from the innards of the toilet bowl and Lila sticks her head out. "Watch it Nina, soon my biotech startup will take off. And I'm very motivated and focused. And by the way, Nina," her voice trailing off acquires a gentle quality, "you say you do not feel happy, but actually you look like an angelic corpse on this marble floor . . . Hmmm, especially with your mouth shut and your eyes closed. But okay, keep talking to me actually because . . ." Lila is actively preparing for the next explosive belch. I am hopeful. In vain.

"Lila, maybe there's a toothbrush you can put deep into your throat. Because I might not be able to wait any longer. Maybe I can help you if I move closer." Lila doesn't respond and I open my eyes and slide my body as close to the lavender receptacle as I can. "But Lila, actually this throwing up together is a special intimate private affair. Don't you think?" Or better, a Puking *Prywatka* for two, I comment in my head. And soon begins again the mantra about Sylvia's Guest WC's plain creamy Swiss vanilla ceiling not being at all inspiring.

Suddenly, Lila is overtaken by a powerful single retch.

"Finally! Lila, keep pushing it out!! But don't rush, rushing is stressful and actually I don't mind waiting a little longer with this balmy cool sensation of the marble tiles under my wretched body. But . . . oh *merde*, seriously Lila, but when will you be *done* . . . because I think I have to go just about *NOW*!"

Lila's head emerges from the toilet for a quick announcement: "Be patient Nina, not quite yet."

I'm back to my circuitous monologue to the ceiling.

"Give me a chance to finish," she says from the depth of the toilet bowl.

"Lila, if you don't let me puke soon, I'll continue boring you with my ceiling observations, and my awareness is more distinct, and to keep myself from puking my focus is more thorough than before, so I can distract myself and not make a mess on this beautiful floor in lovely Sylvia's lavender Guest WC . . . But believe me Lila, this dull plain vanilla ceiling has no character and is especially unimpressive when I'm nauseous and want to see the feathery white clouds traversing the blue sky . . . But Lila, is the inner lining of this toilet at least lavender?"

She does not answer. I am whining gently: "Lila, I know I'm repeating myself but otherwise I may throw up on this exquisite floor, and yes, not everything in here — as is the case in life — has to be in pleasing lavender."

I close my eyes thinking about this scene of *Prywatka for Two* in Queen Sylvia's Lavender Guest WC . . . it's a good title.

"Hey, Lila . . . I hear someone at the door. Martin is here to check on us!"

"Girls, do you need any help?" Martin's restrained voice inquires and I am sure he has his ear plastered to the door. "Hey, girls, so you're not done throwing up yet?" He continues with concern.

The door isn't locked. In a lethargic trance, I say, "No Marti, not yet. It's still Lila's turn in Sylvia's special issue lavender composite original one of a kind toilet bowl." I slowly get up and open the door but only a slit. He doesn't push.

"Hee, hee, hee, a lavender toilet bowl? But shall I come in and help you two girls throw up elegantly? Hee, hee, hee."

He places one foot to wedge the door open. A little flicker of a smile is visible in the fine creases around his eyes behind his unfashionable rectangular glasses.

"Marti, so you intend to be gentlemanly and help us throw up elegantly in this exquisite lavender toilet bowl, which by the way has a real magic Sesame Open button?" I bat my eyelids flirtatiously.

"No! No! Nina, don't let Martin come in!!! I don't want him to see me like this!" Lila's attempt at a desperate whisper fails — she is yelling, in a deeper than normal voice, additionally amplified from within the toilet bowl.

But it's too late. Martin pushes the door and steps inside, then closes the three of us inside together. I return to my spot on the floor. He gives me a quick glance, then smiles sheepishly and stations himself on his not all the way bent knees, near Lila.

"Hee, hee, hee, don't worry Lila, I'll help you throw up elegantly," he purrs reassuringly, a voice he uses rarely (except with our kids and our cat, but almost never with me). The marble tiles feel soothing and I resume my angelic corpse pose, eyes open facing the uninspiring ceiling. Lila is quiet and does not pull her head out.

While Martin, on his knees, is waiting for Lila's signal of agreement to his offer, I ask him about the party fun we are missing, and if anyone else is drunk on *Żubrówka* like us, and if so, is there another Guest WC. And I also ask if there is any *Żubrówka* left, since after all the Invitation said it would be unlimited till the sun comes up.

"I know you don't believe in magic Marti, but this toilet really has a Sesame Open button and once you open it, things happen. Not just abstractly."

"What's the problem now, Nina?" Martin says loudly, lowering himself on his knees nearer Lila, whose head is still inside the bowl.

"Nothing is the problem, darling, I'm just waiting to throw up." I close my eyes and start in on an unemotional monologue summary in my head: Subject: Paradox of . . . Unlimited *Żubrówka* for our exiled case of Melancholia. Can the blade of grass in the bottle elicit it? Or heal it?

Martin is concentrating on Lila, whose head is hiding in the toilet bowl. "Are you done yet, Nina?" he says, not looking at me.

"Done with what, darling? I'm just mumbling an uninspired monologue to the uninspiring ceiling. Waiting my turn. And it seems that Lila is not done yet," I casually report.

Perplexed, Martin looks at me as if he doesn't really see me, and after a long pause, as if he is thinking what to say, he says: "Nina, in most cases you're not supposed to start an elegant sentence with *And*."

"And why not, Marti? Is that an official Oxford Dictionary archaic British rule?" I shoot back in the confrontational tone I use when someone quotes stupid rules to me.

Lila's clear resonant voice comes from one side of the toilet bowl. "You can check it on Google, Martin." And her head disappears back to the full depth of the toilet bowl.

"Hee, hee, hee, Lila, my wife accuses me of being an antiquated patriarch and it's true that I would rather consult an old fashioned hardback grammar book written by an authority. But how can I help you now, Lila?"

From one side of the toilet opening she hardly lifts her head (so he can't see her face) and says loud and clear: "Don't worry, Martin, I'm fine, I'm really fine."

"You're sure you don't want me to hold your head, Lila?" Martin insists.

"But Marti, can one start an elegant sentence with *As*? If you approve of it, I'll put it in my book." I dare him innocently.

"Hee, hee, hee, if it's not too vulgar, try it on me now, Nina."

"Okay. Listen. I'm making it up now: As — note that *as* sounds like *ass*, an ass by the way on which Nina, reminiscent of an angelic corpse, lies, waiting her turn to throw up, face up, trying not to complain that the ceiling is an uninspiring vanilla (with maybe, per Gertrude, a noninvasive coffee hint), when suddenly she experiences a sensation of vomit coming up her throat, but to her horror, Lila, in a prayer position on her knees, her hands protecting the black lace of her décolletage, is not done yet at the, I hope, inner lavender tint toilet bowl . . . maybe Lila can tell you if it is lavender colored and scented . . . if it is, it would be nice to throw up in. Marti, that sentence starts with *As* and covers the essence of this WC scene. Can you guess the title, darling?"

"Hee, hee, hee. Are you going to tell me?"

"*Prywatka for Two*, now *for Three*."

"Just Stop It, Nina, I'm really trying hard . . ." comes out from depth of the toilet bowl.

"Hold off, Nina. I think Lila is almost there." Martin

sounds confident. "Lila, I'll gladly hold your head up. It may help you throw up," he says in a sympathetically cajoling enthusiastic tone.

Quietly I reflect: And my husband will also gladly protect from accidental soiling the pretty lace border of Lila's décolletage.

"Martin, I don't need any help!" Lila yells sharply.

"But Lila, Martin's big cool palm will feel good on your forehead, I promise, and I know because he puts it on mine sometimes when I throw up at home."

"Stop it, Nina!" an annoyed muted directive demands from the toilet bowl.

Somehow I suppress my gagging reflex and move to my original "waiting room" spot farther away from the toilet and sit cross legged to watch Martin down on his knees quite close to Lila, whose head is halfway in the bowl. He gently places his large palm on her forehead; unexpectedly, she does not object nor resist. "It will help you calm down and throw up elegantly," Martin says tenderly.

His free hand smooths Lila's hair away from her forehead.

"Marti, did the Bold Bald creep, leave yet?" I pretend no interest. Lila's hands are protecting her décolletage.

Martin's eyes are fixed on Lila's décolletage but he redirects them at me long enough to say with a satisfied relief, "The bald creep is gone, and good riddance. Couldn't stand the sight of him. But what did he want from the two of you girls?"

"Marti, you guess what," I say. His hand is on Lila's forehead and he takes secret glances at her shapely breasts. I continue, "I wonder if our hosts understand *unlimited*. But can you tell us who is still here? And in what stage of postpartum unpolished nostalgic stupor?"

"Hmmm, there may be a few of the insiders in the kitchen. Not overly polished, hee, hee, hee. I didn't see the Russian couple, but I saw Douglas with one eye closed, hee, hee. Gertrude is not making an idiot out of him again, yet. And the hosts disappeared somewhere, hee, hee." Martin laughs under his nose, both hands on Lila's forehead, tenderly smoothing the sweat. Her hands are covering her décolletage.

"Is Sew there, darling? Is he making jokes in Russian too?" Martin doesn't respond so I say in a pleasing voice, "Marti, by the way, I heard that these Russian Jews were married for twenty years, then divorced, then married again to each other, the second time without any ceremony, and now they live in two different houses and see each other on weekends only and are very happy finally. . . Shall we take their example, darling? Actually Dr. Butterfly did say that at times meager sex in long term marital imprisonment — my term not hers — thrives again when loyal partners are free of domestic wars. Like when there is never a fight about where is my good spatula and lemon zester. They each have their own kitchens. What do you think, Marti?"

Lila doesn't lift her head.

"Hey listen, Marti. And there are three toilets in each

of their two houses. Total six. I can explain why two people need six toilets. Three toilets for each primary partner's house for their weekday threesomes after work, in case each of the three participants needs to throw up privately! They may have orgies. They didn't say."

"Hee, hee, hee, Nina, you actually used *and* correctly in the opening of the sentence — in conversational language. And by the way, that is not a bad joke, hee, hee."

Lila's head comes out of the toilet, halfway. "I'm trying my best to be done soon. But if you go on like this, Nina, it may take longer." Her head hides again.

Through half clenched teeth with lips partially opened and no upper teeth exposed, Martin laughs hee, hee, then says: "So that makes a total of six toilets for the couple — for two people . . . No one in Ireland would believe that. I can understand the extra rooms. I'd just put all my books there."

"Darling, I used the *and* correctly only by accident. But let me postulate, darling, a little more about all the extra rooms in two houses: On Saturday the Russians have a romantic just for two of them candle lit dinner date and afterward they make love with each other, and for novelty and variety they play games with each other in three different rooms in each of their two houses. On Sunday they switch houses. They cook together and flirt minus spatula, lemon zester, and ladle fights in their two kitchens. Dr. Butterfly also very firmly believes that variety of romancing within marriage counteracts marital boredom. Plus an incense scented ambiance and beeswax candles. In the dimly lit glow, the couple can admire each other in silky lingerie in every room of the house. That's six variations times how many total in a month? Practically exponential. Right, darling? But there should be one rule. Not to visit each other out of the blue during the week because who wants to feel jealous and hurt? Trust and maybe a little bit of jealousy is okay. I agree with Dr. Butterfly."

Martin winks. "I think Lila wants you to stop this nonsense, Nina." He gently repositions his palm on Lila's forehead.

"Okay, I'll change the subject. However, Lila, I need to go, seriously. Very soon. Hey, Marti what time is it? Is it still dark outside? I hope not sunrise yet. And I hope some *Żubrówka* is left. O shit!"

"Don't say shit, Nina, it's not polite," Lila and Martin say in near unison. Lila with her maybe not so rare outraged irritation a bit magnified because of the head location, and Martin with his normal advisory educator tone.

"Lila, take pity on me, I really don't want to miss any of Sew's jokes. I want to laugh while there's still time, before it's the end of Sylvia and Alek's Party. And before we die, I mean . . . We need Sex and Laughter. But to change the subject, did you know that Sew named himself The Great? Great What? Sex and Laughter? I asked him that. No, Great Loser, he said. Maybe he gets hard laughing at himself. That's Sew. But he doesn't give details of his losing case. He looks at you saying nothing but his eyes are laughing. But

I'll ask him after our WC *Prywatka* ends. And now actually it's part two of this scene, *WC Prywatka for Three*. And Marti, I'm reminding you again that after I throw up, and have a last goodbye shot of *Żubrówka*, don't drag me out before the sun comes up. Okay, Marti?"

"Hopefully Nina, we can get out sooner and without a final performance by poor Douglas, under Gertrude's direction," Martin intones seriously.

"I wouldn't want to miss that, Marti! I can use it as raw material for my novel."

"Nina, there is nothing to miss. Maybe a few more of Seweryn's crude untranslatable jokes and a few big laughs. And Nina, you shouldn't complain so much. First you had your Triple Kabanasii Orgasms and now you want more laughing orgasms, nothing new, hee, hee, hee."

Their hands are still in the same positions, Martin's on Lila's forehead, and hers on her décolletage as if to protect her breasts from his eyes.

"That's exactly what I didn't want to miss, Marti," I say to the ceiling. "So there still is action in the kitchen, darling?" I'm hopeful.

"Nothing scintillating is going on and you girls are missing nothing," Martin reassures.

I lift my head from the floor. "Unpolished Chosen Ones. So who exactly and what is left? I hope some *Żubrówka*? Yes I know that the bald creep is gone, good riddance to him. And Gertrude and Douggie? Does he have all his eyes open at once? And Sew? He never leaves a good party till the very

231

end. Sylvia and Smart Alek are probably taking a fucking break in her bedroom. Is anyone else in the kitchen? How about the young loving couple who watched you while you were trying not to smell or taste the *kabanos* . . . and I warn you, Marti, that I definitely won't be ready to leave till dawn — and not without a final drop of our Jewish Polish bipolar Melancholia Elixir in exile." I sigh and put my head back down on the floor, closing my eyes.

Lila does not ask what in the world I mean by the bipolar Melancholia Elixir. Martin does not either and I open my eyes and see him smoothing the hair on Lila's sweaty forehead with an attentive soft motion, and he is cooing softly: "There may be some *Żubrówka* left, I bet Smart Alek keeps it hidden somewhere, but I wouldn't recommend it to you girls tonight, hee, hee."

"And darling, did you notice if there is an early morning coffee for the sleepy guests? I hope so. Gertrude says Douggie needs one cup of coffee per each eye before he can drive her home safely, and the third cup is for his third eye." I say all this in a matter of fact voice. Lila is silent and her head not visible. "But Marti, can you go to the kitchen and see what's going on and report back not too soon? I think Lila may want you to go now, because I can tell that she needs to take a breath of fresh air and I will be fine."

"Fine, no problem Nina. Just leave the door unlocked and I'll be back to check on you girls soon." He gets up from his knees and comes over and bends down over my head — which I lift to meet his lips. He gives me a quick very little peck on my forehead, and leaves. Lila (who I bet has been holding it in) produces a massive belch followed by a significantly productive explosion.

Lila and I change places. Finally, yes finally, I have a majorly efficient and productive go at the lavender toilet bowl!!! Is it plain toilet white inside? I am not sure. I stay put. There is more to still come up. A lot more.

Martin is back. Lila and I, having given up all sense of feminine decency, had surrendered by turns to multiple and dangerously powerful retchings while he played nursemaid and supported our heads.

He kneels next to me, both of his large protective palms on my forehead, gently reassuring me with a pinch of a patronizing tone, which normally bothers me, no matter how little. "Hey baby, throwing up can be dangerous against a hard toilet surface, hee, hee, hee." His laughter is restrained and kind.

The touch of his finger pads on my forehead gives me a feeling of security. He pushes my bangs off my clammy forehead. "There is a price to pay if you play around with other men, Nina, hee, hee, hee," he teases me tenderly. "Hey, Lila, my wife thinks she can have the cake and eat it too. Is that the Polish view of reality? Please explain to my wife what should be obvious but that she doesn't understand. You can explain to her better than I can, I bet."

Lila's voice surprises me with its sudden sharpness:

"Martin, in fact Nina seems to think she has a right to have even two or even three cakes, while others like me have none, but I would rather not comment on this subject."

My head is out of the toilet bowl. I look at Lila, who is flat on her back, with her eyes closed, where I was before, on the cool marble checkerboard floor. She looks like a pale angelic corpse. I take three deep cleansing breaths and know that I look as miserable as I feel when I say to Martin, "Darling, sometimes life tastes like vomit, and you can't protect me from that."

Then for the final time I expel what remains inside me of *kabanosy* and *Żubrówka* and *śledzik* and *mizeria,* into what I'd imagined to be the lavender blush of Sylvia's toilet bowl.

DR. ANGELA BUTTERFLY, MSW, PH.D.
INTIMACY SPECIALIST
(8th Session)
8/24/05

As we approach the end of our sessions, some modified impressions / conclusions:

N considers herself an intuitive person but is not fully aware that she chooses to play the victim. Her older sister's pity infuriates N.

N: "Who wants pity?" M: "Only those who have lost pride."

Picking up on something from the last session, N jokingly ponders if M's addiction to the presence of her foot within the reach of his arm in bed before they go to sleep is his pacifier.

Her own pacifier, daytime only, she states (and not for the first time) is marijuana.

When I asked point blank if she loved M, she said she knew and felt that he loves her, and that she did fall in love with him the second time (the first time had been when they had met) when they had good sex on his sabbatical with family in Paris in 2001. "But she always complained it was never long enough for her," M clarified.

N repeats, yet again, that her inability to perform fellatio is her unresolved revenge for him once saying she was a disgrace to the artists.

It also infuriates her and makes her unresponsive to his advances when he tells her what to do, when to do it, and how to do anything. Even when he asks her lovingly "to pet my balls." It has to be spontaneous for Nina.

And yet again she asserts: "He doesn't get it that I just don't find it romantic – a blow job as a barter coin, for cooking a good dinner." Martin actually smiled and said that Nina was a genius at blow jobs.

Impression: N and M in their way (his full commitment, hers not expressed so far) love each other, but N's resentments and sarcasm coupled with M's patronizing unspontaneous style kill N's willingness to give pleasure and cause her to reject his amorous advances. In our work together, M has always been very quiet when discussion focuses on expression of emotion.

Plan: Re-emphasize the need to talk about and get past resentments affecting sex.

———————

FUNERAL FOR ŻUBRÓWKA AT DAWN

"So it is the truth? It is not Unlimited!?"

Nu Alrest — Radio Tarifa

At the oval kitchen counter the mood is not exactly lively. Remnants and spouses sit on the high swivel chairs or lean on the counter, subdued and somber, sobering up with black coffee in paper cups (all the ceramic cups are in the sink by now). The street lights are reflected on the black glossy marble. No one appears eager to leave. Refreshed after our WC session, Lila and I settle in while Gertrude, next to Sylvia, considers us from the opposite side of the counter, her face a studied expression of no expression. "So you are finally done," she says with a twinkle of scorn. Sylvia's eyes are directed at me. "What took you so long?" Martin lets out three shy hee, hee, hee's, his upper lip covering his teeth.

Gertrude gives him a plastered on smile: "But fortunately these two girls sobered up just in time, because Douggie has just opened his second eye and is waking up his third eye with a third cup of coffee."

But wait! With an unexpectedly devilish grin on his face, Douggie slowly makes Eye Contact with each of us. He then stands up, fully erect, a step away from Gertrude (whose hand is no longer inside his cashmere sweater where it was petting the inner aspect of his forearm before).

Out of nowhere, he launches into a monologue: "Hey People! I know you all think I'm an idiot. Maybe I am. Like Dostoyevsky's Idiot!" Without so much as clearing his throat, Douggie has transformed into Cicero addressing the Roman Senate. "Yes, I've read Dostoyevsky. We all know that Polish women choose idiots for their husbands. Idiots with PhDs. And so what if I learn stupid things to please my brilliant wife, who agrees that such idiots are essential as the makers of genius children? If I learn to pronounce Polish," he continues in an uncharacteristic booming voice, "adequately for Gertrude, will I become a satisfactory provider? The question is: Can one become what Gertrude wants if one learns properly? And brings her coffee in bed. What would she be without me? I'm indispensable. And how do I get rewarded? By being made a fool of at parties! But maybe I'm not really such a fool after all?" He waves his arms. "But what do you people think!"

Douggie isn't done: "In fact I am not an idiot. I am not *Głupi Chuj*. In fact I am a genius *Chuj*! Go ahead and laugh at me. I can laugh at you too."

Gertrude is speechless.

Sew is here! He had snuck in late as usual, while Lila and I were literally spilling our guts in Sylvia's lavender Guest WC. He yells out, "I'm sure our Rebbe would have something to say on that subject. But I vote for equality! For all of us genius idiot *Chujs*, medium, big, and fat like kielbasa and even too thin like *kabanosy*. We all deserve Genius Blow Jobs! Douggie first!"

Sylvia's dramatic eyes seemed pinned open.

Martin livens up: "I agree with Douglas and Sew. All men want Genius Blow Jobs."

"Here stand the heroes who make us happy with genius children," Gertrude coldly remarks, taking back control, a general mustering her troops. She seems somehow oddly proud of her husband.

But Douggie is still on a tear. He gesticulates in an exaggerated manner. "There must be a Jewish law requiring the wife to do what *we want* in bed once a week, something for all of us idiot genius husbands! I've been studying the Torah lately, but have not encountered that law. I'll find it yet!"

Gertrude seems to have decided that the winning hand is to telegraph her burst of pride at Douggie's little performance: "My husbie is passionate about becoming a serious genius Jewish scholar!"

Douggie is through, back in his high swivel chair, where he checks if there is any coffee left in his paper cup. It seems to be empty. He puts it on the counter. He closes his eyes again.

Has something changed? The atmosphere in the room? The temperature? At first it seemed like it, but now I start to wonder if Douggie's star turn was all just a dream.

Sew winks at me, with a knowing smirk on his ever observant face. We are in telepathic communion, I can tell, about the promise on the Party Invitation. "Sew, do you know anything about the Unlimited *Żubrówka*?" I ask nonchalantly, flashing him a return conspiratorial wink. His eyes and face assume an exaggerated innocence. He shrugs in helpless surrender.

A "fuck" quietly escapes my throat. "So the *Żubrówka*

is all gone? It was *limited?*"

The innocence on Sew's face becomes mischief and deepens. I make an infinity of sadness face. "But Unlimited was promised in the Invitation!!?"

"So to where did this *Żubrówka* disappear?" he asks, in a combination of mock and real despair.

I say: "Until we find out, I'm not ready to go home yet. But Martin wants to drag me away."

"My advice is don't let him tell you what to do Nina," contributes Gertrude.

Sew inches closer. "Don't despair yet Ninochka — you know what? I wouldn't be surprised if our hosts are hiding more of this Unlimited *Żubrówka* and not telling us about it!" Then he whispers nearer my ear: "But Ninochka, why are your eyes pointing all the way down?" (His eyes give me a hint where to look.) "You think I'm hiding something interesting between my legs?" I smile. Sew feigns a serious look. A faint grin spreads across Martin's face. Gertrude turns her eyes upwards. Lila pretends not to see or hear. Sylvia's eyes are more or less on Sew's crotch.

"I'm just looking at your socks," I say loud enough for everyone to hear. "Today they are red but usually they are blue. And there is also a partial view," I whisper.

Sew's eyes light up and he looks downward. "He is in partial hiding, but later you can have a secret look — he likes the attention," he mutters under his nose so only I can hear. He gives "him" one more fleeting and smiling inspection. "Go ahead Ninochka, check if he is still alive!

But don't let anyone see." Pretending fear he turns his head both ways.

Lila watches us. And, from the opposite side of the counter, Gertrude does too, her expression visibly mellowed perhaps for public display. Nevertheless, when she looks at me, it still contains at least a pinch of some hard to digest additive — a tincture of disapproval of her younger sister. Sew notices Gertrude's look, and maybe to improve the potentially bad vibe situation, plays the entertainer and announces: "Hey, everyone, Nina asked me a question about hiding or not exposing fully some things, and my answer is that I'm very sorry for anyone who has to hide, or for anything that is in hiding." He is not laughing, but looking distantly in space, and recrosses his legs (to obscure the view of his crotch?).

"Nina, please leave Sew alone," Lila discreetly warns me.

But I say to Lila, "In fact all of us had to hide in Poland. And Sew doesn't dwell on it but instead he is a bipolar pendulum, sad to comedic . . . Don't you think it's a better approach than being trapped in the unipolar static sadness melancholia?" And I say louder, "By the way I coined the term Laughing Melancholia."

"I don't really know what you are referring to, Nina." Lila is giving me her usual look of maybe not wanting to know.

I whisper: "Lila, I'm referring to Sew as an example of bilateral melancholia — comedian at a *prywatka*, but in private, he is a painter of sad-eyed portraits, when he's done with his day job. But I have not seen his self portrait yet. Maybe he doesn't have a good mirror," I speedily deliver in Lila's ear before she can stop me.

Lila moves her ear away and her clear blue eyes (surrounded by long eyelashes with a perfect black mascara) peer intently into my wide open hazel ones with a not so perfect eye makeup job (smudged black coal pencil and slightly run off mascara). Abruptly, she whispers, "Nina, I can't follow your thoughts. Are you still stoned? How about for a change let me hear what the others have to say. And I need a glass of water. I'll get you one too, Nina. I'm really thirsty." She makes a motion as if to get up off her high chair, but she doesn't do so.

In a monotone, into space more or less, with an end of life funeral vibe, I return to my major topic: "So is this the truth? It is not Unlimited?" Thinking about the imminent end of the party permeates my being, centered in my gut, with a vague fear. Gertrude focuses on hiding all expression.

With a tolerant superior smirk on her lips, Sylvia trains her eyes on me, and her hands in pretty black lace fingerless gloves are under her chin in a "facelift" pose. (She must know it flatters her very attractive features.) Alek is not in the kitchen. No one says anything for a while. So I break the ice, dramatizing my genuine sorrow: "Hey, is it a silent film here? The *Bitter End of Żubrówka*? But who's the director?"

Gertrude is at Sylvia's ear and she is looking down at me. I can tell that she is probably whispering something about Nina directing, unasked.

Sew jumps in: "Not only that our Melancholia Elixir is not as promised, Ninochka." His face is more deliberately sad, but his eyes brighten as he discreetly points down (again) toward his crotch, then whispers in my ear (maybe so others could hear): "He is still a little bit tired now."

Lila's eyes dart up in irritated disbelief before she looks the other way.

From the opposite side of the kitchen counter, Sylvia takes on a resigned but tolerant expression and Gertrude's laugh is only a mild derision. She says: "Anyway, Sew, why don't you tell us a proper joke because my sister can do only half bakes and has no vulgar decency limits, as we all know. Oh, and why don't you also skip the crude parts, Sew? That would be my advice." My sister, satisfied with her pointed wit, shoots me a look of entitled superiority.

I whisper in Sew's ear: "Give us a joke quick when Lila isn't paying attention because she will get embarrassed and pissed. And I'm afraid we were misled. And it's almost dawn! Shit, Sew!"

"Ninochka, I'm already sad." His eyes drop; again it's as if he's addressing his crotch.

Out of the blue, I make a general address: "Hey, did you know something that Sew knows?" That got their attention. "A Big Laugh is definitely better for us than Big Sex!"

Sew points at me: "We need both together! We need double medicine to distract ourselves from the pain gifted us by our fucked up families, not just fucked up governments! But where is our host, Alek? We need a specialist doctor to administer this double medicine for us!"

Sylvia has been building up to say something. "And nothing will kill the pain of being thrown out of Poland, which we had considered our motherland for centuries," she announces in her clear stage voice.

Sew's eyes get watery again. "But where is Dr. Smart Alek? Who wants to be sad?"

Gertrude primes herself to offer her educated opinion: "Okay. Good idea. So why don't you distract us, Sew."

I jump in: "And isn't it scientifically proven that laughter kills the pain but pain doesn't kill the laughter, which is about as good for you as orgasm is, due to similar endorphins release. But Pain tries to kill Laughter, and Laughter kills the Pain. So we need Sew to win!"

"That's a pretty clever slogan, Nina." Gertrude is congratulating me.

"Don't be so sure, Ninochka, that I am virile enough to provide such orgasmic services to all the beautiful ladies here who need them!" Sew laughs heartily.

"Seweryn the Great — you can do it!!! Make us laugh," I encourage him.

"Okay, but I need help! Maybe Dr. Alek has some *Żubrówka* hidden for the end of the party! So where is *Pan tegu domu*? Our Host? Where is he? Anyone knows?"

"Looks as if there is no sign of our host, nor a calm elixir to toast," I say, hearing it rhyme unexpectedly. They all just look at me in a stop this nonsense moment. Except Sew, who says dramatically, "I support Nina."

"Is this the best joke you can muster Nina? Or is it only half?" says Gertrude.

Martin reaches for my hand, as if he owns me, and gives it a let's go home squeeze. The fine muscles of his forearm tremble (his extreme readiness to depart signal). I resist, in the manner of a rebellious child being spirited out of a party in full swing, and Sew makes a joke about the fiction of change in my husband, and about my need for a daily Triple *Kabanos* Orgasm moistened with Unlimited *Żubrówka*, and that a joke on request is as good as orgasm on request.

"Wait, I need to go to my car to get something. I think it may help!" Sew laughs and leaves the polished black marble kitchen counter.

Sew is back, Alek still nowhere to be seen. (Is Sylvia off looking for him?) Douggie is awake and holds a ceramic white cup with coffee in it. (Sylvia made him a special double espresso before she left.) Gertrude's moderately controlled scorn shapes her lips now and is aimed at me: "Actually, I don't think Nina is funny at all," Gertrude pronounces with full conviction, not looking at me but at Sew, her scorn at me transformed into a friendly encouragement to him: "So Sew, why don't you tell us a better joke." One flat burst of laughter and Gertrude throws me a pointed glance. "And can I advise you about something again, Nina?"

"I'm all ears."

"Well, Nina, in my opinion and in the opinion of others

too I'm sure, first, you could once and for all refrain from disclosing to us your private laundry without being asked to. We've already heard enough of it. Second, don't make a joke of what is not funny at all." My beautiful older sister's glare metaphorically harasses me with an acid harshness all the way into my gut.

Sew and Lila send each other that here we go again look about our sibling tensions. "I refuse to take sides between you sisters," Sew says quietly.

Gertrude laughs a brief bark. "Sew, so how about your Promised Joke?" she coaxes gently. "But I wonder if my writer of the moment coquette sister is going to write it up in her head now, to later pretend it's fiction? And make us her puppets." (She looks quite satisfied.)

"Well, I hope Nina is not going to assassinate everyone's character to make her point," Lila says, not joking at all. In fact, her politeness is off and she suddenly seems angry.

Martin is animated. "Exactly Lila, and I wish someone could explain that to my wife who thinks it's her right to destroy her friends' personalities. Who wants that?"

"A writer has no power like that, Marti. A writer creates personalities with words," I say.

"Martin, it's okay with me," Gertrude says with studied calm. "It's only Nina's perception of reality. I'm just suggesting that we don't let Nina copy and spoil Sew's joke in her book — if she ever finishes it," Gertrude explains to Martin. Lila ignores me.

"But Gertrude," I say, "my reality is pretending to be a

writer so as to immerse myself in creative nothing and smoke joints to enhance it. I work halftime at a job I like. And you Gertrude work fulltime at you real estate law job you hate." (And in my head I continue: But you need a bigger house and elegant designer clothes at charity prices, and you clean your toilets by yourself — not because you can't pay for it but because no one else in the world can clean anything as well as you do. And I am fine with tattered clothes and safety pins, my signature décor item.)

"You two are loving sisters, so can you please stop it?" Sew tries, as my inner tirade keeps going: But I will write about how Lila and I missed hours of the party because we were enjoying a *Prywatka for Two* then *Three* in Sylvia's lavender guest WC, throwing up *Żubrówka* with a heavy content of unrelenting nostalgia. Aloud I say: "*Żubrowka* is a symbol of Polish Jewish nostalgia, and me and Lila expelled it bloated with the *śledzik* and *mizeria*, and according to Gertrude, with antisemitic *kabanosy*. But we missed the fun part of the party and it's our fault. But can anyone give Lila and me a hint of what we missed?"

"But Nina, you didn't have to get dead drunk. Then you'd know what you missed." Gertrude looks satisfied, as if she has resolved the issue. Sylvia nods with studied grace.

"Will you shut up, Nina?" Lila whispers in carefully stifled anger. "I don't remember anything and I don't want anyone to know!"

"But Sew, can you end this with one funny joke?" says Gertrude, in good humor again.

Before Sew can come up with a joke to change the subject, and hopefully the mood in the kitchen, I blurt out, "Oh fuck, Sew! Look! Fuck!!! Look at what is hiding here!! I see it!"

Sew is quick: "What is hiding, Ninochka?" He smiles broadly and looks down toward his crotch. "I don't see anything yet, so tell me what you found?!" He laughs with gusto.

"You're looking in the wrong direction, Sew. Up here, behind some other bottles, over at the other end of the counter!" I point to a bottle of *Żubrówka* next to other empty wine bottles. I get up from my high chair to see better. "But *fuck-ola*, it's almost empty!"

Gertrude's eyes, narrowed by her usual dose of mild scorn or disrespect of who I am, fix on me. Lila is sipping her water. Douggie seems to be observing vaguely with one half open and one half closed eye.

Sylvia appears without Alek, and walks with a sexy swing of her hips all the way back to her high chair.

"Ninochka claims," says Sew, with boisterous joy and the bottle in his hand, "that this *Żubrówka* bottle is not empty yet!" Douggie's one eye is fully open and looking at me blankly. He takes a sip from his white ceramic coffee cup.

"My husbie will need one more cup of coffee to wake his other eye up," Gertrude informs the room.

Smart Alek reappears. From her seat at the counter Queen Sylvia welcomes him with a languid where have you been my husband to be expression.

Sew starts right in: "Hey Smart Alek, our Ninochka wants to know if she can have these sad remnants of *Żubrówka* in this promised to be unlimited bottle?" He winks.

The *Żubrówka* bottle is now in my hand. Gertrude cannot resist chiming in: "Alek, maybe you can talk reason into my sister's head. She wants more *Żubrówka* to feel more of her stupid for the wrong reason Polish nostalgia. Poland doesn't deserve our nostalgia, not the way they treated us, our grandparents, and our parents. But according to Nina's fancy joke, apparently *Żubrówka* is tinted with Polish bison urine found on the meadow grasses from Białowieża Forest near Białystok, where *nota bene*, pretty much all the Jews were wiped out. I don't think that is funny."

Smart Alek settles in next to the previously satisfied and dreamy eyed Sylvia, who now looks anything but at peace. But Alek looks sleepy. He flashes me a curious tired look. Gertrude conspicuously studies the ceiling, then gets up, taking truly pissed staccato steps away, to the other end of the black marble counter, near Sylvia.

With partially regained exuberance, and after taking his sweet time, Smart Alek responds: "Of course there is some *Żubrówka* for you, Ninochka." He comes closer to me and takes the bottle from my hand, locates a shot glass on the shelf, and pours the last drops of *Żubrówka* in it. "See, I saved some for you, Ninochka." He hands me the glass. I inhale the aroma (of my Elixir), and leaning against the black glossy counter I notice the reflections of the street lights on it. Relieved, I whisper triumphantly into Martin's ear, "Notice that the street lights are still on, darling, and there is some *Żubrówka* left, so it's not time to go home yet."

The *Żubrówka* glass rim is just at my lip and I'm about to take the smallest sip possible when Martin, with a firm hand on my wrist, tries to prevent me doing so. "Hey, watch it Nina, you were just throwing up. Drink coffee. It has some water in it. Or drink water, like Lila is doing. Hydrate! Like Lila. Lila is smart."

"I think that our two sisters, Gertrude and Nina, are both right, so there is no reason to fight," Alek says. "And as to this bottle of *Żubrówka* — this is a limited elixir of our . . ."

"Unlimited *Melancholia*," I throw in impulsively.

"But limit means . . ." Alek trails off again.

Sew throws a significant look in Alek's direction and spits out emphatically, "It's simple: It means that there is no more left for us, and maybe the end of this Schmelancholia is not a bad thing, but it also means the nearing of the cruel end of this *prywatka*. Hey, okay, look everyone," Sew continues, making his voice cut through, aiming it at Alek (who is still subdued compared to his normal exaggerated joyfulness at a *prywatka*). Raising his voice, Sew presses on: "Hey, all my friends are here and are witnesses to the fact that our dear host Smart Alek possibly cheated us about the philosophical true nature of the meaning of Unlimited Schmelancholia on the Sacred Invitation, as Nina is suggesting, and even though she is irregular, which by the way is not quite the same as plain weird — we all know the world is weirdly fucked — in this case, it is the promise of Unlimited *Żubrówka*, the symbol of unrelenting Schmelancholia, until Sunrise, as we were assured in print!" Sew isn't laughing audibly but his eyes are; they shine behind a thin layer of tears. No one else is laughing.

Suddenly Lila stands up and takes a few dainty quick steps toward Sew (on her high heel sandals with her pretty toenails painted the same red as her pretty fingernails). She raises her eyes and peers into Sew's, still tearing up, "You seem much better, so don't look sad when you are not sad," she says, standing on tiptoe, straining to be as tall as she can, for despite her high heel sandals she is shorter than him by a head.

"But why shouldn't I look sad when I feel sad because the fun is about to end?" Sew says in earnest.

Marti gently reminds me: "Just drink your coffee Nina. It's good for you — it has some water in it. And get yourself ready. Do you need to pee before we go home?"

"No I don't need to pee!" I apply firm pressure on his forearm, to calm it down. (It's trembling with a paper cup of coffee near my lips.) "And the End of Party Scene is just starting." I point to my shot glass with hardly a miniscule teaspoon of *Żubrówka* in it.

Lila and Sew sip their water from paper cups. I move my head toward Lila, confiding, "Be serious. You really do not remember the bald guy?" She shakes her head. "First, I and then you danced with him."

Sew is listening in, his eyes opening wider.

"Stop it, Nina," Lila warns in high pitched whisper words truncated by a censored but not entirely dainty anger.

Sew leans toward her from his high seat, hugs her hard (maybe too enthusiastically) and kisses her with effusive affection on the cheek, and he addresses Lila and me with an air of import: "I'm warning you two to stay away from that bald cantankerous character! Don't say I didn't warn you that he is a specimen of inflated ego!"

I stand to face the suddenly serious Sew eye to eye and challenge him: "So, give us an example of his inflated bold bald ego, Sew!"

Lila also has lifted her eyes to meet Sew's and quietly says, "In general, I think that most people are not that bad."

Sew pulls his hands out of his navy blue sweatshirt with a hoodie and takes a step toward my husband. "But Martin, let Nina be Nina. I'll bet even if she wants to she cannot stop her addiction to moving rugs and chairs all over your house because she is a true bohemian, a movement and ambiance artist, and it's something she gives you every day, so don't complain, Martin!" Sew's hand emphasizes the point. "So let her be a mover of this and that in your house, Martin, and also the poetic coquette of words that live outside the Oxford Dictionary! Is that how you say it good in English, Professor Martin?"

Martin perks up. "Hee, hee, Sew, for me the only Polish poet is Wisława Szymborska, and as for other poets, there's

Dylan Thomas. And definitely a word is not a word unless it is in the Oxford Dictionary."

"I love Szymborska because I can understand her despite not being an intellectual. And Marti understands her and he *is* an intellectual, but not only, though he doesn't like to boast in public, so I will boast for him that he also is a poet, a Poet of Equations living in an organized Chaos Theory Studio where he tries to extract an essence of abstraction. Of Absolute Truth. He is an Abstract Chaos Poet of Equation genius. And only six people in the world fully understand him. And if I'm lucky, only six people in the world will read my Word Coquette Ninaism book." I look at Sew, whose eyes light up as if he is about to make a joke, but I'm quicker on the draw: "No, no, Sew, I know what you're thinking, it's not an Onanism Book . . . it's Ninaism!" I say with a straight face. Gertrude and Sylvia turn their eyes upward. Lila looks like she is holding something in as usual.

"But maybe Nina can write distilled poems on her deep subject too, " Sew offers, boisterously.

"Yes I can. As an Occupational Sex Therapist, I taught a very disabled woman to masturbate," I say seriously.

"Stop it, Nina, that's not a subject for a party," Lila practically shouts, a reddish blush on her cheeks.

"And what do you, Sew, as a painter of close up portraits of universal melancholy, have to say?" I provoke him.

"Yes, Sew, you are also a high school teacher and an artist. So what do you preach to your students?" Martin throws in.

255

"Professor Martin, I don't believe in anything, so I can't preach and maybe that's why I'm not a professor at a university like you are. Is that the right way to say it in Irish approved English?" Sew laughs wholeheartedly and Gertrude almost does too. Sylvia is very quiet, covering her mouth (in fact, yawning at times). Alek has disappeared again.

I give Sew a light pat on his shoulder. "How about a change of subject at this very present moment. About us Jews with Polish souls that vibrate when sufficiently saturated with *Żubrówka*? For example, my soul needs more *Żubrówka* before this party ends." For effect, I wipe an imaginary tear under my eyes and take a tiny imaginary sip.

Sew gives a light pat on Martin's shoulder without Martin ducking away. "See, Martin, your wife laughs and cries, which means she gets the essence of life. But where is our Smart Doctor Alek? He is a doctor, so he definitely knows the essence of many conditions. Where is he? We need to drink *L'chaim* — to life, to this party!"

"To this *prywatka* before it ends." I raise my empty glass. "Marti, toast with us. Even if it's water, darling."

"Nina, you should know that a real Irishman never drinks water. W.C. Fields said he never drank water. Why? Because fish fuck in it." (He whispers the last part in my ear.) "But here I feel like a fish out of the water, hee, hee, hee."

Lila raises her paper cup with water. "Nina would you stop your whining? Let's all drink pure spring water from our local untouched virgin forests. To clear our heads."

Smart Alek appears. "Our Nina knows what she is

talking about, but our Gertrude, her older sister, and my Sylvia — oh where is my dear wife soon to be — they are older and wiser, so they know even better." Alek holds an empty *Żubrówka* shot glass, and raises it in a *L'chaim* gesture.

Like a graceful cat, Sylvia settles herself next to Alek. In her sexy, languid, suggestive pose, with one hand, in a fingerless black lace glove, parked thoughtfully under her chin, she puts a mysterious smile on her pouting lips, and her wide open questioning eyes are fixed on me and Lila or maybe on our lips — we both have French Rouge lipstick on, which we helped ourselves to at the end of our visit to her lavender Guest WC. In a queenly manner, Sylvia accepts an empty shot glass from Smart Alek and raises it in a *L'chaim* gesture. "To Life! *L'chaim*!" she says loudly, smiling broadly, puts her shot glass down, and her fingertips touch each other in black lace gloves also caressing the underside of her chin, in a self flattering self loving pose, perhaps a little self consciously so.

"So why not have some more fun my dear Sylvia?" Suddenly Alek is in an almost jovial mood.

The sobering guests lazily raise coffee and water cups.

"*L'chaim*!" Sylvia repeats with a self satisfied slightly skewed smile on her lips, the one that implies she is the happiest of all women.

"But since my wife Nina claims to be a writer of the moment, I think she should write up this scene and explain to us who do not understand what's so special about this Zuperovska Shmelancholia Hoopla. Hee, hee, hee."

"Darling, the absolute truth is that in Puszcza Białowieska, the *Żubry* roamed centuries before. Then they were almost extinct . . . don't interrupt, Marti, I'm in the middle . . . but they're back, roaming the pristine meadows again. But the Jews of nearby Białystok, who also lived there centuries ago, side by side with the Catholic God fearing Poles, don't roam anymore. All gone, seven official Jews left in total as of now. All others from the *Shtetl* gone."

Sylvia interrupts: "Nina, you probably don't know how many there were. Sixty thousand Jews lived in harmony with fifty thousand Poles in that big *Shtetl* town. There are still a few more Jews left, but they are hiding in the shadows." She sighs with resignation and her gloved hands leave her chin and she sends a wide eyed look to Gertrude, who glares at me before she opens her mouth: "Nina, can you stop right here before you misrepresent the truth?" She sneers. "And be careful, Nina, or you'll end up like our philosopher father who achieved nothing. And you will turn people off if you keep hanging out your dirty laundry at this party and anywhere you have an audience."

"But her laundry machine is broken!" Sew's laugh shatters the tension. "So let Nina tell us about this *Żubrówka*, even though she does not have all the information! Sylvia and Gertrude can straighten her out with the other side of the story."

"Is it a *Rashomon* story?" Lila injects.

"And we're all here to help figure it out," Sew says and opens his arms wide.

Lila puts her cup of water on the counter, then immediately picks it back up. Gertrude leaves the kitchen, her heels making an elongated self righteous tap tap tap.

"Sew, but I didn't make up the legend of *Żubrówka*'s magic blade of grass which flavors the whole bottle with an aroma of melancholic scent which is never the same from one bottle to the next. And by the way the color differs depending on *Żubry* piss acidity . . . "

Sew interrupts me: "Ninochka, and where does this Piss Legend comes from? The single blade of grass is responsible for the pissed upon amber color?"

"And the hint of Polish jungle juniper intensifies the bittersweet experience of collective nostalgia," I say quickly.

"Juniper is okay in *bigos* too," Martin contributes. "A nostalgic Polish dish I like."

Sylvia opens her eyes and, as if we're all characters in a play she's watching from her private box in a theater, addresses us in a soft but clear and distinct full attention requiring voice: "Guys, we are talking of irreparable loss, yes, but also of pure joys *na wygnaniu*, in exile, in our new country. That's us. And others. Anywhere, anytime." She sighs deeply.

"Sylvia, I know a thing or two too," says Sew, holding the almost drained bottle of *Żubrówka* — with a single blade of grass stuck to the inside of it on the side — upside down. He peers into it intently. His face radiates a disappointment. "But look what is happening inside this *Żubrówka* bottle!" His voice is permeated with dramatic emotion. "What is sad is the fact that this glorious Kitchen *Prywatka* is about to end with a note of a limp blade of *Żubry* pissed upon grass lifelessly stuck in this bottle. See?" He points to the bottle and ends on an extra simulated sad note: "This — according to Ninochka — magic blade is pretty dead or definitely it is not moving like it was before, when the bottle was full."

I say, not really knowing why, "This innocent and once buoyant blade of Puszcza Białowieska grass once upon a time was swimming freely in the golden liquid, but Sew, don't lament, there still is hope."

"Okay, so let's ask Dr. Alek!" Sew livens up; his sad expression is gone. Sylvia's eyes shoot up, as do Lila's. Alek is in midyawn. "But maybe there is another bottle?" I ask in half pretend hopefulness.

Alek, who had taken off his multicolored tie, yawns again. Sew addresses him: "Dr. Alek, wake up, I want your medical doctor's opinion. Hey, Dr. Alek? Aren't you responsible, with your home remedy medicinal cellar, to cure the specifically hysterical Polish or Jewish female condition of Schmelancholia?" Sew asks, suppressing a smile.

Alek makes a resigned face and I say, "Are you serious, Dr. Alek, that you have no more *Żubrówka* in your cellar? It was advertised to be Unlimited, right?"

"She is right, it was written in the Invitation! So what's up, Dr. Smart Alek?" (Sew does his mock lament.)

To demonstrate the sad state of affairs, Sew turns the bottle upside down again. Nothing comes out. "I also want to know the truth, Dr. Smart Alek," Sew says confrontationally, with the bottle in his hand, almost yelling: "No, no, don't look at me like that! It's not about me, I'm fine, but our Ninochka wants to know why there is a discrepancy in the availability of *Żubrówka* as promised in the Invitation. You know that we Polished or UnPolished Jews take things very seriously!"

Sylvia's eyes are closed again. Gertrude is back and waits till Sew is finished before putting in her three pennies: "Well, no one prevents Nina from being responsible and drinking moderately with everyone else and having fun, but she prefers to miss the best of the party by throwing up as part of this occasion. Serves her right. You yourself chose to suffer, Nina, so don't make a victim out of yourself." (Gertrude's three pennies have been contributed in a patient condescending voice.)

"Oh, don't be so hard on your poor sister, Gertrude," Sew chides her, "she is already punished: she missed almost all the fun," he declares and takes a tiny sip of *Żubrówka* (which he'd patiently dripped out from the nearly empty bottle into a shot glass he'd found). Alek yawns again, and Sew administers a friendly wake up slap to his forearm: "So Dr. Smart Sleepy Alek, what is it with that Unlimited *Żubrówka* Promise?"

Sylvia seems half amused and is watching. Douggie is not quite asleep. Lila picks up her water cup and puts it back down again without taking a sip: "It's too sad to talk about. In some situations it is better to be quiet."

"Lila is right. What's the point of looking the truth into the sad eye if we can't change anything about it?" inserts Sew, who has just drained the last miniscule sip of *Żubrówka* from his shot glass. He puts it on the counter with gusto and loudly inquires, "But can someone besides Martin please tell me about that cake of the absolute truth, including its definition and who has the right to eat it without limits?" He speaks rapidly and his voice reaches crescendo forte intensity. "But the most important thing is if I'm allowed to eat it too!" He laughs heartily and his eyes glaze with tears. Alek's laugh resonates, and Gertrude, as if she has trained her face to resist expression, looks blankly into a neutral space.

"I would really like to solve this problem for good, so my wife and I stop having fights about it in our kitchen, hee, hee."

Smart Alek, back to his normal jovial self, excitedly spits out, "But the good thing, my dear friends, is that my beautiful soon to be my wife and I are going to try a very good cake tonight when all of you are finally gone to your own houses." Sylvia giggles lightly. She rests her arm on Alek's neck.

"And what cake are you intending to try tonight, Alek? So, how many cakes are you going to eat all together?" Sew giggles.

Lila takes a step toward me and whispers, "Nina, I wish Sew stopped this cake nonsense."

"I like you, Sew and Nina, but our bedroom is none of

your business," Sylvia says, yawning.

"The cake limit rule is not to get fat," Gertrude states flatly. "I use it on my husband. And I think Martin should not let Nina have it — she is getting too fat. And her cat is also getting too fat. It used to be more elegant before."

I pretend not to hear and Martin poses a question to all and sundry: "But who can finally tell me what's so special about this . . . this . . . Zu-prewk-ska that causes all this Hoopla?"

Sew's entire muscular well shaped body is in its element and he speaks authoritatively: "Professor Martin is talking about the power of this urine colored liquid which his poetic tantric wife calls a magic golden piss elixir or Zuperowska (he is imitating Martin), which is brewed in Białystok." Sylvia seems on the verge of saying something.

"This Zuperofska by the way is impossible to find in our big local liquor store," Martin says good humoredly, "and is difficult for us foreigners to pronounce. So am I saying it right? Zu-prewk-ska?"

"Martin, you can do better than that. I already told you and your wife how," Gertrude throws in casually.

I walk away to the mirror in the foyer to refresh my lipstick and when I return, Martin is still in good humor. "Hee, hee, hee, but I still don't understand why this Zuperovka is so special. As far as I can tell, it does have a hint of juniper, which is good for you if you like peasant smells."

I whisper in Martin's ear: "Before I forget, I wanted to, privately in your ear, so no one can hear, poetically distill the unhappiness of a limp lifelessly suspended blade of grass in the bottle, which previously — maybe thinking that its time was unlimited — was floating carelessly in the bottle before its contents were drained, that is. Marti, are you not listening already? Despite my spontaneous poetic insights? And the other relevant question is if more than one cake is allowed and should it be eaten in secret, or is it okay to openly enjoy another cake of a different taste and consistency. Among other novel features found in different cakes . . . by the way I think a feature of modern polyamory is equality of choice," I say into space.

Lila and Sew don't seem to hear; their heads are close and they are talking to each other *sotto voce*.

Gertrude is in her high seat, and looking in no one's direction, she says, "This is a recurring problem. Is my sister back at it?" Then Gertrude barks amusedly, "Nina, remember that your husband's training is your responsibility." Lila lifts her eyebrows.

Sew pokes Martin lightly on the side. "Don't run away, Martin, I'll try to explain to you something your wife cannot because she is highly irregular like me and we understand how honestly a Professor of Theoretical Abstraction cannot stomach his irregular stoned artistic wife's ideas. A Professor Poet of Elegant Equations! The fluff we artists feel is not your thing! But we need artists and writers to expose our vibrating emotional souls to those who hide theirs, so the rest can vibrate too. Otherwise, who will?" Sew pokes Martin again, in a friendly way, and Martin takes a small cautious step away and laughs, hee, hee, hee, without covering the bottom half of his face.

Smart Alek and Sylvia are back from somewhere and Alek suddenly produces a deep exuberant ha ha ha ha. "My dear Professor Martin, there is nothing wrong with being a numbers poet, but I feel that Nina, your wife, is quite qualified to please you, her husband, not just with the true words of heart, but more than that!" Smart Alek makes a move to slap Martin, but Martin eludes him, taking a dignified step away to where Alek's big hand is out of striking distance. Alek continues: "So Nina, dear, in my experienced medical opinion, you are still too young to know the truth, but as I said earlier, your smart and beautiful older sister Gertrude and Queen Sylvia, my beautiful wife to be, most certainly know what we don't know!" Alek's proclamation ends with a victorious flourish, after which he turns toward Sylvia and Gertrude, whose heads are now in close proximity, conjoined in secrecy. Maybe Sylvia is whispering to Gertrude, "Would you please tell your younger sister to shut up? Tell her it is not her party?" Gertrude, her freezing contempt infused gaze fixed on me, is giving me an unpleasant vibe.

Sew dives in: "Hey, isn't our Alek terribly smart, even for a Professor Doctor? In fact, I know that Doctor Smart Alek knows an awful lot from his careful and deep examination of mature women as his professional subjects. And he claims that mature women know the truth! And our forever young and wise mature women are not only smart but also beautiful like our forever young and spirited Sylvia and Gertrude and Lila! . . . And Nina too sometimes, when she doesn't bullshit too much. And I'm not saying that she is full of shit at times, ha ha ha. But the truth is that no one would look that good if they knew the truth of what's waiting for us!"

"That's nothing to joke about." Gertrude averts her eyes. Sylvia, after a moment of reflection with her eyes closed, opens them and says simply, "Hmmm."

"That's why I'm calling myself a writer of the moment, which means no future, no past, only present," I say.

Gertrude immediately retorts: "That's an unoriginal slogan, Nina. Can't you be more creative?"

"So, this is a Funeral for Unlimited *Żubrówka* — right?" I say louder than I intended.

"Here she goes again," Gertrude says with an above it all smirk. Sylvia says nothing and moves her head farther away from Gertrude. Alek comes closer to Sylvia and she puts her hand into his and leans her breasts on the black reflective marble counter. Her free hand is under her chin in another flattering facelifting pose, her lips pursed in a knowing she's special way, and she starts in very slowly formed words with her rather perfect American accent: "Hey, all of you, stop bullshitting. I know the real truth about *Żubrówka* and Białystok and I'll tell you if you'll listen. You want to know the truth about *Żubrówka*?

Żubrówka is said to come from Puszcza Białowieska. It is now the only ancient forest in Poland where wild bison are found. Near Białystok, which was one of the biggest *Shtetls* in Poland." (Sylvia's words as always carry the tone of indisputable truth in perfect English pronunciation.)

Lila raises her paper cup with water. "So I think we all should finish off in a good mood. Let's drink to preservation of all the noble species. So they survive. Every creature has a right to live."

I raise my shot glass with a virtual drop in it. "But let's get to the point: Is this for real a Funeral for *Żubrówka*? But it's not dawn yet! And what about the Unlimited *Żubrówka* until Sunrise promise? We need to drink a toast for the freedom of all species!"

Sew and Alek laugh, putting their hands on their shoulders and start singing "Sunrise Sunset Sunrise Sunset la la la la la la Sunrise Sunset la la la," loudly, but not in a harmonious unison. Douglas opens and closes his eyes.

While they whoop it up with their la la la's, I say, "So how about that last toast before Sunrise . . . "

"With this limp symbol stuck hopelessly to the wall of this empty bottle here?" Sew completes the sentence for me.

Sylvia is quiet again. (She is probably thinking about some of her family who had lived in Białystok before the Holocaust and perished.)

After the la la la peters out, Gertrude challenges me: "But Nina, can't you explain your affected limpid melancholic symbol a little better?"

"To me it's obvious, Gertrude, but of course it is only my reality. The *Melancholia* is symbolically represented by this blade of Białowieska Puszcza grass stuck to the inside of empty *Żubrówka* bottle."

Gertrude gets up from her high chair, and approaches Sew, addressing him formally: "Seweryn, why don't you just acknowledge that this blade of grass which Nina made so soulful is from who knows which Polish forest. But I know that this antisemitic grass is for sure generically and genetically engineered, and stuck to the inside of this *Żubrówka* bottle is a symbol of Nina's melancholia. I wonder if being stuck is optimal for her as well." Gertrude is pleased with her humiliating retort and emits a short burst of self satisfaction. "But it would be helpful to my sister if someone else besides me and Martin told her that her pseudo-philosophy is getting weary." She looks to Sylvia for confirmation. Smiling Alek is now sitting next to Sylvia.

"That's rather cruel what Gertrude is saying," Lila whispers in my ear. Gertrude is on alert.

"Hee, hee, what I see is that the Zubrewsky is gone, everybody is tired and it's time for all of us to go home. Where is your coat, Nina?"

"But Marti, the sun isn't up yet and I'm feeling purified after throwing up all the miserable parts of my *Melancholia* with *mizeria* and *śledzik* assistance," I announce, my rebellious child tantrum impulse in check.

Sew jumps in practically yelling: "Hey Professor

Martin, don't you know your wife *needs* this kind of Polish Nostalgia with miserable explusions that *Żubrówka* combined with a *kabanos* and *śledzik* can give us a case of. But if more purification is needed, I'm sure Alek has more pure clear Polish vodka!"

"And it's a well known fact that Polish vodka is a universal Polish disinfectant!" I throw in.

A controlled displeasure twisting her delicate features, Gertrude presses on: "Don't believe my sister that antisemitic Polish vodka will disinfect our Jewish insides!"

Sew points his finger at Martin: "But pay attention to your wife, Professor Martin. She plainly is not ready to leave yet for your domestic bliss. And to tell the truth, I myself am actually thinking that maybe it is my turn to take advantage and purify myself in the famous guest WC!" He laughs heartily.

Sylvia's sensual face has suspicion painted all over it. But Sew is encouraged: "So I also need to empty myself of all the unnecessary *sheisse,* so I can get drunk again and have fun! Hey, Dr. Smart Alek, our dear host! For real, don't disappoint poor Ninochka. Isn't there another bottle of this Pissy Nostalgia Before Sunrise Elixir? And Nina is right in demanding an explanation!"

Sylvia bestows an enough is enough expression on him.

Gertrude turns to me: "But Nina, could you tell me why are you letting your husband hide your coat and dictate to you when and what you need to do? Can't you decide for yourself? And your safety pin is still working?" she barks.

"Marti, darling, where did you put my coat? And where is my Coach bag?"

"I can get it for you no problem, Nina."

"No, Marti, please don't get it! I'm not ready to go! And from now on I'm hanging my coat so I know where it is, and I'm getting it when I want to," and in his ear I whisper, "and I'll have with me not just three roaches but also three extra safety pins just in case. And by the way, I married a responsible genius to have children with. I didn't marry an overprotective mother father hybrid to look after me."

Martin throws a few fearful glances around the kitchen.

Alek is back, with an empty shot glass in his hand. He points at me and Martin. "See, these two pretend not to, but they still love each other! Look at these whispering love birds!" Alek's jovial voice is infectious and he raises his glass. He actually has a drop in it. I watch him drink it all the way to the end. He puts his glass on the counter and approaches Martin, who, with a polite instinct, quickly sidesteps Alek's path.

Suddenly Sew administers a restrained out of nowhere swat to Alek's shoulder (as if to show that he can do it before Alek slaps him), and says loudly, "Hey my friend, Doctor Alek, I see you were just getting ready to slap Professor Martin on the shoulder! But he ducked just in time! He is a brainy and agile handsome young fellow!"

"Sew is about to tell a crass joke at your cost, Marti," I whisper in my husband's ear. Alek, visibly excited, without skipping a bit, returns an affectionate slap onto Sew's shoulder and more or less yells, "Sew, my friend, actually I was about to tell our Professor Martin to let his wife try a good medicine! Let her have a drink of *Żubrówka* every single night at sunset! And Gertrude and my wife to be Queen Sylvia in my professional opinion need the same advice. A shot of *Żubrówka* at sunset! And *nota bene*, *Żubrówka* is well known in medical literature to be of benefit with cases of dramatic intensity Eastern European Jewish hysteria in females, which likely is a form of insatiable dissatisfaction!"

Martin's interest is awakened. "Hey, it happens that my genius wife coined a similar diagnosis for her own, and possibly her older sister's condition. I think she calls it . . ."

"Darling, Expandable Extra Large Double Bag of Insatiable Dissatisfaction!" (And Gertrude has an infinity of insatiable dissatisfaction, I say to myself.)

"Ha Ha Ha." Everyone is laughing except Gertrude. Sew and Alek laugh the loudest.

"In my opinion," Alek says between paroxysms of laughter, "your very experienced wife should receive a doctorate in this condition. What do we men know?"

"Don't provoke your wife, Martin, or she will give you a diagnosis too!" says my sister, letting out a warning little bark.

"I already did. But Gertrude, what about *your* self diagnosis?" She just stares at me with an expression revealing nothing. I continue, "I gave Martin a dual diagnosis that amends his academic title: Professor Didn't Notice Always Right."

Sew is laughing so hard he coughs. Martin covers up his triplet. Meanwhile, Alek approaches my husband: "Hey, but our Professor Martin is straight on right about girls. In fact, girls are women of all ages. And I know what I'm talking about. I'm an experienced doctor." Then he yells out with gusto: "But frankly, you don't have to study medicine to know that a woman, a drunk woman, Polish Jewish Blue Black Yellow or other, provided that her hysteria is under control, is a good woman in bed!" For once, we all share a laugh.

Alek is still guffawing when his intended gets up from her high chair and approaches him with an all the time in the world sway to her hips and a knowing, even double knowing, smile on her bright red lips. With a seductive gesture of ownership, she puts her arm around Alek's neck. "Shut up, Alek!" She produces an inviting and charming pearly giggle.

"My dear Sylvia, my wife to be is always right — so we don't fight. Instead we go to our bedroom and have some fun, don't we, Sylvia? Ha ha!" Alek looks at his wrist watch. "In fact it's about that time," he strongly suggests.

Sew looks like he wants to say something. And does, loudly: "Hey, you guests, listen to me! Our host is most impolite. He wants this party to be over so that, in plain direct language, he and his chosen one can go to their comfortable bed and in any language, fuck!" Sew slams his empty shot glass on the black marble. The glass doesn't break.

Martin, with nothing to drink (water doesn't quench an Irishman's thirst) is visibly anxious. There is a mild tremble in his forearms. "So the party is over, right?"

Sew continues in a loud accelerated manner: "The Invitation clearly states Un-li-mit-ed *Żubrówka* from dusk till dawn. And Doctor Alek confirms with authority that a *Żubrówka* shot at dusk — and just a symbolic droplet at dawn — is a desirable ritual that dilutes the Eastern European Girl Hysteria . . . But look out the window!" Sew suddenly yells, excited. "The street lights are off! It's dawn! But quite a doggone foggy morning. So, dear Ninochka, let Martin get your coat because he needs to do that. But Martin, please don't strangle your poor wife with that long black scarf! She needs to breathe this fog so she has something foggy to write about after you take her back home to boring domesticity!"

Douggie opens his eyes and stares into space. Alek looks around as if in distress and yells, "Sylvia! Where is Sylvia, my beautiful wife to be!? It's finally time to have fun, just the two of us!!" he bellows in the direction of the lavender Guest WC.

In an exaggerated regretful gesture, Sew tilts his empty *Żubrówka* glass, and his eyes allow me a glimpse into his, not at all laughing. "So this is the way it is. In plain language, our dear host just wants us to go our way into the bitter freezing fog! And why are we the guests treated so badly?! Because the lucky husband to be wants to have some fun with his Beautiful Queen!" He whispers in my ear, "Nina, *Oni nas chcą wygonić ze swego wygodnego domu. A przecież tak nie jest ładnie gości wyganiać!*"

I translate for Martin. "Sew is upset because our hosts are about to throw us out from their comfortable house and it is not nice to be throwing out one's guests."

"But really Lila, you don't remember the bald head and our WC session?" I quietly say.

"Who? What? I don't know what you're talking about, Nina! Is that bald guy here?" Her whisper is very perturbed.

"He is not here Lila, he apparently left when we were throwing up."

"And how about the Russians?"

"I think they are still in the living room. Maybe they fell asleep on that plush couch, you know where the abstract painting hangs and . . . the bald head . . ."

"I danced with a bald head?" Lila's eyes open in disbelief.

Sylvia and Alek are busy with private jokes and Gertrude's face is softened with her eyes closed as she pets Douggie's forearm under his soft cashmere sweater. "Gertrude looks happy and Douggie looks as if he is in seventh heaven," I say quietly to Lila. "If you want, Lila, I can tell you what Sew heard about the bald one. But not now. Later on the phone."

"Get to the point, Nina!" Lila says unexpectedly loudly.

"The bald bold Casanova confided to Sew that he wouldn't try to get you because you were too delicate of a bird for him, Lila."

"Stop Nina, I've had enough!"

Martin, already in his Irish wool herringbone jacket and his colorful scarf, and I, without a coat, scarf, or bag, are at the door, when suddenly he fishes out a slip of paper from the side pocket of his jacket and turns around, and when it is silent at the kitchen counter, with tears in his eyes he starts to recite in a quiet voice (but for everyone to hear):

True love. Is it normal,
is it serious, is it practical?
What does the world get from two people
who exist in a world of their own?

True love. Is it really necessary?
Tact and common sense tell us to pass over it in silence,
like a scandal in Life's highest circles.
Perfectly good children are born without its help.
It couldn't populate the planet in a million years,
it comes along so rarely.

I'm moved to the marrow of my bones.

Let the people who never find true love
keep saying that there's no such thing.
Their faith will make it easier for them to live and die.

Hiding my tears.

Dr. Angela Butterfly, MSW, Ph.D.
Intimacy Specialist
(9th Session)
9/7/05
(Solo session w/Nina)

N states that M threatened her with divorce last year unless she would remove an oval mirror from the dining room wall. It bothered him to look at himself while he ate his steak. She believes the oval mirror brings in light and the stars at night and happy people's faces when they eat good food. They solved the problem, after a fashion. She took his "patriarchal seat" at the table across from the mirror and has sat in it ever since.

However, in the "before and even after the kids early days" of their marriage, they were sexually more or less compatible. M and N enjoyed it, even though both had wished he could last longer.

It is apparent that M loves N deeply, and N is deeply attached to M, claiming that she does love him, but as we typically do not change our styles during the course of our lives, I question N's ability to express deep feelings for M at this point, and his ability to fulfill her current needs.

She feels that their incompatibility starts at the cellular level. He is defensive on a tactile level, while she could have a massage every day. When she suggested that every human being needs it and deserves it, he said: "I don't need a massage. I need a blow job."

N is still not able to let go of her anger at M for long ago yelling that she had no right to call herself an artist and was a disgrace to other artists.

I feel a sense of failure, in that I still do not have the full picture after so many sessions. These two very different and complicated individuals are simultaneously mismatched but drawn to each other. There is more beneath the surface than just sexual incompatibility, I suspect.

THE PARTY'S OVER

"Say it better, Nina."

Sin Palabras — Radio Tarifa

Martin seems sheepish (due to his outburst of emotion upon reciting Szymborska). He has my black coat on his arm.

I feel the jolt of a minor terror like sensation. "But I'm just not quite finished with the last of *Żubrówka*, darling." I hold up my glass with a drop of golden liquid in it.

"Nina, I want to sleep," he insists, putting my black coat over my shoulders despite my taking a step away from him.

My long black scarf is dangling off his arm, a scarf I knitted for myself of soft alpaca wool. He is about to wrap it around my neck. Another jolt. "I'm not ready yet, Marti, I still have to kiss everyone before we leave," I protest as he wraps the scarf around my neck. "Hey stop it, Marti, you're going to suffocate me!" I snap, trying to muffle desperation.

"Nina, I have to keep you safe from this bald scoundrel," Martin nervously mutters as he continues wrapping the scarf. I tilt my head this way and that to avoid being tangled in my own creation. On the third wrap around my neck, I have it figured out. Innocently, casually, I will ask Sylvia for the Bald Bold Man's cell phone number and pretend I'm asking for Lila, who is single and shy . . . I could say she needs a man to hold her but is too proud to do anything about it.

Martin, finished with the third wrap around my neck, says gently, "Ready now?"

I kiss him perfunctorily on the mouth. "Not quite yet, darling."

In the kitchen, Sew is leaning against the black marble counter. He misses nothing. He smiles and says, "Professor Martin, please don't strangle our Ninochka, I'm telling you again that she will never be ready to go back to your domesticity."

"Marti, shit, the scarf is too tight." I tug at it. "It's morning already. Is that why you look so satisfied?"

"And why is that, Ninochka?" Sew says, his eyes curious not mocking.

"To me, the reflections on this black marble meant the night was still young. But Marti is happy because there is a final objective proof that it's morning."

"An undisputable end of the party." Sew sounds more tragic than comic.

"Is the party really over?" I say in a mournful voice.

Gertrude yawns. "The party is not quite over. Douggie may still need another cup of coffee. Look, his third eye actually was open for a short while, but now it is closed again!" With half affection and half tenderness, she regards her husband, still slumped on his high chair, but awake enough to be slowly sipping from his white porcelain cup. As if his recent bout of defiance never happened.

"Of course our Douglas has to have another cup to keep at least one eye out of three on the road!" Alek yells from his position at the kitchen counter, so close to Sylvia that he is almost touching the side of her cheek.

Sylvia puts her head on Alek's chest. "It's time for bed! I am depleted!" She smiles broadly, sighs and lets out a few pearls of her languid provocative laughter, maybe a bit contrived.

In the foyer everyone is kissing each other goodbye, on both cheeks, then a little peck on the mouth or another one on the cheek, Polish style. (This will go on for a while.)

My coat is already buttoned and my black scarf is not suffocating me too badly when I open the heavy front door. Dawn has just begun to break and it's hard to see beyond a few yards. I breathe in deeply three times. The air feels trapped in the dense fog. In the dark gray sky the clouds are unmoving, as if stuck in the foggy gloom. The cold dripping fog seems to be entering my nostrils.

At the half open massive oak front door, I am hoping to feel the movement of the air on my face. But nothing is moving.

Martin is already in the driver's seat of our reliable red Toyota hatchback, patiently waiting. Reluctantly, I walk toward the car. The door on the passenger side is open and I poke my head inside, but stick it back out and put my hand above my ear to hear the noises from the house better. "Darling, but actually the party is not quite over. We are the first to leave. Listen . . . Don't you hear? Or you don't hear or see what you refuse to hear or see — but I hear and see very well."

"What do you hear? But please can you get in, Nina?" My husband's kept in check impatience doesn't fool me. He looks at me like I'm temporarily insane.

"Darling, don't look at me so weirdly, because I'm not imagining that right now I can hear Smart Alek and Queen Sylvia calling out the last *Żubrówka* toasts, no matter that the shot glasses are empty, half empty, or half full. Imagination is not your thing, I know," I say once I am finally in the passenger seat.

Martin is already focused on the printed directions, the reverse of how we got here.

"I bet, darling, that as soon as we drive away they will be opening a new bottle, a full bottle of *Żubrówka*. There is always some left for the few truly Chosen Ones. The insiders. And I am not included. Gertrude prefers a private space without me, her younger sister. It's how it always has been. But Marti, feel the air. It's so thick," I say calmly.

The engine isn't warm enough yet. Martin examines a small speck of dry white bird shit he just noticed on the driver's side window. He puts his hand on mine. "Hey Nina, let me know if you see a gas station with a car wash, so we can get rid of this bird shit," he says and with controlled annoyance removes my hand from the top of his. "And stop panicking Nina, there is nothing wrong with the air, you're imagining things." He pats me reassuringly three times on the top of my left thigh, feeling the silky Victoria Secret nylon stocking (like the ones his mother wore).

I'm irritated, by any man in my life, with this kind of reassuring patronizing tap tap tapping on my knee or thigh. I retaliate, touching Martin's nose, three light tap tap taps in return, and he ducks a little. "Stop it Nina, that hurts."

"I just wanted to wake up your focused attention, darling, away from bird shit, before we drive off and you start worrying over directions, because I wanted you to feel what I'm feeling, which is called Empathetic Validating Sharing. Did you know that intimate relationships feed on that?" I feel tears coming. "I wanted you to feel this heavy gloom of fog freezing the inside of my nostrils."

"You can put the heat on, Nina."

"But then you will not feel what I feel and the cold mist will just be dripping out of your nose, which is not that sexy." I give him a look. I feel angry. He looks away.

"Nina, in a few minutes the sun will be up and you will be happier, so cheer up." He gives me a cajoling parentally reassuring little peck on the cheek, which makes me more sad than angry. I am quiet for a few deep breaths.

"I think the engine should be warm enough. Let's give it another minute, Nina. Without complaining."

"You make me feel lonely, because you don't want to experience happy or gloomy things with me. Your fear of the unknown prevents you from spontaneously feeling the spontaneous with me, like dancing together, which is intimacy, which is what we don't have, yet you want me to service you because you served me a good dinner, so in order not to cry or leave you, I need to fortify myself with a full size joint . . . my soothing mood enhancer. My pacifier. My true friend." The tears haven't come yet but are threatening to.

"Hey Nina, I'm really tired. Can't you wait until later

to start in on me again? And I have an enhancer for your mood fortification. In my opinion you could just touch me here — he points to his crotch — "and see how easily it gets enhanced, hee, hee."

"What I need is my Special Purple Shit . . ."

"What??? You're going to make me choke from the smoke."

We are still waiting for the engine to get warm. Martin is quiet, as I perseverate about the last bottle of *Żubrówka* being opened in the kitchen without me. Suddenly he kisses me tenderly but too quickly on the lips and I want more, but his attention is already back on the written directions. "It's about two miles till we have to make the first right turn," he says.

"I like that kiss, Marti," I say but I'm resentful and my consciousness becomes occupied by the hot breaths the Bald Bold Man delivered into my ear lobe near the cubic zirconia earring — a birthday present from Martin — and for a while a part of me is back in the living room with the hot breaths in my ear.

I am calmer now, but not really. "Darling, the kiss you planted on my lips felt like a proof of planned spontaneity. I need to counteract the disappointment I suffer from in such circumstances, and that's why I have preferably three roaches in my bag, in my tarnished cigarette case, a present from you, just in case an outbreak of unexpected and unspecified angst may afflict me. Like right now. Two angstrums worth." I'm about to search for the tarnished cigarette case in my scuffed up Coach bag. "I need two or three roaches, depending on the size." I attempt a smile.

"Hee, hee, Nina, this is a good joke. Are you trying to tell me that to be satisfied you need three roaches, one symbol for each dick or what? Or maybe you need three dicks to keep you happy?" (There is a painting by Alice Neel, a portrait of Joe Gould, that we saw at the Metropolitan Museum of Art in New York. In the painting, Joe Gould has three penises. Martin had to drag me away, I stood in front of it for so long.)

He turns his head to briefly look at me, renewed fear in his eyes. "What's the problem now? Don't you have your roach?"

Finally he pulls away from the curb and creeps through the fog on the long and straight fresh black asphalt suburban street without sidewalks or trees, at no more than five miles per hour (a third of the speed limit). I open the cigarette case. "Can you see anything through this fog, darling? As if there is anything to see . . . I do have my very nice roach, but I don't know if it will cure my wordless — *sin palabras* — bitter melancholic nostalgia of this moment."

"Hmmm . . . describe it better, Nina, aren't you a writer of the moment? But it seems that you're having a bit of a post party depression. Postpartum, hee, hee. By the way, the Irish cure is to have Guinness in the morning. And I have a bottle in the fridge," he says tenderly as he continues to navigate the wide empty fogswept steel gray, almost black, asphalt street.

"This murky grayish fog soup is in mourning, darling . . . and we're stuck inside it . . . or are we trapped or strapped in the sticky mist of this empty street moment . . . which is why I need to smoke my pacifier so I won't distract you with my irrational foggy of the moment thoughts which I'll quietly write in my head so you can find the way home, ignoring me," I say as I'm feeling the almost unbearable pressure of my suppressed tears (ever since the end of the party) inside my nose.

"But don't smoke yet Nina, please, let's find our way home first. He picks up the page of directions but doesn't look at them.

I don't know the Bald Bold Man's name and have no idea how to get it from Sylvia without revealing my true motive. If I tell her I need his number for Lila, who is shy . . . and what if Lila finds out? Friendship over. Her honor. Betrayal. And as far as *Żubrówka Prywatki* in the future? They may never invite me again if they find out about my selfish manipulation (to get hold of the Bald Bold Man's number for myself). I bet they are in the kitchen right now, saying don't you think Nina is a bit off and not to the point with her points — and her need for attention with her crude dirty laundry talk and the ripped dress and an ankle strap hanging literally on a safety pin that looks like it will break any moment . . . And if I have an affair with the Bald Bold Man, somehow they'll find out . . . So Lila is too delicate of a bird for a sex only affair, but I am not too delicate of a bird? What does the Bald Bold Man think I am, if not a delicate bird?

When I zone back in, Martin is talking about the Bald Bold Man. I'm so tired that I think I must have told him something and forgotten. "Don't tell me, Nina, that you want that creep for yourself? And Lila needs a decent man, not a creep. I feel like punching him out, in fact. And you shouldn't lie to Sylvia — it'll come out sooner or later and no one likes to be deceived, Nina." (Maybe everything I've been saying in my head has been said aloud instead?)

"I'm not planning to deceive anyone. I'm not into cheating. I'll call Sylvia to get his cell number and offer it to Lila. And if Lila likes the creep and the creep likes Lila, she can call him or wait for him to call her. If I were interested myself, I'd tell you. But don't you think that people need from time to time a passionate sexual expression, not just brief marital pecks and paternalistic tap tap taps on the shoulder? Or on the thigh? And darling, didn't a famous wise male philosopher, a real one, not a fuzzy woman philosopher, conclude that a man — a woman by the way I'm sure was not mentioned — is entitled to take what he can get at the moment he can, provided he causes no harm . . . The more pleasure for everyone the better, and there is only one real life, and it excludes dream or fantasy, which only exists in the head and is not real . . . though imagination can induce reality. And sadly the *now* is a very limited affair, which ends when one dies. Right? And you and I have no romantic dates because we are already married, have a house, good jobs, and two beautiful sons. But don't we have a right to have passion in our lives? Marti?" I'm calmly reflective, not yelling.

Again, he doesn't seem to hear. (He is studying the directions intently.)

"In my opinion" — sarcasm is slipping into my voice — "our marriage, darling, is a prime example of a self imposed marital prison of two opposites. And I feel sometimes that you have more interest in Alexis than in me. She purrs and I complain. I hear you calling Alexis for her dinner with sweet affection and for me it's only a sharp irritated, "Nina, dinner on the table." I raise my voice. "And later, after you've had enough to drink, you tell me that actually it would be a good idea if I sucked your dick. Not very sexy!!!" I finish my yelling with a flourish.

"Please Nina, I'm driving. I'm exhausted. And your red lipstick still turns me on, so don't say that I don't notice. I notice. And don't yell at full volume in this fog — I'll miss the turn. I can't drive when you're ranting, raving, and complaining."

He pulls the car to the curb, stops, and glares. Says nothing. I don't storm out of the car as I have often done when accused of ranting, raving, and complaining. Instead, I take three calming breaths. "I didn't really yell, Marti, I was dramatic just so you'd understand my point. So keep driving. The suburbs unnerve me. Let's get the fuck out of here. That's why, darling, I'll need the Purple Shit Roach,"

I say quietly to try to calm him down. I know I've hurt his feelings. I exaggerated. But then I controlled myself. Like I should.

In my handbag, I find the Merlot Wine lipstick, flip the car mirror, apply the lipstick with my finger, and with provocation in mind ask him, "Like this, darling?" I turn my face toward his and he throws me a quick suspicious glance: "Don't distract me. I have to find my way out of here."

"Darling, I could direct you if you let me. And notice that I put red lipstick on for you, since your masculinity and maybe femininity, is disappointed when it is not on my lips. Too bad that I don't excite you properly *au naturel*. And why, darling, do you never slowly blow hot air in my ear so the hairs inside it move and pleasantly tickle? It's so erotic, but you find it unappealing and awkward and ticklish or grungy? Actually, darling, I have a diagnosis for your condition: How about the Proud of It Pedantic Paranoid Patriarch who likes to cook and serve his wife but will not dance with her?"

The highway is not yet visible and my sobbing impulse has subsided. Martin puts his hand on the inside of my thigh and caresses the silky nylon black stocking.

"Just like your mother wore, right, darling? So I'm a mannequin for your fetish? I want to tell you something. Something Unedited, Uncensored," I announce, though I don't know what I am going to say. I hear myself yelling again: "It's about us: We're going home to boring domesticity, with you in the kitchen where you never put anything back in place, then tell me that it's somewhere. And it's about your alcohol breath and your beer stomach heavy on me when we try to have sex, and my ranting, raving, and complaining . . . and yes, I would like what feels good for sixty erotic minutes! And I'm not thinking about that bald creep whose phone number I don't have, and that I will have to lie to Sylvia why I am getting it." (Did I say too much? I did. Maybe he's not listening, as usual, I hope.)

Martin takes his hand off my nylon stockinged thigh and without taking his eyes off the road, in abruptly crisp syllables infused with anger says: "Nina, don't pretend! You don't want it for Lila at all, you want it for yourself only, admit it, Nina."

"Marti, I will not yell but speak in a pleasant voice. So you can drive safely. You said that I'm a hedonist capable of anything if it feels or tastes good. And it is true. By the way, Dr. Butterfly told me privately that a shared joint is best for shared slow sex, but you're afraid of shared anything, except whiskey and Guinness, and are always against fuzzy hedonistic perceptions . . . No, darling, don't look at me now, you may lose your way, but admit you are a red lipstick and old fashioned nylon stockings with seams like your mother wore fetishist, and in addition you are extremely stingy with Emotional Dialogue Response." I become quiet for a moment. "But don't listen to me, darling, so you can get us safely home. Hey, Marti, what the fuck?! I thought we were out of Sylvia's suburb, but we're not out of anywhere yet! There's *another* gate ahead! Shit, is this a double gated hypocritical upscale community at the end of the straight empty road?" (I try to control my dismay.)

He doesn't respond, and I flip the car vanity mirror to study my eyes. The black mascara is smeared around them. I put my finger in my mouth, get saliva on it, and make the area around my eyes clean, like a cat would.

The fog is back again, wisps of it. No morning traffic. We're on the larger two lane bare of real trees avenue leading to the ugly highway; the clearly visible sign says the entrance is two miles ahead. We inch along, as Martin glances at me and yet again puts his hand on the top of my thigh, a bit reluctantly. He gives my thigh a reassuring tap tap tap. How much I hate his automatic paternalistic tapping, but I know he thinks he's being empathetic. Tears of disappointment come to my eyes again.

His eyes are on the road, but he extends a life rope — a concerned protective glance, then breaks the silence: "Nina, I see that you look sad now, and there is no reason for it. I think you really need your roach."

He throws a quick admiring look at my Victoria's Secret silky feel stockinged thigh before he takes his palm off it. "Nina." He says my name with more feeling than usual, not his normal sharp impatient "Nina" (as if I were his daughter who is not coming to dinner when it's ready). "Do you really want that creep that bad, Nina?" His eyes are back on the road.

I wipe my tears in the car mirror and try to remove the remainder of the black mascara smudges on my cheeks. "Marti, I don't know what I want. But maybe the Purple Shit will help."

With worry on his face, Martin briefly takes his eyes off the road (a freshly asphalted wide two lane street with no sidewalks, no shade trees, no houses). He looks at me and says, "Is something else the matter now, Nina? Just put on some more of your nice bright red lipstick and you'll feel better. And you should wear a stylish bright colored scarf, not just black all the time. Black is good for funerals," he says with conviction.

The fog is denser again. The worry on his face and his advice unnerve me as usual, but I control myself. "Darling, don't look at me with such a grave gravity. I don't feel that close to the grave yet, darling," I say, conscious of the extra darling, while wiping the last of the black mascara smudges from around my eyes.

"Then, Nina, describe to me how you feel now, in detail," he says in a sympathetic manner. But I'm aware of his technique: he is cajoling me, and in the process bestowing upon me a glance from above the steering wheel. "Nina, you look kind of blemished, but I'm sure your nice bright red lipstick will fix it, so why don't you put some more on?" he says with an air of self assurance added on to his confidence.

More tears. He is silent and his eyes are stuck to the

perfectly black new asphalt. He does not notice? Or pretends not to notice so he does not have to talk about what he doesn't want to know . . . "So darling," I say, "in your opinion a very bright fresh red lipstick will fix it all? It will fix that I want to cry for no reason?"

I break out in quiet sobs.

Another mildly disturbed glance is shot my way. His voice tries to pacify me: "Say it better, Nina, more poetically, you know you can," he encourages me earnestly without lifting his eyes off the road. "Nina" — he keeps saying my name — "think of a clever metaphor for a good title for the end of Zuperofska Party. For example: Who Is That Creep?" He is trying to entertain me because he does not like to see me crying.

We pass another sign for the highway. Half a mile to go. My tears are under control.

"Marti, how about A Funeral for *Żubrówka* — incidentally, please promise me that you'll buy Unlimited *Żubrówka* for my funeral *prywatka*. I want to be happy when I'm dead. And a day before and the day after, I'll take a pill of Ecstasy. Guests can try it too."

"Nina, why dwell on morbid thoughts? For sure a bright red lipstick will help you describe even more poetically your present emotional state. And put it in your book, but please not the private details about Martin Didn't Notice. Those, in my opinion, you can skip." He leans toward me and without looking at me bestows a little peck on my forehead. The car swerves mildly, but he recovers.

A few more tears of vague disappointment come into my eyes.

"Okay, Marti, I'll try. But I'm not a poet. I don't distill like you do with your Elegant Equations. Feeling words with salty tears are to be distilled. This fog has to be distilled. So you want me to distill the miserable salty fog of how I feel now? Really, darling?" I wipe the tears, close my eyes and take three very deep calming breaths. "How about this: I feel as if I am veiled by a clammy opaque shawl heavy with this suburban melancholy fog. The opposite of the feeling evoked by a blue sky with feathery white clouds, the sun peeking out at sunrise, a delicate breeze motivating the lacy clouds . . . What do you think? Needs polishing, I know. Or is it overpolished in your opinion? Is it at all poetic, darling?" I look at him, anticipating a response.

The highway entrance sign is just ahead but not yet readable. "Okay, Nina, it's not quite Szymborska, but keep working on it. But please don't talk to me now, I have to concentrate, we're almost at the highway, so go ahead and smoke your joint, but I hope you don't smoke when we get home, because the kids may be back early from their sleepover."

"Hey Marti. I think I have it. A clinging weighted shawl of limp cold wet and suffocating foggy melancholy is enveloping me . . . and may suffocate me . . . but you are not listening, darling."

He is concentrating, looking for the highway entrance.

So I write in my head: A sign for the ugly highway appears. Somber immobile clouds gather on the flat gloom of dark gray sky on this wintry November morning. But the sun will show its rays later, illuminating things in our kitchen.

He removes one hand from the steering wheel and pats me on my left shoulder in what is meant to be an emergency gravely reassuring manner. "Hey Nina, you really will be better when we get home. Our kids and our cat need us. And Nina, take my advice and just forget about that creep. Cheer up. We'll have a nice breakfast in bed with the boys and Alexis . . . I got a special cheese for all of us. And why don't you practice some nice Bach on your new Alto recorder? In my opinion neither you nor Lila need a creep like that. So smoke your still viable roach, as you call it. Just open the window a little so I won't choke from the smoke."

I am surprised by his lengthy response and resigned permission. He leans from his seat and places a very quick fatherly kiss on my cheek. I do not respond. I'm holding back my tears again. He does not notice. I am thinking about how to get the phone number of the Bald Bold Man.

DR. ANGELA BUTTERFLY, MSW, PH.D.
INTIMACY SPECIALIST
(10th Session)
9/21/05
(Scheduled as couples session — M canceled)

While N was driving here, M texted that he had an "emergency department meeting." N displeased at his lack of commitment to this process.

N defiantly informed me she would have an affair if the opportunity presented itself. I emphasized the issue of trust and not lying or cheating, as that is what holds the marriage together.

N pushed back, insisting that if she reveals it to M, it isn't cheating. We discussed jealousy and pain. She knows she may be causing him pain, which is not what she wants.

N became strangely silent – unique in my experience with her – barely whispering that she was "exhausted from my indecision." To shift gears, I suggested she close our work together by sharing something personal about her own aspirations as a writer, which I know is a burning desire within her. She perked right up and read from her Moleskine notebook (which she said she always had with her and also wrote in it in her dreaming head).

"I'm a writer of a present moment and at this moment I

am neither drunk nor stoned. I have constipation so I have privacy and time to write here, on my personal "throne." I write scenes in my head al fresco and a few notes in my Moleskine unruled notebook, a rule free notebook where I write whatever comes to my head in elegantly undisciplined cursive with my Pelican pen. (Marti gave me this pen.) Is it correct to write Stoned Writer of the moment in a moment, or the moment? Is that correct English? And off the subject: how much should one trust a decision in the moment? M says it should be an important moment worth writing about. I provoked him: as a foreigner writer of random moments, don't I have a right to tell the story of a random moment of my choosing with random mistakes life is full of? M says if the story is not based on verified by others facts, but is only imagined in one's head, it's always fiction. Period. And when one imagines an equation in one's head, is it fiction too, darling? I asked him with a big grin."

DECISION-MAKING: N to decide to stay or leave the marriage. (Their two sons will be off to college soon.) I wished her luck.

End of Notes

———————

AT THE CROSSROADS

*"She had to let all that wanted to
leave her brain leave."*

Bamba Bamba — Orchestra Baobab (Senegal)

She always felt free alone in her little red hatchback, which she'd bought for its Phillips speakers and paid for with her own money (and in which she lugged around her home health Occupational Therapy equipment and soccer stuff for the boys). The *Bamba* CD from Senegal was on, with its soulful rhythm and silky male voices, which soothed her anguish. She was on her way to cheat on her husband. She had woken up with sexually charged feelings that intensified when it hit her that she was really doing this.

She had managed to get the phone number from Sylvia, without raising too much suspicion. She cranked up the volume, remembering how she'd told Martin she had a yoga workshop and would be gone for most of the day.

While Martin liked soprano opera arias, she preferred a deep male bass voice. They were not like the lucky couples who danced together in the same rhythm. On the contrary, when Martin saw her dancing in the living room, he walked by without stopping, throwing her a quick approving smile of paternal understanding, then gliding into the kitchen to put on the potatoes.

She restarted the disc, turning it up even louder, dancing in joyous abandon within the confines of her seat belt. A joint would enhance this experience, but she knew that as soon as the music stopped, her enhanced awareness could possibly freak her out. "Bamba Bamba," her favorite track, ended, and it happened: the unpleasant tightening in her gut. She did have three good roaches in her cigarette case for when an unspecified random angst might afflict her. In fact, she always needed at least one roach in front of her parents' apartment door, to fortify herself from their various camouflaged and uncamouflaged humiliations, with Gertrude piling on, at dinner thank God without the kids. Now she definitely felt the need for a calming roach, because here she was again, this time by choice, on the very highway she vehemently hated. (She liked onomatopeic words like vehemence and made a mental note to not use inadequate in expression English words; sometimes she dreamed new words up in both languages.)

On a positive note, she was thinking, this ugly highway gets you where you want — or think you want — to go. For Martin, the direct route in a safe car to a destination with a statue of an important mathematician was a joy of life.

"Bamba Bamba" was on again — how many times? But she couldn't ignore the dark gray filth colored industrial warehouses with mostly broken windows, not a tree or a church steeple. The same blackish dust covered tall somber cement walls separating generic housing developments from the intense noise and impure air produced by the never ending ten car wide river. To confirm and not to exaggerate her description, she counted the lanes. Five in her direction, five in the other. Traffic thickened. She was painting with words but repeating herself too much, and thinking: it will bore the reader if it bores me, and the worst nightmare of a writer is to bore the reader.

She still had half an hour to go, and she played two

tracks from her music of Mali CD, and following that, two tracks of smoky Ethiopian 1970s café jazz and after that the "Super Tentemba" from Guinea. At the moment, she was entranced by the sensual saxophone and the rhythm which matched the beat of her heart.

Once more a sensual "Bamba Bamba" was playing at full volume as she passed through the gates of Rustling Creek. She stopped the music and addressed herself in silence: Here lives the Bald Bold Polish Jew who acts like a *cham* (a rude dude in English). He held his hand on my waist and I couldn't resist, and didn't walk away from him while to the rhythm of elevator muzak he was puffing hot breaths in my ear . . . just next to Martin's cubic zirconia stud earrings — an anniversary gift for being together twenty years.

She slowed to a snail's pace along Rustling Creek Way. So where is the rustle and where is the creek? Only wide and empty windswept newly resurfaced black asphalt. Just like where Sylvia lived. *No* sidewalk. *No* people. *No* dogs taking their poets for walks. A few big cars parked in oversized driveways of oversized one level houses, she was writing in her head while crawling along with the window rolled down to listen for a rustling creek sound. A pleasant warm breeze caressed her face. The sun was out but not too bright yet. Three deep cleansing yoga breaths. A nice roach would be just the thing.

But the sun became too bright, and an eerie unsettling

feeling overcame her, forcing itself into her awareness at solar plexus level, but not grabbing it yet. Is this windswept street alive at all? These poor trees are only the *pretense* of trees, mere scrawny dwarfish growths with brownish leafless branches, no birds, just these measly saplings planted according to a sterile master plan at a precisely measured distance from each other. She really hated things pedantically rectangular. Her purposefully ripped style had not developed just to irritate Martin. She felt like a teenage punk. Me, the mother of two teenage sons about to have an affair without telling my husband! Identical rectangular ranch style houses in the same shade of cement gray. Nothing round. But Martin probably thinks the well rounded ladies here do not complain. They are curvaceous and wear a nice red lipstick and he is sure they service their husbands without skipping a beat. Maybe *he* should have an affair here.

She slowed to five miles per hour. A few dusty brown leaves from the nearly bare branches of anorexic drought nonresistant excuses of trees swirled in the wind.

And on went the monologue in her head: On the positive side, these young trees will get bigger and have fresh green leaves in the spring twenty years from now. And what if there is a real creek rustling someplace in the distance? Optimism is a good thing. But these sadly identical trees are wearing exactly the same dusty brown uniforms, producing mirror image noon shadows on the blackish asphalt. Martin would love the no potholes here.

She was getting bored with her wordy street painting. She slapped her cheeks to wake up, regretting not having brought any coffee, and returned to observing the ranch style houses, the fronts of which were predictably neatly manicured, uneventful rectangles of crisply cut lawns, or fake green polyester lawns extending all the way to the curb. But no lazy front door cats. How could people live without sidewalks or cats? And where are the kids on three wheeled training bikes? Nowhere to be seen were dogs taking their poets for walks! No cascades of red and gold nasturtium, since here they are considered weeds . . . no wildflower meadows. No wild fucking *anything*.

She tried the Positive Frame of Mind method: But maybe there is a real creek after all? She listened more intently, but didn't hear any rustling water; the growing disquietude constricted her esophagus further.

"What if *nothing* is real in a place like this?" She turned right, as per the Bald Bold Man's directions, onto a street that looked just like the other street, except for the wind, which grew louder and more eerie, roaming unrestricted against the stark new black asphalt, flanked by the same dwarfed skeletons of trees attacked by the bright sun. Not a soul around. She opened the window more than halfway to immerse herself in this soulless landscape.

The harsh noon sun was fighting its way through gray clouds. She was acutely missing the glorious shade trees on her own street, which formed a live green cathedral ceiling, with the sunlight filtering through its roof of leafy lace . . . where dogs and cats rub themselves on a friendly leg, and birds sing their mating songs, and the woodpecker peck peck pecks and the squirrels *Basia* and *Kasia* (she gave the squirrels Polish names) chase each other on this live roof of branches reaching from one sidewalk to the other. (All this she was writing in cursive in her head with Martin's blue ink Pelican pen.) Where happily shrieking children play with abandon. And the woodpecker, whose name is *Tadzik*, pecks on the tree trunk right in front of our house in early spring — and Martin notices; in fact he is the first one to hear *Tadzik*, who returns every early spring to peck on that tree trunk.

She turned the corner and started a bout of anxious reflection accompanied by a slightly different variety of discordant constriction still at the level of her solar plexus. Yes, she needed a good roach and she was quite sure that there were three in her tarnished cigarette case.

Above the harsh sun drenched black asphalt, the wind blew even more unnervingly. A viable roach really would be a good idea. But what if it amplified the uncertainty of not quite knowing what she is doing? A second roach might rectify or amplify the effect of the first. And the third roach? Depends. On how it burns, how thick it is, how long it lasts. She laughed at her own joke. They were waiting — in her tarnished silver cigarette case, a gift from Martin.

Narrating in her head, on a Moleskine page, in third person (with the Pelican pen — even in her dreams she wrote cursive with it), Nina let the feeling of discord invade her body; to study it, she slowed to a crawl. She was compelled to experience even things she feared. Her solar plexus was already fully invaded — and it was hard to take the calming yoga breaths or even keep the relaxed pace of her natural breath.

She pulled up to the curb, stopped the engine and lit her first roach, hoping to organize her thoughts. Puffing, she pondered: Could the rational brain, if it exists and if it is focused, prevail and have a curbing effect on an unspecific free floating and fleeting irrational thought? And is such a thought a thought? And if a foreigner is writing a book in English, will she be excused for making up new words if she can't find one in the Oxford Dictionary? According to Martin it's illegal to make up your own words. What should be illegal is these suburbia street names conjuring real images. This is the Real Lying Fiction. And where are the precise or made up words for indescribable inner reality? The roach was about finished. Names like Whispering Creek are marketing ploys of developers who rip out real trees . . . Nice names sell. Hmmm . . . Refreshing Rumbling Creek? Is Lying Real Fiction working on me?

The roach was history and she still felt cheated. A false promise was delivered by the Rustling Creek — a Hallmark promise of happiness. She turned the key in the ignition to continue to her destination, as per her own handwritten directions.

More Hallmark promises: Hampton Court, Hunter's

Point Creek, names that carried scents of gracious hospitality, of a cool respite by a bubbling stream. So maybe the people in these perfect suburbs do not miss the richness they were promised — promised and denied. The fake street signs produce illusions to help them accept where they are, or maybe to forget rather than to hope for what is missing in this sterile stage set of suburbia paradise for which old forests had to be ripped out . . . Oh, why upset myself at this point?

She took three focus defining breaths. Whatever method, she had to tame her angst . . . like a dog that needed to be tamed, so she could experience an excitement, not fear . . . And thank God there were still two good roaches in her tarnished silver cigarette case.

On the next street, Bubbling Creek, she passed the first white speed bump. More sprawling ranch style houses imitated each other in size, color, and shape, irritating her more, but here and there she spied a joyful splash of color. Bright orange and green! At every house at each left corner by the garage door there was an identical young orange tree, fecund with late crop miniature oranges. So, she thought, happiness is possible here, despite the monotony of gray. All it takes is a splash of bright orange. Despite the sharp noon glare, this thought put a smile on her face and she put on her polarized sunglasses.

Martin was right after all. With these pretty miniature orange trees, people living here could be capable of at least momentary happiness. She listened. But no bubbles, no birds, not even crows like it here, no bees, no flower scents no joyous children's shrieks . . . no inspired dogs who take their poets for nature walks . . . And shit — no cats, worst of all. Was this her suburban refrain on a loop?

She drove over the next white speed bump. Actually, Rustling Creek might once have been a Promised Land when Indians lived here. These suburban builders are hypocrites, who entice with a promise of beauty and deliver nothing but dark gray asphalt streets with white bumps. She couldn't stop this lament of a refrain: No mothers or fathers pushing strollers. No green fields with grazing cows, no cats, no dogs, no visible sign of life except the little oranges in front of each house.

She parked two blocks from the Bold Bald Man's street, listening to the silence, which was less than serene. Again it filled her with an unsettling foreboding, and yet she was also in the grip of anticipatory excitement, despite something literally still grasping her not just at the level of her solar plexus. Her heart was beating wildly and she was breathing in and out cautiously as if the air were laced with sticky angst.

Unsettled, in her Coach bag she located her red Bic lighter and her second roach. In and out she took steady and slow puffs. She needed to be lulled into a stupor to face whatever was to come, instead of boring herself with fuzzy rhetorical questions with or without a thinker. Either way, she had to let all that wanted to leave her brain leave. Three deep calming breaths, eyes closed. The conclusion came to her: One can breathe easier without troubling thoughts and isn't life also about the unknown moments we allow ourselves to have?

The second roach was finished, and she was inhaling cleansing breaths through her nose, exhaling through her mouth when another clear thought struck her! She could of course go back home, turn her red Honda Fit hatchback around, with all her Occupational Therapy Visiting Home Nurse equipment in the trunk, and her sons' soccer balls and junior league outfits, plus her husband's old tweed jacket with buttons she'd promised to sew on during the boys' next soccer game.

One more cycle of three cleansing breaths. After the last one, freed of her guilt, she smiled. She was not going to turn around. Just like she didn't leave the dance floor when the Bald Bold Man hissed in her ear.

A wave of the same kind of uncontrolled anticipation now fluttered inside her belly. She didn't feel constricting anything anywhere anymore, and focused on the involuntary waves of pleasure. They were accompanied by voluntary pulsing Kegel contractions, and she was aware of her need to pee, which luckily was more or less under control thanks to Kegels; involuntary flutters were intensified by the voluntary ones. She touched her breasts and nipples in a spontaneous impulse and put her hand between her thighs, thinking of the first boy she was in love with in Poland at the Jewish summer camp. They are on the train in an old hardwood second class compartment where eight other kids are dozing. Going home from summer camp. Her head is on his lap and she lets him touch her under her skirt. No one else saw it. She was touching herself now the way he had done.

The contractions became spontaneous trepidations. The Kegels were more forceful. But she was not going to let herself have an orgasm yet. The pissing urgency returned and had to be stopped before she got to the Bald Bold Man's door. She stopped contracting her Kegel muscles. And let go of her nipple (which very much liked being lightly pinched, like her first boyfriend had done it when she was fifteen). Breathing slowly in and out through her nose, she was trying to alleviate the peeing urgency. It would be embarrassing if the first thing after the Bald One opened his door, she asked in a panic where is the WC. She imagined him hissing and pointing down the hall, her running in that direction, pressing her hand into her crotch to stop the piss.

No, not like that. After he opens the door, I'll study his eyes. Is he going to be studying mine? Running to the toilet is not the thing to do on the first date of hopefully an eye to eye affair. So she continued the Kegel contractions. She will not permit herself a spontaneous touchless orgasm in the car on this windswept street, so as not to deplete her libido. It will be more intense . . . what's his name? Weird, nameless sex will be more intense?

No matter what, she was tempted to play with herself

through the hidden hole in the crotch of her spandex leggings. In fact she was *terribly* tempted, so she did put her long middle finger through the hole in her spandex leggings as far as she could reach. The throbbing intensified. No one on the street. She closed her eyes. (This small opening in the crotch of her tights had ripped in the seam and she hadn't sewn it for a practical purpose — it provided an opening for ventilation to prevent yeast infections, and also to let her pee in her private garden, and for a quick access, when alone in the car like now, after a joint. She could make herself come.)

The access with the middle finger of her right hand was comfortable and she was able to reach the spot where the most sensitive and well lubricating receptors were and sexual perfume was emitted abundantly. She pulled out her middle finger and smelled it. She always liked her natural smell.

But I'm not going to make myself come yet, she said to herself quietly once more, not here in the driver's seat of my own little red car, even if no one is on the street. (She could make herself come in a few seconds if she put her finger back in.)

She exercised an unusual level of restraint. Better to wait for a greater reward than have another one of these solo orgasms. (She also preferred to forgo the so called "charity orgasm," where after a quick fuck, the man, already satisfied, is obliging but not too enthusiastic, since he wants to go to sleep, as he magnanimously offers it to the woman with his tongue or his longest finger, but being spent himself, performs mechanically, like a duty. It's not his fault if a man is tired and lust free. But still . . . After his orgasm, the sensuality of a man goes to sleep with him, and very soon he starts snoring and his finger inside a woman stops moving and a woman, unfulfilled, is left all to herself.)

Parked dangerously near his house, she was in control till in her ear the unabashed hissing of the Bald Bold Man appeared and entranced her again, cleansing her conscience of the fact that she and Martin did have an agreement not to lie nor cheat behind each other's back.

The pulsing throbs didn't stop even though she was no longer touching herself. She opened the car window fully. There was not a soul around.

Her black scuffed up leather Coach bag from the years before marriage was on the seat beside her. She snapped open the magnetic clasp, and saw the third and last roach in her tarnished silver cigarette case, and in the silence of the wide and empty windswept street she put on, not too loud, a South Indian soothing flute CD and lit the roach.

Her purple cosmetic case was also in her scuffed up Coach bag and she unzipped it, finding her new deep black curly eyelash mascara wand. She flipped open the car mirror. Indian bamboo flute music was providing a sensual ambiance as she took little puffs and applied mascara lightly, since she did not want it to smear later on in her abandonment. A little jar with shea butter lip balm was in her purple cosmetic case too, and she dipped her fingertip into it and slowly smeared it over her lips. "Great for the upper and the lower lips," she said aloud, like the star of a commercial. "But I have to save myself for later," she reminded herself as she applied a good dose of the lip balm through the small opening in her black tights.

With the roach in her mouth she was looking into her eyes in the car mirror. She pulled her finger away before it would be too late. Her libido must stay at max. She finished the third roach.

Next, off her feet came the sneakers she'd jogged in that morning. The Ross plastic bag she had taken from home, hiding it from Martin, was on the back seat. Her frilly bottom Paris skirt was inside. Starting to rip too much in some places, it still showed off her ass and hid her stomach. Also, a black spandex top with a low boat neck that flattered her breasts.

No one was around, no moving cars either, so she took off her jogging T-shirt and pulled the sexy spandex top over her head and pulled her skirt on by lifting her hips in the driver's seat — a kind of pelvic tilt bridge. She smoothed her black yoga leggings with sexy black lace at the ankle.

Her silk black skirt from Paris, with subtle floral design, and not yet too ripped, flowed softly over her hips — the very skirt Martin had watched her try on, admiring herself, in their bedroom mirror last night; he'd commented that the skirt was tattered and she looked like a homeless person in it, but he would go with her to Victoria's Secret and buy her a new one. I *like* the tattered look, darling, she'd told him. And to herself she'd said, Okay darling, then I will not wear it for you, the tattered look is for me. It *is* me. (This morning, when Martin left the bedroom to make breakfast, she had defiantly taken the skirt and her sexy black spandex not yet too stretched out top with three quarter sleeve, which showed off her breasts but was too stretched out for his taste, and stuffed them in the plastic bag from Ross and put the bag in the back seat of her car.)

To complete her transition, she slipped on her black BeautiFeel medium heel dancing shoes with an almost falling off ankle strap (the same ones she'd worn to Sylvia's party, the right strap held with the safety pin, which irritated Martin and her mother and her sister every time they saw it).

She was combing her fingers through her unkempt black shiny curls, watching herself in the car mirror, careful not to tame the curls arranged in an artful mess, because they were also hiding her unattractive profile and short chin. She turned her head to the side, examined her chin, then from the other side; it wasn't any better, so she moved some curls to hide her unattractive chin better. She hoped that the Bald Bold Man wouldn't notice her chin. She tossed her curls around a bit more.

Examining her eyes in the car mirror she concluded that she trusted her eyes and that they were more dramatic with a little makeup. She actually admired the green color and gold speckle in them, now in the sun. Was she a narcissist? (It was her daily ritual to look into her eyes, maybe even multiple times, in the foyer mirror of their house, in filtered sunlight.) Now she was studying her eyes even more intently, hoping to see in them her essence — literally speaking, what the fuck is essence? The essence at the end is fucking? Will the Bald Bold Man notice my eyes? Isn't the essence to trust and to be trusted before fucking?

It turned out that there was one good long puff, after all, left of her third and last roach! She was wondering if eyes can also lie to their owner and if the Bold One smoked weed.

Done applying her mascara, eyeliner, and subtle iridescent shadow, she felt relatively pacified. One more look into her eyes revealed a wistful melancholia; a black Kohl pencil lined it dramatically.

A new wave of uncensored anticipation arrived and was growing seriously unrelenting between her thighs. She turned off her cell phone, started the car and crawled along, looking for the Bald Bold Man's house number. The spontaneous pulsing just about everywhere inside her quickened — and she didn't just imagine but could actually feel his breath near Martin's cubic zirconia earring. She could hear his bold raspy whisper, his mouth touching her ear near the cubic zirconia. (But she didn't hear the elevator muzak which had no soul of any sort.)

The Indian bamboo flute music ended and now his warm breath seemed loaded with sinister, victorious, self flattering conviction. And there was his whisper in her ear: *Do you want to have an affair?* Out of the blue. Causing her to lose her voluntary capacity for a rational response,

314

to say NO and walk away. The contractions went on as she ruminated loosely. Paralyzed by his hot breath. The breath of a man whose eyes I don't know. Shit. This is not romantic. But I'm here. The contractions almost stopped.

She flipped the car mirror back to its resting place and drove twice around the Rustling Creek cul-de-sac but couldn't find the house number, so she turned her cell phone on and called him.

His *Hellllo* was sinister. Like a winner already relishing his conquest. There was silence on the line. He waited. He didn't say who he was.

"This is Nina. I am here, but I cannot find your house," she said in Polish. "I've been driving around and around and there is no number 1659."

"Oooh." He prolonged the word, with more than a hint of cocksure satisfaction. A long moment and he laughed stiffly and then minced his words in English with a strong Polish accent. Calculated indifference: "Sooo, Nina, you seem not to understand my directions, but I never give wrong directions, for your information, and my house is on the other side of the main road. And you'll see the *mezuzah* at my door. It's the only one around here. So Nina . . . you must have turned right instead of left. You should pay more attention, Nina."

Asshole, didn't even apologize, she thought as she flipped the cover of her cell phone. But she was driving back to the Rustling Creek subdivision, on the other side. Right not left.

At the next road crossing, the highway was fully visible. The highway that led to home. She needed to collect herself. She pulled over, turned off the engine, and listened to the wind sweeping over the black asphalt. She could really feel her heart's unsettling beat when unbidden, disconnected lines from Szymborska's poem "Labyrinth" that she didn't even know she had memorized violently coursed through her mind pell mell, helter skelter:

This way or that if not the other. Więc tędy albo tędy, chyba że tamtędy. By intuition by premonition na wyczucie na przeczucie by chance by common sense na rozum na przelaj. This way or that . . . if not the other . . . by intuition . . . by premonition . . . by chance. Road after road . . . twist after twist, gasp after gasp . . . ucieczka . . . albo nie . . . run away . . . albo nie . . . or not.

CODA

Libiamo, ne' lieti calici — Verdi

"Let's drink from the joy."

Dear Dr. Butterfly,

It was nice to run into you in the CVS! And you remember so much from our sessions! Big congratulations on your retirement and finally having time to work on your book on Intimacy.

Martin and I are still together, despite our endless differences. That may be an Eternal Mystery, but here we are! Our sons are grown and now we have a beautiful grandson. He is a real American: Irish Jewish Polish Palestinian, a true melting mix!

About Martin: Abstract Mathematics remains his Pure Love. And I'm anything but pure or abstract.

About me: I have had some success in curbing my tendency to mercilessly confront Martin. I'm not sure how but I learned to add humor to end a fight. In private and among good friends I address my husband with a note of affection as Professor Martin Didn't Notice.

About us: We actually have dates! Martin met me more than halfway. My concession is to wear the silky leggings he likes to touch in dark theaters. Each morning he brings the breakfast tray to bed, which we share with our two cats. We are at a fragile stage of a fragile life, and apparently we need each other. (He needs to hold my foot to fall asleep.)

I long ago forgave him for calling me a disgrace to artists. He brings me tea when I'm at my writing desk.

In the modern language of my older son who declares himself Polyamorous, Martin and I are Monogamish. I also have dates with my American Jewish and unbearably narcissistic "boyfriend." Martin treats him like an always hungry immature teenager and often cooks for him. With my "boyfriend" I smoke weed and philosophize on fuzzy subjects and Jungian dreams. I can tell that he also gets exhausted from listening to me, and only sometimes responds to my impertinent questions.

I've gone on too long and will end this here by saying Martin sends his fondest hello.

Warmest wishes,
Nina

PS: On our forty years of marriage anniversary I offered Martin a new "contract": if he dances with me on Sunday nights to Leonard Cohen's "Dance Me to the End of Love" while looking into my eyes, maybe I will, you know what, before he falls off to sleep.

You asked about my stylish forever young older sister. I am so impressed that you remember that too, after 20 years! I took to heart your advice. The only thing you can do is to distance yourself from those that try to place you below them. We see each other now and then, no questions asked. Will we forgive each other for whatever before we die, knowing that Revenge carries no benefits?

That would be something to celebrate.

ABOUT THE AUTHOR

In Poland, Eva Gerszon's high school literature teacher encouraged her to write because of her apparent ability to express subtle emotions. Long after, in the US, following an epiphany on her way to work, she took fiction classes at a community college and wrote an essay on the *Optimal Dose of Soulful Melancholia*. She writes in English "with a Polish accent." This is her first published novel.

Childhood Memories of Eva Gerszon

I am three years old in the courtyard of the small apartment building where I grew up, in the sandbox, with a friend. We are making sand *babkas* with little buckets. "I can't play with you because my mother said you killed our Jesus Christus," she says to me. I go to my mother and repeat the accusation. She doesn't explain anything.

*

Along with some preteen kids from the building, I play "house, mother, father, doctor," in the postwar ruins adjacent to our apartment house. We take joy in hiding from our parents. Furniture in the hideout consists of boxes and crates to sit on, covered with old blankets stolen from home. For us it is cozy. A home in the ruins with a roof. We even make a warming fire. We bake potatoes in it.

*

I am afraid of going up the stairs alone to our third floor apartment, because I believe there is a bomb left over from the war that could explode at any time. My heart beats crazy every time I pass that part of the staircase. I wait till someone else is coming up. Sometimes I wait hours.

*

I am alone in the coatroom at elementary school. A good looking popular boy, Maciuś, is chasing me among the many aisles of coats, yelling *Brudna Żydówka* (Dirty Jewess). No one else is there, no supervisor. Maciuś chases me, waving a sack of heavy shoes (kids keep their street shoes in fabric sacks, and change into *papcie* — home shoes — when in school). Maciuś is throwing the heavy sack at me, hurting my arm, my side, and I'm running as fast as I can among the rows of coats as he yells *Brudna Żydówka* over and over. I tell no one. I'm too shy.

*

It's March of 1968. The Jews are being expelled from Poland. My grandfather, a devoted Communist Party member, goes to his last Party meeting where he throws his Party membership card on the floor, spits on it, and crushes it to the ground with his foot, before turning around and walking away.

*

It's late October in 1968 and we are leaving Poland for good. We are on the train to Vienna. We see Russian tanks on the Czech border. My family, seven of us, are in the second class compartment with two hard wooden benches facing each other. We have one suitcase apiece. A small suitcase on the luggage rack is partially open — maybe the lock is broken. It's held together by an old leather belt. A distinct, not quite familiar, smell permeates the compartment where we sit across from each other: we three sisters, my mother and father, my grandmother and grandfather. My grandfather is crying. I had never seen him cry before. Everyone else is very quiet.

The sadness of the moment is impossible to convey. My grandfather's weathered face is covered by his worn hatmaker's hands. The smell coming out of the suitcase is becoming more distinctly identifiable. It's not quite that of *kabanosy*, although the suitcase is full of them, for the next month of our meals. My grandmother starts to cry. The smell turns out to be a curious, not overly pleasant, mix of *kabanosy* and my grandmother's cherished perfume, the only scent she ever used: Chanel N°5. Perfume has spilled all over the *kabanosy*.

In Vienna (my first time out of Poland), in our small hotel room we hang the *kabanosy* from the ceiling to air them out, but it doesn't help much. So we eat the perfumed sausages, making a face each time, along with delicious hot little Vienna rolls and tea. That is what's for breakfast, lunch, and dinner.

*

The Jewish organization (HIAS) in Vienna gives us two dollars per person per day. My older sister and I won't spend it on a tram ticket. Instead, we walk all over Vienna with one orange for both of us and a *Milka* chocolate to share. We are exhilarated and free, in transit to the unknown. My mother is a pediatrician and doctors are needed in the US. We get a US visa. My grandparents will go to Israel.

*

In the hotel room in Vienna, after a dinner of the Chanel N°5 infused *kabanosy*, my father says to my older sister, "You have a good brain and you're flat like a board, so when we get to New York, you will go to university, so you can support yourself. With such breasts like a board, you won't find a husband." To me he says, "You don't need to go to university, you've got big breasts." To my younger sister he says, "And you, you're a silly chatterbox."

ACKNOWLEDGMENTS

To my husband for everything.

To my editor Kurt Lipschutz for guiding me.

To my publisher Mark Weiman for getting me into print.